THE CO

"He found Mrs. Pritchard in a state of great agitation. She was, as usual, lying on her invalid couch, and she had a bottle of smelling salts in her hand which she sniffed at frequent intervals.

" 'George,' she exclaimed. 'What did I tell you about this house? The moment I came into it, I felt there was something wrong! Didn't I tell you so at the time?'

"Repressing his desire to reply, 'You always do,' George said, 'No, can't say I remember it.'

" 'Well, as I was telling you, this woman knew at once! She actually blenched—if you know what I mean—as she came in at that door, and she said, "There is evil here—evil and danger. I feel it." '

" 'What else did she say?' he asked.

" 'She couldn't tell me very much. She was so upset. One thing she did say. I had some violets in a glass. She pointed at them and cried out. 'Take those away. No blue flowers—never have blue flowers. Blue flowers are fatal to you—remember that.' "

—From "The Blue Geranium" by Agatha Christie

MORE MYSTERY COLLECTIONS FROM
THE BERKLEY PUBLISHING GROUP . . .

SENIOR SLEUTHS

edited by Cynthia Manson
and Constance Scarborough

BERKLEY PRIME CRIME, NEW YORK

SENIOR SLEUTHS

A Berkley Prime Crime Book / published by arrangement with
Dell Magazines, a division of Bantam Doubleday Dell, Inc.

PRINTING HISTORY
Berkley Prime Crime edition / April 1996

The Putnam Berkley World Wide Web site address is
http://www.berkley.com

ISBN: 0-425-15258-8

Berkley Prime Crime Books are published
by The Berkley Publishing Group,
200 Madison Avenue, New York, New York 10016.
The name BERKLEY PRIME CRIME
and the BERKLEY PRIME CRIME design
are trademarks belonging to Berkley Publishing Corporation.

PRINTED IN THE UNITED STATES OF AMERICA

10 9 8 7 6 5 4 3 2 1

CONTENTS

INTRODUCTION

For mystery fans of all ages we have put together a collection of stories featuring amateur sleuths who are over fifty years old. The "golden years" for these senior sleuths does not imply serene or retiring years. In fact, the senior sleuths in this book are active, alert, and strong-willed characters determined to solve the crimes in which they find themselves involved.

Our impressive lineup of authors includes such well-known writers as Lilian Jackson Braun, Agatha Christie, Dorothy Salisbury Davis, Loren D. Estleman, and Michael Gilbert.

These sleuths include a wide array of colorful characters such as Hugh Pentecost's Pierre Chambrun, the manager of a luxury hotel who prevents a diplomat staying at the hotel from being poisoned. William Brittain's Mr. Strang is a science teacher who assists a detective in tracking down a murderer. In Mr. Estleman's story, an elderly book collector solves the theft of a missing rare book as well as a murder. Mr. Gilbert's Dr. Arnold Lethbury is a pathologist about to retire who figures out a complicated murder case. For comic relief, turn to Robert Arthur's story "Larceny and Old Lace" featuring two elderly ladies who inherit their nephew's house and stumble into blackmail and murder. They never lose their cool and by their wits alone solve the mystery. For those readers who need a more exotic locale, please note Ed Hoch's "Waiting for Mrs. Ryder" in which a retired CIA operative meets up with a double agent while on vacation, on an island off the coast of Kenya. Finally, this collection would not be complete without the most famous senior sleuth of them all, Miss Marple. In Agatha Christie's story, Miss Marple puts her skills of detection to use in relating the mysterious tale of an invalid tormented by a fortune-teller.

While the clever senior sleuths in these stories will entertain readers of all ages, their energetic application of the wisdom and experience of their years should prove an inspiration to those of you who share that life experience.

—The editors

SENIOR SLEUTHS

THE HONEYMOON MURDERS

VINCENT McCONNOR

The howling gale roused George Drayton before dawn. He cursed as he listened to the driving rain, knowing that he would be held prisoner in his flat for at least 24 hours after the weather cleared. His only exercise would be a short walk, morning and afternoon, around the iron fence that enclosed Knightswood Square. He pulled the covers over his head to shut out the sound of the storm and slowly sank back into a dreamless sleep.

Seven o'clock breakfast, in his study as usual, at the work table facing the tall front windows. He prepared his own breakfast every morning. Today he broiled a rasher of bacon and heated yesterday's scones. His appetite always seemed to improve on a stormy morning.

As he poured his third cup of tea George glanced through the rain-spattered windowpanes across the street to the gale-lashed Square. Bare trees appeared ghostlike behind slanting curtains of November rain. He shivered as he gulped the hot tea. Was he catching cold? At 73 he was increasingly aware of his health. The gas heater, glowing in the fireplace, had not yet driven the night chill from his book-lined study.

He put on his reading glasses and opened the morning paper to check the latest London crime news. Another smash-and-grab job on Regent Street. A fire in a Chelsea antique shop that smelled of arson. Juveniles with razors had attacked a man near Soho Square. No new developments on the honeymoon murders. He wondered what the Yard was doing about them. Surely they knew that the killer was about to electrocute another young bride. They must have noticed that the three murders had been at six month intervals and always on a Saturday night.

George tossed the paper aside and reached across to his desk for a small stack of clippings. He spread them out among his breakfast dishes and, once again, studied the photographs of the three young women: Bessie Gray, Emily Lynch, and Doris Midgely. Their three faces had one thing in common—a kind of sad innocence, discernible even in these gray newspaper clippings. All dead in their baths, electrocuted, on their honeymoons.

"He usually waits six months between murders." George realized that he was talking to himself. "And it's now going on seven. So he's overdue with his next victim." If there was going to be another victim . . .

Each of the three deaths had occurred in a second-class hotel located in a seaside town. Folkestone, Bristol, West Hartlepool. Bessie, Emily, Doris. All dead in their tubs because an electric appliance had fallen into their bath water. Radio, hair dryer, portable heater.

Local authorities had written off the three deaths as accidents. Death, they said, by misadventure. The sorrowing husbands had buried their young brides and faded from the news. Until Doris Midgely's father turned up last month and demanded a further investigation. That was when an alert local constable noticed a curious similarity in the deaths of Doris Midgely and Bessie Gray.

The constable's report to New Scotland Yard brought a CID investigator to West Hartlepool, and almost immediately the papers announced that there was a similarity in all three deaths. Bessie, Emily, Doris. Their husbands had signed different names on the hotel registers. Charles Gray, Timothy Lynch, William Midgely. But the newspapers hinted that it was now suspected they were all the same man and that the three brides had been murdered.

George ran his eye down the most recent clipping, two days old, which described the missing husbands. All three possessed completely ordinary faces according to the few people, mostly hotel employees, who had seen them. The sort of man in each case who would fade into the background. In Bristol, Timothy Lynch had worn spectacles and in Folkestone, Charles Gray's hair had been blond. In West Hartlepool, William Midgely wore a small mustache. So it would seem, if it were one man, that he did attempt to change his appearance from bride to bride.

The only odd thing reported about him was what two people described as his "awful peculiar" eyes. "They seemed to hold you," one maid was quoted as saying. "Like they hypnotized you."

George Drayton's thoughts remained with the honeymoon murders as he dressed for his morning walk. He imagined the murderer had found those "awful peculiar" eyes useful when he was persuading his victims to marry him and, almost immediately, hand over their savings to his loving care for investment. Later he would certainly use them, his "awful peculiar" eyes, terrifying his victims as he stooped across their tubs with his deadly electrical appliances.

George's charwoman, Mrs. Higby, would straighten the flat and wash his breakfast dishes. But she would not arrive for several hours, so he could leave the clippings spread out until he returned from his walk. He wanted another look at them.

As George came down the shallow marble steps to the

sidewalk, the wind slashed under the portico and struck across his face. He headed east, keeping close to the long line of Regency buildings with their identical columned façades. The wind whipped his waterproof and thrust him forward in spite of his heavy stick, forcing him to walk more quickly than usual.

He wondered if it was raining at the seaside town where the murderer had taken his newest bride. Were they held captive in their hotel room because of this same storm? Would they be asleep at this hour or enjoying breakfast in front of a cozy fire? The poor girl, whoever she was, probably had only one more day to live. Tomorrow was Saturday—and the murderer was behind schedule.

George turned north along the eastern edge of the Square. He gasped for breath as the wind struck him full in the face. By the time he took the elevator up to his flat he was completely exhausted.

The doorbell rang as he hung his waterproof in the bath. He kicked off his rubbers and went to open the hall door.

"Saw you come back from your walk, sir." Fitch, the building caretaker, stood in the hall. "Somethin' personal I'd like to speak to you about."

"Come into the study. I've a fire lighted in there."

"Very good, sir."

George sank into his favorite chair, rubbing his hands together to restore circulation. "Storm gave me a bit of a battering."

"Wireless claims it won't let up before evenin'." Fitch hesitated, uncertainly, in the center of the Persian rug.

"Was there something personal you wanted to speak to me about?"

"That's right, sir. Family matter, you might say. It's the Missus' niece—Cora Penton. Ever since you solved that Clarkson murder and saved old Mrs. Heatherin'ton's life—

well, sir, the Missus has told all the relatives about you. That's how her sister knew. Came in from Hornchurch last night. Begged us to speak to you and ask you to find her son-in-law."

"Find him? What's happened to him?"

"Clyde's disappeared, sir. His wife ain't heard from him in weeks."

"She'd better report it to the proper authorities."

"She did. But they've not found him."

"Then I'm afraid there's nothing I can do. Tell her the police will be in touch. After they've sent out a description of the missing man, made inquiries, and placed items in newspapers all over the country."

"There *was* a piece in the paper. Said Clyde was reported missin'—"

"In that case you can assure his wife that everything is being done."

"We was hopin'—the Missus and me—you might have a minute to see Cora. Hear her story. When you take your afternoon stroll."

"Well, now—"

"She lives on Walton Street. Just up the way a bit. Mrs. Cora Penton—I've written down the address." He brought a slip of paper from his pocket and set it on the table. "Or I could have Cora come here. If you would talk to her."

"I'm afraid that's quite impossible. With the police already working on the case I wouldn't dare interfere. They would resent it. And quite rightly!"

"See what you mean, sir. Well, I'll explain to the Missus and she can tell her sister. Good day, sir." Fitch bowed slightly and headed for the hall.

George pushed the slip of paper aside and, once again, turned his attention to the newspaper clippings scattered among his breakfast dishes. Bessie, Emily, Doris. And the murderer who connected all three of them.

Reminded him of George Smith. Hanged in 1915 for drowning three brides in their baths. In as many cities! But Smith had always returned to his dear wife and the small shop they kept in Bristol.

He wondered if the current honeymoon murderer had a family hidden away in some quiet corner of England. Would he hurry back to them next week after doing away with his newest bride? At least he didn't grab their feet the way George Smith had and pull their unsuspecting heads under the bath water. He was more modern than that with his deadly electrical appliances.

He sneezed. Damn! He was catching a cold.

George got to his feet, and moving away from the windows he crossed to a small sofa near the fireplace. He stretched out and pulled a wool coverlet over his legs. Then he turned to the waiting piles of new books. Since his retirement several publishers, old friends, continued to send him copies of their latest publications. Where was that new book on Egypt? Perfect morning to read about sand and sunshine.

George found it and settled down to enjoy the handsome photographs of towering statues in the Valley of the Nile. The entire valley would be flooded when that new dam was completed. Under water like those poor brides in their baths. He chuckled at the image of a mammoth Egyptian statue, smiling mysteriously, disappearing under the sudsy water of a gigantic white porcelain tub . . .

After lunch he started a new paperback detective novel but the names of the characters were confusing. Other names seemed to float across the pages. Bessie, Emily, Doris. He tossed the book aside and prepared for a second walk in the rain, picking up the scrap of paper that Fitch had left on the table and thrusting it into a pocket of his waterproof.

George hesitated on the marble front steps, as usual, and looked across Knightswood Square. The storm seemed to be letting up but it might be another two days before the ground would be dry enough for him to sit on his favorite benches. It was less than a ten minute walk to Walton Street, he told himself, and he might just have a quick look at the missing man's home. Nothing more.

It was a street of toy houses, joined together, with a few small restaurants and shops. Most of them were well kept. Brightly painted doors. Gleaming brass knockers. He checked the slip of paper and discovered that he was standing within a few steps of Clyde Penton's front door. There was a small, crudely hand-lettered *VACANCY* sign in one of the windows. Without even considering his action, George Drayton pushed the button and heard a bell chime inside.

He glanced at the houses on the opposite side of Walton Street and noticed curtains moving slightly at an upper window. Somebody was watching him.

"What is it?"

George turned to face a plump young woman wearing a damp-spotted apron over a flowered house dress. Bright eyes in a pleasant face. "You have a vacancy?"

"Oh! Thought you were another one from the police."

"Police?" He hoped his pretense of surprise sounded genuine.

"Do come in." She motioned for him to enter. "I'm Mrs. Penton."

As he stepped into the house George decided it might be wise not to tell her who he really was. "My name is Timmers." It was the first name that popped into his head. "Ernest Timmers."

"You're the second to inquire about the room, Mr. Timmers. Placed that sign in the window only yesterday. Didn't like the look of the other gentleman. One must be careful, don't you think? If you'll follow me—"

She led him through a narrow hall toward the carpeted stairs. The parlor door was closed but he noticed a glow of light from a back room as he climbed behind her to the second floor.

"I've never had a lodger before," she was saying, "but then I s'pose there's a first time for everything. You're a businessman?" Her manner was hesitant, as though she had never before asked a stranger such a personal question.

"Retired. I was a publisher." No reason not to tell the truth.

"Here we are." She opened a door and ushered him into the room, switching on a light.

The furniture was plain but comfortable. He walked to the one window, pulled aside the curtains, and glanced down at a back garden, forlorn in the rain.

"You do like it?"

He turned, realizing that she was waiting for his decision. "It's exactly what I wanted." Why had he said that? While he tried to think of an answer to his own question he paid a week's rent in advance.

"If you would care to see the bath—" She led the way up the hall. There were two other doors. Mrs. Penton motioned to the one on the opposite side. "That's our bedroom, my husband's and mine. But he's—away." She opened the third door, clicked a light switch, and stood aside for him to look in.

The bath was small but satisfactory—except that the gleaming blue-white porcelain reminded him of that other tub waiting in some seaside hotel for tomorrow night. "Everything seems just right. I'll go and fetch my luggage."

Back in his own flat he left a note for Mrs. Higby to find when she returned to cook his dinner. He wrote her that he was dining out with friends. That would not arouse her suspicions because he did precisely that several times every month. He would come back in the morning, before Mrs. Higby returned, and muss up his bed so that she would not suspect he had spent the night elsewhere. He packed a small bag, including the paperback detective novel and the clippings about the honeymoon murders, phoned for a taxi, and rode through the rain back to Walton Street.

Mrs. Penton opened the front door as he was paying the cab driver. "Forgot to give you a key." She handed it to him with a fold of paper. "And that's the receipt for your first week's rent. Would you care for a cup of tea?"

"I would, indeed."

"Just fixing it. If you'll join me in the back parlor—"

George carried his bag upstairs and quickly unpacked. When he came down again, he could hear Mrs. Penton moving about in the basement.

The small back parlor was crammed with furniture. A gas fire burned on the hearth and lamps were lighted. Two rear windows were covered by heavy lace curtains which allowed only a faint chalky light to filter into the room.

"Here we are!"

George turned, startled, to see Mrs. Penton with a tea tray.

"Our kitchen and dining room are downstairs but I always like to have my tea up here." She placed the tray on the table not cluttered with bric-a-brac. "Do sit down. I was wondering, would you mind looking after the house while I go out for a bit of shopping?"

"Certainly not!" Mind? This would give him an opportunity to inspect the place without arousing her suspicions.

"That's ever so kind. Please help yourself to these biscuits." She set his tea in front of him and poured her own. "Don't know what my husband's going to say when he finds out about you."

"Hadn't you better tell him? Right away?"

"Guess you didn't read about me in the newspapers. My husband's disappeared."

George tried to look his most credulous.

"Clyde's a traveling man. Jewelry, mostly. Goes on long trips. Eight or nine weeks usually. But this time he's been away nearly three months! That's why I went to the police. I know something's happened to him. Something terrible!"

"Did the newspapers print a picture of your husband?"

"They couldn't. I didn't have one. Clyde hates to have his picture taken."

"When was the last time he wrote to you?"

"He never writes. Says he's much too busy."

"Where did you meet your husband? Here in London?"

"No. I was working as a waitress. Tea shop on the pier at Bournemouth. He was on one of his selling trips."

"Does he have a regular itinerary?"

"I couldn't say. Keeps his schedule in a little notebook. Name of jewelers he does business with. Often checks them over in the evening."

"He must have a case of samples. The items he sells."

"Leaves that at the office. Never brings it home."

"Then he has an office? Here in London?"

"Victoria Street, I think. Though he's never told me exactly."

"Too bad. You could check with them if you had an address."

"That's what the police said. Of course, I have seen some of the jewelry he sells."

"Have you?"

"Clyde's given me several lovely pieces. More tea?"

"This is fine. Thanks."

"Then you rest here while I slip out. Now that you've paid your week's rent I can get some food in. Clyde always leaves me money for the housekeeping, but this time he's been gone so long I've spent it all. That's why I decided to rent our spare room." She got to her feet. "No, you sit there till I come back."

"I'll just finish my tea and then go up to my room." George peered around at the gimcracks scattered across the tables. Sea shells, a bisque figure of a sailor, paperweights which held down no papers, ashtrays of bizarre shapes. Would there be something hidden in the house that might explain Clyde Penton's disappearance?

"Back in half an hour!" Mrs. Penton was getting her coat from the hall closet.

"Take your time." He watched her hurry down the hall and out the street door into the rain.

George got to his feet and headed for the front parlor. The first thing he noticed, in the fading twilight, was a massive rolltop desk between the two street windows. He carefully raised the top and saw that the desk was completely bare. Not so much as a bent paper clip. He rolled down the top again and began to open the drawers.

The first was filled with cheap writing materials. The next was crammed with old jewelry catalogues. George lifted them out, carefully, flipped through the faded pages, but nothing caught his eye. He placed them back exactly as he had found them. The bottom drawer held an assortment of junk: galoshes, a pair of spectacles in a plastic case, an empty candy box, and worn leather gloves.

There was no other possible hiding place in the parlor. Most disappointing, he almost said aloud.

He then went upstairs to the Pentons' bedroom, leaving the door ajar so that he could hear, immediately, if Mrs.

Penton returned. The room was large, with an old-fashioned double bed. There was a dressing table between the two windows facing Walton Street and a heavy chest of drawers between the back windows. The chest would belong to Clyde Penton.

George searched through it, drawer by drawer, fingered the few articles of male clothing, poked into every corner. Nothing. He opened the single closet door and saw that it was almost filled with feminine clothing. At one end was an empty space where Clyde Penton obviously kept his wardrobe when he was home. One old tweed jacket hung on a wooden hanger. He examined each pocket. Nothing again.

He suddenly realized he'd been a fool to come here. Whatever made him think he could be a real detective? Preposterous! The best thing he could do now would be to get out of the house as quickly as possible.

He went down the hall to his own room to pack his bag and steal away while Mrs. Penton was still shopping. But the bed looked so inviting that he decided to relax for a few moments. And while he was resting, he thought: why not try to sort out the meager information he had uncovered about the missing husband?

Just what had he learned about Clyde Penton? Very little, to be sure. The man did not care to have his picture taken. He never wrote letters home to his wife. And he had avoided telling her where his office was located in London—that is, if he had an office. Scotland Yard would certainly be looking into that.

Anything else? Oh, yes! Clyde Penton had met his wife at Bournemouth where she'd been working in a tea shop. But there was nothing to explain why he was detained longer than usual on this trip. George frowned as he stared at the ceiling. Cora Penton seemed a good sort. Was it possible she had quarreled with her husband?

Must be something here, in the house, that would explain Clyde Penton's absence. He had a feeling that his unconscious mind had noticed something. Now he must force his conscious mind to identify it. Was it something Mrs. Penton had said? Some object he had seen?

His thoughts were interrupted by a brisk knocking on the door.

"Mr. Timmers? I've something to show you."

"Come right in!" He swung himself up from the bed.

Mrs. Penton entered with several small boxes of various shapes. "Did all my shopping. Still raining out. Thought you might care to have a look at these." She arranged the small boxes on the bed cover. "You seemed interested in the kind of jewelry my husband sells."

"I am, indeed."

"These are presents Clyde brought me. One from each of his trips."

"You showed these to the police?"

"They didn't seem interested. Clyde always brings me a bit of jewelry when he comes home. Each time in a box from a different city. Nothing really valuable, of course. But quite pretty." She selected a slim box and opened it. "Brought this back from his first trip after we were married." A single strand of pearls nested on blue cotton. "They're imitation, of course."

George could tell at a glance that they were nothing of the sort. Only the genuine article glowed like that. Why would Clyde Penton say they were imitation? "May I ask— how long have you and Mr. Penton been married?"

"Bit more than two and a half years. This box of pearls came from a shop in Portsmouth." She turned over the lid, to check the address. "You see? Says so right here—

Portsmouth. Next trip Clyde brought me a bracelet." The second box held a simple circle of gold etched with a neat floral design. "Isn't it sweet? Came from Folkestone." She was opening other small boxes as she talked. "This square box is from Bristol. Garnet brooch. Quite nice, don't you think?"

"Very nice, indeed."

After Mrs. Penton carried away her collection of boxes and jewelry, George turned off the light and again stretched out on the bed. In the fading twilight he went over each separate bit of information he had learned about the missing Clyde Penton—went over each one again and again . . .

He wakened with a start and reached for his familiar reading-lamp button, but it was not there. He felt a moment of panic before he remembered that he was not in his Knightswood Square study but in the house on Walton Street.

He got up and felt along the wall until he found the switch near the door. When his eyes had adjusted to the electric light he checked his watch. Past eight o'clock. Better slip out and find some dinner.

He retrieved his hat and waterproof from the wardrobe and carried them downstairs. Muffled sounds from the basement. The mouthwatering aroma of chops frying. George went to the head of the stairs. "I'm going out for a bite of food. Back in an hour."

Mrs. Penton came to the foot of the steps. "There's a pub at the corner of Pelham Street. Clyde says they serve the best food in the neighborhood."

"Thanks. I'll try it."

George found the pub and settled into a comfortable corner with a dry sherry. As the waiter handed him a menu he felt in his pocket for his reading glasses. Blast! He was getting forgetful. The spectacle case was sitting on the bedside table of his rented room. Spectacle case? The spectacles in the desk drawer of the Pentons' parlor. Was there something about them he should have noticed?

He explained to the waiter that he had forgotten his eyeglasses. What would he suggest for dinner?

"Oysters, perhaps? Fresh from the seaside. Only this mornin', sir."

"Splendid."

"Then we've an excellent steak and kidney puddin'—"

"I'll have that. With a half bottle of Medoc. Glass of Chablis with the oysters."

"Very good, sir."

Oysters from the seaside? Spectacles in the desk? George finished his sherry as he tried to pin down what was troubling him. Spectacles? Seaside?

The oysters reposed in their gritty shells like succulent gray pearls. George studied them as he tasted the Chablis. Pearls? Mrs. Penton's imitation pearls that were not imitation! Did she say her husband brought them from Folkestone? No, from Portsmouth. The gold bracelet had come from Folkestone.

Folkestone . . . Bessie Gray was murdered in Folkestone! Didn't Mrs. Penton say the brooch in the square box had come from Bristol? Where Emily Lynch had been electrocuted in her bath. And the murderer had worn spectacles in—was it West Hartlepool or Bristol? The spectacles in the rolltop desk!

He nearly choked on the oyster he was swallowing.

Was it possible? Could the missing Clyde Penton be the missing honeymoon murderer? George sat dumbfounded, his hands suddenly cold, and stared across the crowded pub. Was Clyde Penton also Charles Gray and Timothy Lynch and William Midgely? Could the small house on Walton Street be his hiding place between murders? Did he return to Cora Penton each time after he had killed his latest bride?

Certainly London was perfect for the killer's home base because of its easy access to every seacoast town. And Cora Penton had met her husband at Bournemouth—another seaside town! Had he married Cora with the idea of killing her in her tub?

Perhaps there were others he had killed whose deaths had gone unnoticed. Death by misadventure again! Were there still other items of jewelry left by the brides he had killed? Pathetic baubles which Clyde Penton brought home as gifts for his wife who waited for him so innocently in London.

What about that pearl necklace from Portsmouth? And the boxes Cora Penton hadn't opened?

George ate his dinner with increased appetite as he examined every possible connection between the missing husband and the missing murderer.

When he left the pub the rain had stopped. Low clouds scudded above the roof tops but there was a sprinkling of stars in the west. He felt like going straight home to Knightswood Square, to the familiar comfort of his own bed, but he knew that he must return to the house on Walton Street.

Perhaps, first, he should ring up Fred Trewe at New Scotland Yard. Years ago, George's firm, Drayton House, had published a definitive history of London crime. Was it ten years? Chief Inspector Frederick Trewe had written the introduction and they had become good friends, frequently meeting for a drink at the Savage Club. Fred Trewe had handled the investigation when the Yard cleaned up that Clarkson murder which George had solved from his bench in Knightswood Square. Perhaps Fred would know whether a bride had died in Portsmouth about six months after the Pentons were married . . .

George crossed the Brompton Road and stepped into a public phone kiosk.

A brusquely official voice at the Yard informed him that Chief Inspector Trewe was not in his office.

"This is Mr. Drayton. Friend of the Inspector's. Could you tell me if he might be in later?"

"Couldn't say, sir." The voice became somewhat more cordial. "He's out on an investigation. No tellin' when he might get back. Is there a message?"

"Would you tell him I called?"

"Certainly, sir. Mr. Drayton, wasn't it?"

"George Drayton . . . Hold on! You might ask him to check something. Was a young bride electrocuted in her bath about two years ago in Portsmouth?"

"Very good, sir." There was no change in his voice at the surprising request.

Mrs. Penton called down the hall from the back parlor as he closed the street door. "Won't you join me here by the fire?"

"Thank you." He hung his hat and waterproof on the newel post. "Bit raw out tonight. I'd like a hot tub before bed."

"Thought you might. I turned on the electric heater in the bath."

"Your husband's right about that pub." He sat in a low chair, facing her, near the gleaming gas heater. "They gave me a first-rate dinner."

"We eat there at least once whenever Clyde's home. I've always found it quite satisfactory." She was working at some embroidery as she talked.

"Unfortunately, I went out without my reading glasses."

"What a pity!"

"Waiter had to read the menu to me." He hesitated before he asked the important question. "You don't wear glasses?"

"Oh, no."

"And your husband?"

"His eyesight's even better than mine."

George wondered how far he could go, with his questions, without arousing Cora Penton's suspicions. He certainly didn't want to frighten her.

Fortunately she talked freely, rambled on, without having to be prodded. And, mostly, about her absent husband. ". . . kindest man in the whole world. So thoughtful. Such a good provider, as they say . . ."

He realized that she was embarrassed at having confessed, earlier, that she had been forced to rent him the spare room because she had run out of money.

"Of course, Clyde thought he would be back much sooner. First time he's ever stayed away so long. I really don't understand it."

She would never believe him if he told her that her husband, whom she thought so kind, had married several other young women—married and murdered them. And that tomorrow night he might be killing still another.

"I do have a bit of money of my own," she was saying. "Though I can't touch it. Papa left it to me. Better than a thousand pounds. But all I get is the interest. After we were married, Clyde and I went to my solicitor. Asked if I couldn't take at least part of the money to start a little business. Clyde was furious when he found we couldn't touch a shilling! First time I saw him lose his temper."

So Clyde Penton had married her for her money and discovered, too late, that he couldn't get his fingers on it. That, probably, was what had saved her life.

"It would have been ever so nice if we could've opened a little shop of our own. Clyde wouldn't have to take these long trips away from home. Perhaps a shop to sell his jewelry." She held up her arm to look at the circle of gold around her wrist.

"That's the bracelet he brought you? From Folkestone, wasn't it?"

"Yes. I wear it more than any of the other pieces. Although it does feel rather strange. Wearing something with somebody else's name inside."

"What's that? What do you mean?"

"As I told you, these presents he's given me were all samples of what Clyde sold. That's how he could get them wholesale. This bracelet had an inscription to show customers how it would look. A girl's name. Of course, there was no such girl and nobody ever sees it while I'm wearing it. Clyde's meant to take it somewhere and have the name removed, but—"

"What is the name?"

"It says, *To Bessie with love from Charlie.*"

There it was! The final proof. Bessie Gray dead in her bath at Folkestone. And the murderer had signed his name as Charles Gray when he registered at the Folkestone hotel.

"I'm rather tired," he said, getting to his feet.

"I do hope you sleep well."

"Thank you. And good night."

"Good night, Mr. Timmers."

George suddenly felt bone-weary as he went down the hall. He would talk to Fred Trewe first thing in the morning and tell him all that he had found out. The Yard could take over from there. He picked up his hat and waterproof and carried them upstairs.

The bedroom was freezing. If the bath was warm enough he would soak half an hour in the tub. Perhaps even read for a while. That always helped him relax.

After he undressed he found the paperback detective

novel in his bag. Under it were the newspaper clippings
about the honeymoon murders. He set them on the bedside
table. Have another look at them after his bath, he thought—
to refresh his mind before he talked to Fred Trewe tomorrow. He slipped his spectacles and the paperback into a
pocket of his robe and headed up the hall.

The bath glowed with warmth from the electric heater.
As George closed the door he noticed it was without a lock.
No matter. Mrs. Penton would hear him running his tub. He
selected a thick towel from a fresh pile and draped it over
the rack above the tub. Then he inserted the plug and turned
on the hot water. Almost immediately it was boiling. He
added cold water until the temperature was what he wanted.

Then he placed his spectacles and the paperback novel
on a chair which he pulled within arm's reach of the tub,
and hung his robe on a wall hook. After testing the water
again, he turned off both faucets and lowered his aching
body into the steaming water. Delicious warmth flowed
over him, but he still had a strong feeling that he was catching a cold.

As George soaped himself his thoughts returned to the
new bride. Was she asleep? Far away in some seacoast
hotel? Or was she, at this very moment, kissing her husband, unaware of what he might be planning for tomorrow
night . . .

Scotland Yard would have all the facts in the morning.
Fred Trewe would save her. Mrs. Penton would give them a
more detailed description of her husband. Surely, with that,
they would be able to track him down. If only Trewe had
been in his office!

George had discovered at least half a dozen incriminating facts about Clyde Penton. But the most damning piece
of evidence was the inscription on the bracelet.

To Bessie with love from Charlie.

Those words would surely convict the scoundrel. Tomorrow he would tell Fred Trewe all he had learned. Fred would have to do the actual work. Send out bulletins describing Clyde Penton. He and his associates at the Yard would capture the wretched man . . .

George dried his hands and reached for his spectacles. He settled down into the tub with his paperback novel and opened it to the page where he had left a thin ivory bookmark. The first thing that caught his attention among the printed words was the name of Ernest Timmers. So this was where he had gotten it! The name he had given, out of the blue, to Mrs. Penton. He had remembered it from this detective novel he had been reading after lunch.

But now, as he tried to read, George found it difficult to keep up with the fictional pursuit of Ernest Timmers. His plight was not as real as that of the unknown bride who, at this moment, might have only one more day of life, unless Clyde Penton was apprehended.

The steam from the water was clouding his eyeglasses. He took them off, set them on the chair with the paperback, and settled down again into the hot water. Some of the aches seemed to be soaking out of his weary body. He wished he had remembered to pack his cold tablets. Maybe a good night's rest would get rid of this feeling of impending pneumonia. At his age even the simplest head cold could be serious.

The closing door wakened him.

George opened his eyes to see a man, a complete stranger, approaching the tub. "Can't you see I'm taking a bath?"

The intruder kept coming.

"Get out of here!" George started to reach for his glasses but the man's eyes held him.

Those "awful peculiar" eyes. The sudden shock of recognition made George shiver.

"You're from the Yard." Clyde Penton's voice was low.

"What's that?" His body seemed immersed now in ice water.

"You're a copper."

"No! I'm nothing of the sort!"

"Then you're just a nosey meddler! Askin' my wife all those questions."

"What questions?" George's teeth were chattering. "What the devil are you talking about?"

"And what are these?" Penton held up the newspaper clippings about the honeymoon murders.

George clutched at the edge of the tub. His fingers slipped on the damp porcelain. He clawed at the rim but could not get enough of a grip to support himself.

Penton let the clippings fall from his hand and they scattered over the linoleum. "What are you trying to do?" The eyes moved closer. "You don't think you're going to get out of there? Do you?"

George tried to shout but his voice choked in his throat. He used his elbow as a lever in a desperate effort to lift himself; but he slipped and fell back into the water. It sprayed across wall, floor, and Clyde Penton.

Penton was soaked but he did not retreat. "Never thought you'd catch up with me." His voice was calm, without the slightest trace of emotion. "You or anybody else."

George was held by the staring eyes and hypnotic voice.

"How did you find out about me? Tell me that!" Penton was reaching down to pick up the glowing electric heater. "What was it brought you here?"

"Had no idea you were that other one. In the clippings—" Penton was holding the heater in both hands, ready to toss it into the water. One of those brides had been electrocuted in her bath by just such a heater.

"You're goin' to die, old chap. Police'll think you pulled this into the tub by accident. Cora will say she thinks you called out but when she came upstairs you were dead. They won't find me here. And they still won't connect me with those others. Lucky I read in the newspaper that Cora had reported me missing. Caught the first train down to London. If that hadn't brought me back you might've—"

George suddenly plunged both hands into the bath water. Scooped it up. Sprayed it at Clyde Penton—and at the gleaming electric heater.

There was a flash of sparks. The bathroom light went out.

Mrs. Penton called something from downstairs but her words were not clear.

Two powerful hands clutched George's shoulders. He felt himself thrust under the water. Breathing became an agony. He swallowed soapy water in great gulps. In some now-forgotten book he had once read how long it took for a man to drown. Complete insensibility came within one minute. Or was it less? He couldn't remember.

The water was churning. Great flooding waves of it.

Voices calling. Dozens of voices. Voices rolling and roaring, almost drowning out the sound of the rushing flood that was sweeping him into a black maelstrom. Finally there was only one voice. Far away. "George!" It echoed through the revolving darkness.

He tried to fight his way to the surface, up through the cascading torrent, higher and higher. "George!" The voice was coming closer. "George . . ." Light was seeping down from far above. He was choking. Gasping for air.

He made one last effort and felt his weary body rise to the top.

"George!"

He slowly opened his eyes.

Fred Trewe was looking down at him, his long face solemn. "Well, old friend. You've had a close one."

His body seemed to be wrapped in blankets. He was in bed. In the house on Walton Street. This knowledge helped him to say the name. "Clyde—Penton."

"We caught him."

George sighed. "How did you—know—I was—here?"

"Rang your flat when I got your message about Portsmouth. No answer, so I drove over to Knightswood Square. Caretaker told me he hadn't seen you since morning. That he asked you to come here—to talk to his niece. We'd already found you'd called the Yard from that public kiosk around the corner. When we got here the neighbors across the street had already phoned the police. Mrs. Penton was screaming bloody murder. Thought you were killing her dear husband."

"Is she—all right?"

"She will be. And Clyde Penton's been taken in charge. You were right about Portsmouth. There was a bride. Died there about two years ago. Nobody suspected foul play."

"Looks as though—I've solved those—honeymoon murders—for you." So many things to report. The garnet brooch from Bristol. The inscription on that bracelet.

"We found a return ticket to Blackpool in Penton's pocket. Key to a hotel room. Rang up Blackpool and had them check. Bride in the room waiting for her husband to return from London."

George relaxed into the warmth of the blankets. What was Fred saying? Must pay attention.

". . . solicitor arranging for her funds to be turned into cash. Some legal delay. That's why Clyde Penton was away from London longer than usual. Money only just came through. He would have killed her—tomorrow night. You saved her life."

George sneezed. No question about it. He was getting a cold. Dangerous at his age. He really must be more careful of his health.

He let the first dark curtain of sleep cover his eyes.

TRAGEDY ON NEW YEAR'S DAY

LILIAN JACKSON BRAUN

Early New Year's Day

Dear Tom,

Blessed New Year, and may God protect you wherever you are. It's four o'clock in the morning—strange hour for a mother to be writing to her son, but—Tom, dear, I'm so upset! A terrible thing has just happened on the back street behind our apartment! I'm here alone—John is working tonight—and I've just got to talk to somebody.

(Excuse the smudge. There's a *cat* sitting on the table, pawing the paper as I write. Just a stray cat that wandered in. That's part of the story.)

John went on special duty tonight with the Clean-Up Squad, so I curled up on the sofa and read a mystery, and at midnight I opened the window and listened to the horns blowing and the bells ringing. The street looked like a Christmas tree—green lights on the corner gas station—red neon on Wally's Tavern across the street—traffic lights winking. The cars were moving cautiously—we'd had a freezing rain, then more snow—and I said a little prayer that John would get home safely.

After that I put on the pink woolly robe he gave me for Christmas and had a snooze on the sofa, because I'd promised to wait up for him. Every few minutes the sirens would wake me—police cars or ambulances coming in to the hospital on the next block. Then I'd doze off again.

Suddenly a loud noise jolted me awake—like a shot or an explosion—and then I heard a bumping, creaking, crashing, and the sound of shattering glass! It came from the rear of the building.

I ran to the kitchen window and looked out, and there was this black car on the back street—up over the sidewalk—rammed into the brick wall of the warehouse. All the car doors were flung open, and the inside light was on, and a black figure was sprawled out of the driver's seat with his head hanging down in the snow.

I was stunned, but after a moment I came to my senses and telephoned the police. When I went back to the window, everything down on the street was ghastly quiet. No one had come running. There were no lights shining out from any of the apartments in our building. And there was this stranger, this man, hanging out of the wrecked car—dead or dying—and nobody cared.

I thought about you, Tom, and how I'd feel if you were helpless and alone like that—and so I went down to him. I grabbed John's hunting jacket—first thing I laid my hands on—and ran down three flights—didn't bother with the elevator—and out the back door and across the street.

When I saw how young he was, I thought my heart would break. He was about your age. His head was covered with blood, and the snow was stained, and I knew he was dead. There was nothing I could do—nothing—but I just couldn't leave him there alone, so I waited and prayed a little—until the blue light from the patrol car flashed into the street.

Then I realized I was standing in the snow in my fuzzy slippers—with a hunting jacket thrown over my pink robe—

so I ran back to the building and watched from the doorway.

An officer jumped out of the patrol car and looked at the man in the snow and yelled to his partner, "This one's had it! Better radio for a wagon."

And that's when I saw the cat—a black cat walking through the snow as if his feet hurt. He came to the door and mewed pathetically, and I let him in. Then he started rubbing against my slippers. I picked him up. My, his little feet were like ice! I was shivering, too, so we both came upstairs to get warm.

As I watched from the kitchen window, the ambulance came and they put the body on a stretcher and took it away. I shuddered! He was so young, and I couldn't help thinking of his mother and how the police would wake her in the middle of the night and take her downtown to the morgue.

I wonder who he was. Maybe it will be in the newspaper. I just noticed there are two telephone poles knocked down, too.

I wish John would get home. I'm writing this at the kitchen table. The cat sits here staring into my eyes and then looking at the letter, as if telling me what to write. He's an unusual cat—black as midnight—with empty yellow eyes. They're so deep you can see way down inside them.

That young man—I suppose he had been drinking too much at some New Year's Eve celebration. Maybe he lives in this building. I haven't met any of the neighbors yet. John says some of the tenants are real kooks, and he thinks it's best if we keep to ourselves. This is a run-down neighborhood, but the apartment is comfortable, and the rent is low, and it's close to the precinct station.

When John retires next year, we'll get a small house in Northport. I miss our little hometown—don't you?—but

I'm happy to be here with John. I never thought I'd be married again—and to a detective! Remember how you and I used to devour those stories about Hercule Poirot and Inspector Maigret?

I think I hear John coming. I'll finish this letter later.

New Year's afternoon

Here I am again! John is having a nap. I told him about the accident, and he said, "Another drunk driver! He was asking for it."

I didn't tell him how I went downstairs in my robe and slippers in the middle of the night (he wouldn't approve), and I had a hard time explaining how I happened to acquire a cat. The kitty is still here—follows me around like a shadow.

There! . . . I just heard it on the radio—first traffic fatality of the year—car rammed into a warehouse after hitting two utility poles—driver's name Wallace Sloan. He lived at 1830 Hamilton, and he was only *twenty-five!* Probably a single man, whooping it up on New Year's Eve. I'm thankful he didn't leave a wife and children.

This morning they towed the wreck away, and now the phone company is fixing the poles. I asked the superintendent of our building if anyone had lost a black kitty, and he didn't know.

Dear son, take care! We think of you constantly and pray that the fighting will end soon and you will be coming home.

Love from Mother

January 4—Wednesday afternoon

Dear Tom,

Glad the fruitcake arrived in good condition. Would you like more? Are they giving you decent food?

Did you get my letter about the accident? Well, I have more news! When John heard the victim's name, he said, "Why, that's the young fellow who owns the tavern across the street." John wasn't very sympathetic. Apparently the tavern is a real dive. John says Wally inherited it from his father a couple of years ago.

The next day I got the newspaper and read the obituaries, and that's when I learned the shocking news. That young man left a wife and four children! My heart went out to his family. I know what it's like to be a widow with a young son to raise, but imagine being left with *four* little ones to bring up. That poor woman!

Tom, you may think this is strange, but—I decided to go to the funeral! Of course, I didn't tell John. He thought I was going downtown to shop the January sales.

It was a terribly depressing funeral—hardly any flowers—and his wife looked like a mere child. My heart bled for them all. Afterwards, I learned something *very* interesting. Outside the funeral home I got into conversation with a neighbor of the Sloan family, and she said, "People think Wally was drunk that night, but I know he never touched liquor—not a drop. He worked hard—worked day and night. Must have been dead-tired and fell asleep at the wheel—that's what happened."

Doesn't that strike you as peculiar? He comes out of the tavern, cold-sober—starts his car—and immediately falls asleep!

You see, he was traveling east on the back street, so his car must have been in the big parking lot behind the gas station. Would he fall asleep after driving only half a block? Hardly! Besides, that street is full of frozen ruts that almost jolt you to death.

I don't know why I'm so concerned. Probably because I

read so many mystery stories. (Do you have time to read, Tom? Shall I send you some paperbacks?)

At any rate, I asked a few questions at the grocery store this afternoon and there are two facts I was able to verify: Wallace Sloan always parked in the lot behind the gas station, *and* he never took a drink!

The cat is still here—interested in everything I do. He's good company for me. I've named him Midnight, because he's pitch-black except for two yellow eyes that shine like electric lights.

Now I must set the table for dinner. John has been switched to the day shift. We're having meat loaf tonight—your favorite.

Love—Mother

Thursday, January 5

Dear Tom,

I've been listening to the news bulletins and thanking God you're in the ground crew. Are you all right? Is there anything we can send you?

I must tell you the latest! Today I called on Wally Sloan's widow. I told her a fib—I said I knew Wally at the tavern—and I offered my sympathy and gave her a home-made fruitcake and a large jar of my strawberry jam. She almost collapsed! I guess city folks don't expect things like that.

I thought it might comfort the young woman to know how I stood by on the night of the accident. When I told her about it, as gently as I could, she squeezed my hand and ran crying into the bedroom.

They have a nice house, rather expensively furnished. Her mother was there—a bossy, disagreeable woman.

I said to her, "Do you think your daughter will be able to manage?"

"She'll manage," she said, "but no thanks to *him*. He left nothing but debts."

"What a pity!" I said. "And Wally worked so hard."

She snorted. "Running a bar? What kind of work is that? He could have had a respectable office job downtown, but he'd rather associate with riffraff and spend his afternoons at the race track."

I thought, aha! The plot thickens! So Wally was a gambler! Well, Tom, I must admit I was beginning to lose sympathy for that young man, but I still felt sorry for his family. I came home and made an apple pie and tried to figure out a plan.

The cat was hanging around, getting his nose into everything, and I said to him, "Midnight, what would Miss Marple or Hildegarde Withers do in a case like this? I think they'd go snooping around—the way you do."

And so—after dinner when John left for his Lodge meeting—I started ringing doorbells in our building.

My first try was apartment 408. An elderly man came to the door, and I said, "Excuse me. I'm your neighbor in 410, and I picked up a stray cat on New Year's Eve. Somebody said it might belong to you. It's a black cat."

"No, ma'am," he said. "Our cat's ginger, and she's right there behind the radiator."

Well, I rang about twenty doorbells. Some people said no and slammed the door in my face, but most of the tenants were friendly. We'd exchange a few pleasant words, and then I'd mention the accident. Quite a few of them knew Wally from going to the tavern.

Then I rang the bell at 503. The middle-aged woman who answered looked like a floozy. She seemed quite interested in the young barkeeper and invited me in for a drink.

John would have a fit if he knew I accepted, but I just had a tiny beer.

She said, "The blankety-blank tavern's closed now, and you gotta do your drinking at home. It ain't decent!" Her eyes were glazed, and her hair was a mess. "Yep," she said, "Wally was a cute kid—and a big spender! That's what I like—big spenders."

"His bar business must have been very successful," I said.

She looked amused at my innocence. "Oh, hell, the kid had something going on the side. Don't we all?"

"I know Wally liked to play the horses," I said.

"Play the horses! *Play* 'em?—why, he was a bookie!" I must have appeared shocked, because she added, "You didn't know that, did you? Well, he kept it quiet. He'd lose his liquor license if the cops ever found out. He used Gus for a pickup man."

"Gus?"

"You know Gus—the mechanic at the gas station. He picked up bets for Wally. Dincha hear about the big hassle at the bar New Year's Eve? Gus was too slow in paying off one of his customers, and the guy tried to take it out of his hide."

"Was Gus hurt?"

"Just a shiner. Wally threw 'em both out before it got real bad. The guy bet two hundred bucks, and the horse paid off fifteen-to-one. That was Larry. You know Larry on the third floor here? Big guy. Male nurse at the hospital. Could've broke Gus in two!"

"Oh, yes. Larry," I said.

Later I went down to the lobby and looked at the mail boxes, and there was an L. Marcus in 311. So I went up and rang his doorbell (to see if he had lost a black cat) but he wasn't home.

I wonder why Gus was slow in paying off. Fifteen-to-one! My goodness! That would come to $3000. Tom, do you suppose Wally "welshed," as they say? I'm beginning to wonder if his accident had anything to do with that bet!

If I hear more, I'll write.

Love from Mother

P.S.—Now it's Friday. I didn't get a chance to mail this yesterday, so will add the latest information. This morning I was stroking Midnight and thinking about the accident on the back street, and I could recall the scene plain as day. Everything was black and white—the black blood on the white snow—the black warehouse—snow-covered cars parked here and there—black tire tracks where Wally's car had swerved up over the opposite sidewalk—two black telephone poles leaning every-which-way.

And then I remembered something about Wally's car. It was all black against the snow, and it should have been partly white! Even if the collision knocked off most of the snow, it should have had *some* on the roof—if it had been parked behind the gas station all evening.

Tom, do you remember Uncle Roy's accident with his car three years ago? Do you remember what caused it? Well, I got to thinking about that, and it gave me an idea. So I went to see Gus.

John had ridden to work with his partner, so I took our car to the gas station and asked Gus to check the fan belt because it was making a funny noise. (Another fib.) He still had a lavender circle under one eye. While he was looking at the fan belt I started talking about the accident.

"How do you figure it happened?" I said. "We all know Wally didn't drink. Maybe something went wrong with his car. Maybe he lost control of it."

Gus took his head out from under the hood. "Yeah," he

said, "that's what happened, all right. He told me something was wrong with the steering, and he left the car here for a checkup. But before I had a chance to work on it he drove it away and wrecked it."

"I don't understand much about cars," I said. "What could go wrong to cause an accident like that?"

"Could be a steering knuckle got loose. Hard to tell exactly what happened after a car's smashed up so bad."

Tom, I think the time has come for me to speak to John about this situation—to tell him everything I know. Don't you agree?

I'm mailing you some brownies. Hope they stay fresh.

Love—Mother

Monday, January 9

Dear Tom,

A quick note to let you know that my suspicions were correct!

After dinner Friday night I had a serious talk with John. I said, "John, dear, do you believe in Providence? When Wally Sloan was killed, Providence arranged to have a detective's wife looking out the window—a snoopy old gal with nothing to do but meddle in other people's business."

He looked at me as if I was losing my mind.

"I've found out a few things, John," I said, "and I think the police should take Gus in for questioning—I mean Gus at the gas station on the corner. Isn't there something a mechanic could do to a car to make it go out of control at the first bump in the road? Couldn't he loosen something in the steering arrangement? Because I think Wally was murdered!"

That was Friday night . . . Well, five minutes ago John telephoned from the station. He said the Homicide men got a confession from Gus! He took Larry's two hundred dollars and lost it in a crap game—never placed the bet at all! And when Larry put the pressure on him for the $3000, Gus tried to wiggle out of the mess by blaming the bookie. Then he rigged Wally's car for an accident, which he hoped would be fatal.

Just thought you'd like to know the outcome. John is quite proud of me. He says I made a deduction just like Sherlock Holmes or Ellery Queen. It was the snow missing from the top of Wally's car that convinced me Gus was lying—he *had* worked on the car, and indoors! John says I should go right on reading mystery stories!

Love from
Mother

P.S.—John is going to buy me a pedigreed kitten to keep me company. Midnight has disappeared. He must have jumped out the window—or something. We haven't seen him since Friday night.

LARCENY AND OLD LACE

ROBERT ARTHUR

A crossing bell clanged. Headlights of waiting automobiles glinted into the coach car. The train began to slow down. Grace Usher looked up from her book.

"We must be coming into the Milwaukee station," she said. "High time, too. It's nine p.m. We're four hours late."

"Mr. Bingham will be wondering what happened to us," Florence Usher agreed. She straightened her black jacket and tidied her hair. Florence prided herself on her youthfulness—she was 70, two years younger than Grace.

"Anyway," Grace said with satisfaction, "it gave me a chance to finish both John Dickson Carr's and Ellery Queen's latest. My, they were exciting! I do love a good mystery."

"I must read them next." Florence made a note in a small red notebook which she carried in a voluminous leather purse almost big enough to be a briefcase. "Did you ring for the porter, Grace?"

"And have to tip him a dime? Nonsense! We can carry our luggage quite well by ourselves."

"But I thought he would help us find a taxi and tell us how to get to Mr. Bingham's office."

"Florence, please don't be provincial. After all, Milwaukee is only a city. And though we've never been in a large city before, we know a great deal about every large city in the world. Why, my goodness, we each have read more

than a thousand mystery novels, haven't we? We know
about London from Agatha Christie and Margery Alling-
ham, about Miami from Brett Halliday, about Chicago from
Craig Rice, about Paris, San Francisco, New York—"

"Yes," Florence interrupted, "it's true we know a great
deal about life from reading so many mysteries—but just
the same—"

"Just the same fiddlesticks! I consider we are fully
equipped to meet almost any situation, all due to the liberal
education we have acquired through reading mysteries,"
Grace said. "Now we had better get off this train. Mr. Bingham will be waiting for us—at least, I hope so."

Mr. Bingham was. He had been waiting for several
hours, consoling himself from frequent nips from a bottle in
his dingy office, whose glass door bore the legend *E. Bingham—Attorney at Law—Real Estate and Insurance*. Now
he was chewing mints as he poured tea for Grace and Florence Usher. The tea had been brewed over a hot plate
whose sole prior use had been for brewing coffee strong
enough to help him over a night-before.

"How thoughtful of you!" Grace said, sipping her tea.
"Nothing like a nice cup of tea to refresh one after a long
train trip. We broke down, you know, fifty miles west."

"I was worrying about you, dear ladies," Bingham assured them, slipping another mint into his mouth. He
showed yellow teeth in a smile the effect of which was
spoiled by his large nose and his small eyes, set too close
together. "I feared you had decided not to come to claim
your little inheritance."

"We have burned our bridges behind us," Florence assured him. "When we received your letter informing us that
our nephew Walter had left us his house and furnishings,
we sold the lending library we had run since we retired

from schoolteaching, said goodbye to everyone, and came to stay."

"You see—" Grace's bonnet nodded as she leaned forward—"for seventy years we have lived in a small town. And now we are anxious for broader horizons."

A bit of mint lodged in Bingham's long, scrawny throat.

"Quite so. Kaff—kaff—quite so. Er—I thought that as soon as you sold your nephew's house you would return to Kiskishaw and—"

"Heavens, no!" Grace told him. "We want to *live*, Mr. Bingham! We are going to transform Walter's house into a boarding house for writers and artists."

"We'll meet such fascinating, creative people," Florence chimed in. "The talk at the dining table will be like music to our poor, starved ears."

Mr. Bingham set down his teacup, went over to the bottle, turned his back, and poured himself more than just a nip.

"Really," he said, his tone hollow, "I advise you to sell. The house is run down, taxes are high, the neighborhood unsavoury—"

But Grace merely shook her head.

"We will cope," she said. "Now please tell us something about poor Walter. After all, we haven't seen him in the last twenty-five years."

"How did he die?" Florence asked, pressing her gloved hands together in eager interest.

"Well—" Mr. Bingham rubbed his high forehead distractedly—"he died of a form of heart failure—"

"I suppose," Grace agreed, "that you could call three bullets in the heart a form of heart failure. However—"

"*Two* bullets in the heart," Florence corrected. "The coroner's report said the other missed by several inches. You see, Mr. Bingham, we read all about it in the Milwaukee paper before your letter arrived. We follow all the crime news. Of course, we didn't know then it was our nephew who had been killed. We weren't very much surprised to find out, though. We always felt Walter would come to a bad end."

"As a boy he used to torment puppies," Grace added. "And he was expelled from three colleges, like his father."

"Our brother Henry, you know. He disappeared years ago." Florence sipped her tea daintily. "We suspected he was in the penitentiary. But if he was he didn't use his own name. Henry always did have family pride."

Mr. Bingham, having finished another medicinal snort, wiped his lips with a handkerchief that was not quite clean.

"Of course," he said. "Well, Walter called himself Walter Smith, and until I found a memorandum among his papers directing his property be left to you I did not know his real name, or that he had any relatives.

"He was—ah—well, to be frank, a man of mystery. His source of income was not—ah, known. His house is a large one on the edge of town, but how he acquired it no one knows. One night last month he was entering his home about midnight when he was shot to death on his own doorstep by a mysterious assailant. The police have been unable to catch the killer or even find a motive."

"I'm sure whoever did it had a very good reason," Grace said, patting her lips fastidiously. "When Walter was young we often wanted to kill him ourselves."

Mr. Bingham mopped his brow.

"Er, yes, of course," he said. By now he was having difficulty focusing on the two little old ladies, bright as crickets for all their sober, small-town dresses, their old-fashioned bonnets, and gray hair.

"But again, dear ladies, let me urge you to sell your nephew's house. It is really in a shady neighborhood—

tainted by a murder—and I have a purchaser who wants to tear it down and build a gas station—"

"No. We intend to live there and run a boarding house for intellectuals," Grace told him firmly. "Now, Mr. Bingham, please let us have the key and the address and a taxi will take us there."

Mr. Bingham, who had once had an iron-willed aunt, produced the key and wrote down an address.

"There," he croaked unhappily. "I do hope you have a—ah—a peaceful night. I do hope so."

"Why shouldn't we?" Grace asked. "Come, Florence, I'm all eagerness to see our inheritance. I've been thinking of a name for it. Do you suppose we dare call it The House of Usher?"

They rustled out. From the window Mr. Bingham saw them lift their umbrellas and hail a taxi. He groaned, poured another drink, and went down the gloomy hall to another door on which he knocked timidly, then entered.

Inside, a large man in a discreetly tailored suit lounged in a leather chair, smoking a cigar. The room was furnished with a great deal more elegance than Bingham's and the door bore the legend *Gordon Enterprises, Inc.*

Harry Gordon blew a smoke ring as Bingham entered.

"Well, Ed, how much did the house cost me?"

Bingham mopped his brow again. "They won't sell, Harry."

"Won't sell?" The big man brought his feet down solidly on the floor. "Maybe you didn't persuade them right."

"They're going to open a boarding house called The House of Usher."

Bingham lowered himself into a chair.

"They're tired of hick towns," he sighed. "They want to reside in a metropolis like Milwaukee and live the life artistic. They're two little old ladies and they have whims of steel."

"You told them about their nephew being bumped off."

"Yes. I told them the place had a sinister reputation, their nephew was a man of mystery—all that stuff."

"You didn't tell them he was the smartest blackmailer who ever put the bite on Harry Gordon?"

"Of course not."

Harry Gordon scowled. "I wish I knew where the devil he hid those ledger sheets he lifted," he said. "They've got to be in that house someplace—he wouldn't have trusted them very far from him. But three times we've been over that dump and still we can't find them. Damn it, if they ever got into the hands of the special prosecutor—"

He clamped his teeth down on his cigar. Bingham used his none too clean handkerchief for another face-mopping job.

"If we couldn't find the papers they'll stay hid. Those two old bats will get tired of that gloomy morgue soon, then we'll be able to buy it cheap and tear it down. There's nothing to worry about."

"Maybe we should rough them up a little."

"No, no, nothing like that! That would really start the cops boiling. Newspapers and the public always go for little old ladies like that. They remind everybody of somebody's mother."

"Anyway, they'll get a scare that may send them chasing," the big man grunted. "I sent Tiny to the house tonight for another look around. If they bump into him they may decide to sell, and sell fast. Tiny isn't the kind of guy two little old ladies would care to meet in a dark old house late at night!"

*   *   *

"Well," Florence Usher said doubtfully, "it *is* a big house, isn't it? And awfully dark."

"All houses are dark until the lights are lit," Grace informed her. "Let's go inside and put on some lights."

They picked up their suitcases and went up the flagstoned walk that led from a dimly lit street to the old, brown, somehow sinister house that sat back amid scraggly trees. A shutter creaked and Florence gave a little gasp.

"Please, Florence," Grace said, "control yourself. Every mystery story is full of sound effects like creaking shutters. They mean nothing except that some hinge needs a little oil. Give me the key and we'll go in."

Florence handed her the key. Grace inserted it into a very modern lock in a very heavy front door, and the door opened. This time there were no creaks. They stepped into a hall and fumbled until Florence found a light switch. The overhead light snapped on.

"Well!" Grace said approvingly. "Very nice furnishings. Walter was certainly getting money from some source, though I doubt if he was earning it . . . Florence, what *is* it?"

"I heard a noise," Florence said in a strained whisper. "There's someone upstairs."

"You must not let your imagination . . . There *is* someone upstairs." Grace lowered her voice. "It must be a burglar—someone who knew the house was empty and took the opportunity to search it."

"Let's leave at once," Florence whispered between trembling lips. "Let's send the police and—and spend the night at a hotel."

"Don't be a chicken, Florence! After all, we know all about the technique of trapping burglars—it's thoroughly explained in many mystery novels. Remember your Arsène Lupin and Raffles. Besides, it is well known that burglars abhor violence—every criminal sticks to his trade, and burglars burgle. Follow my orders and we will teach Mr. Burglar a thing or two!"

"I—I'd rather not," Florence objected, but Grace was already tiptoeing toward the stairs. She removed her shoes, motioned to her sister to do the same, and in stockinged feet, only their skirts whispering, the two slowly climbed the stairs.

As they reached the second floor the sound of someone moving about became louder. The sound came from behind a closed door near the head of the stairs. Grace and Florence tiptoed toward the door. Grace looked confident and Florence looked unhappy.

"No noise. Let me peek through the keyhole." Grace bent and put her eye to the old-fashioned keyhole. Inside a light was on. A short, heavy-set man with a face like a dish of scrambled eggs was tapping the walls with his knuckles. Tiny Tinker had been a heavyweight prizefighter, but not a good one.

"There's a man in there looking for something," Grace reported. "We must get him to come out."

"I don't *want* him to come out!" Florence wailed. "Please, let's *go*."

Grace ignored the plea.

"After reading all those mysteries we certainly know how to handle this," she retorted. "Practically all of them agree that the heel of a woman's shoe makes a splendid weapon. As we wear Dr. Borden's Sensible Shoes, with extra heavy heels, I'm sure we're well equipped. Now I'll stand on one side of the door, you stand on the other. We'll each hold a shoe in our right hand. Then I'll toss my other shoe down the stairs—"

A moment later Tiny Tinker, inside the room, heard a clattering noise. "Rats," he muttered to himself and went on rapping the walls. But the noise was repeated a few moments later (when Florence, after some urging, threw her left shoe down the stairs). Tiny, never a great brain, decided the time had come to investigate. He opened the door and stuck his head out, blinking into the darkness.

"Whazzat?" he asked. Then all the knockouts he had ever suffered came back to haunt him. Even a skull like his was not made to withstand the impact of two heels on Dr. Borden's Sensible Shoes.

Tiny went down for the count.

"Well, we're making progress," Grace Usher said determinedly.

She looked down at Tiny Tinker, who lay on the floor of the room. They had been able to drag him in but not to lift him onto the couch. So they had stretched him out and with a lot of brightly colored neckties from a rack beside the door they had lashed his legs to the couch and his hands, stretched up over his head, to a handsome cherrywood desk. Snoring on the floor, Tiny Tinker looked like a cannibal's Thanksgiving dinner ready for the pot.

"*Now* can we call the police?" Florence asked.

"Certainly not. Take a look at this burglar. See how well dressed he is. He's no ordinary burglar." (He wasn't. Tiny was Harry Gordon's bodyguard.)

"What of it? He's so ugly it makes me nervous to look at him."

"Florence, I am very disappointed in you." Grace surveyed her sister disapprovingly. "After all these years we've talked about living life and having adventures, and now that we're really doing it you keep wanting to call the police. I *really*—"

The phone, which sat on the desk, rang. It rang again. Grace started toward it.

"But Grace—"

"Maybe it's for us."

"Who would be phoning us? Really, Grace—"

But Grace picked up the phone. "Hello?" she said pleasantly. Then she covered the mouthpiece. "It *is* for us! It's Mr. Bingham!

"Yes, Mr. Bingham?" she said into the mouthpiece. At the other end Mr. Bingham sounded as if he might be breathing hard. He asked if they were all right—if everything was quiet—he just managed to refrain from asking if they had heard any unusual sounds.

Beside him, Harry Gordon was chewing a cigar and growling in his ear, "Damn it, Tiny just has to be there! They must have bumped into him by now."

While Florence listened in disbelief, Grace assured Mr. Bingham that everything was quiet, the house seemed lovely, and thank you for being so thoughtful. She hung up, leaving Mr. Bingham and Harry Gordon staring at each other with disbelief.

"Damn it," Gordon swore again, "maybe Tiny left before they got there. We'll give him half an hour to check in. Then we'll go over there and see what gives."

In Nephew Walter's house of mystery, Florence and Grace were also staring at each other.

"Grace, how could you tell such lies? He could have brought the police and taken away this—this criminal on the floor."

"But we don't *want* him taken away." Grace summoned all her patience. "We have to question him first."

"Question him about what?"

"About Walter's death and what this man is looking for—something Walter must have hidden. My goodness, don't you see? This is a real mystery! We're plunged right into the middle of it. It's a chance we never dreamed we'd have."

"What in the world are you talking about?"

"I mean this is our chance to solve a mystery, like all those amateur detectives we've read about."

"But hardly any of them were women," Florence pointed out.

"Stuart Palmer's Hildegarde Withers is a woman. Also, she is a schoolteacher. I see no reason we shouldn't be able to do anything she could. We'll start by searching this room."

"Well, all right," Florence agreed, a faint flush in her cheeks at the excitement of the chase. "But first we must scan the room for possible places of hiding."

Together they scanned the room. It was a sort of library-den, with Walter's bedroom beyond. It was furnished expensively—the cherrywood desk, several new easy chairs, a shelf of books, all mysteries, hand-blocked wall paper, an Oriental rug. On the desk was an expensive pen and blotter set—which had been ripped apart—and two framed photos. One of them was of a busty young lady wearing a scanty costume. Across it was tenderly inscribed *To Walty with love from Peaches*. The other one brought a tender expression to Florence's face.

"Look," she said. "The picture of you and me with Walter when he finally managed to graduate from high school twenty-five years ago. I confess I've always felt a little guilty about giving him a passing grade in Civics."

"As things turned out, he certainly didn't deserve it," Grace agreed, studying the faded photo of themselves, with Walter, a head taller, standing between them. Walter had had a rather narrow face, with a rather thin mouth and sharp eyes set closely together. He had had fine wavy hair, however. "I'd forgotten how close together Walter's eyes were.

But we were quite good-looking, then. Yes, and our figures were hardly inferior to that of this—this female with whom Walter seems to have been so friendly."

"Please, Grace!" Florence cast a scandalized glance down at Tiny Tinker, who was groaning softly on the floor. "It isn't like you to be indelicate with a strange man in the room. Anyway, it proves there was some good in Walter. He did remember us even after all these years. And he thought enough of us to leave us his house. Perhaps we always thought too harshly of him."

"Perhaps," Grace said, her features softening. "In spite of his mischief he always did seem fond of us. But back to business—this room has already been searched. The desk has been ransacked, the chairs examined, the rug taken up, the couch almost turned inside out—the work obviously of this individual on the floor. Perhaps we should make him tell us just what he is looking for."

Together they looked down at Tiny Tinker. His face twitched with the pain of approaching consciousness.

"Florence," Grace remarked thoughtfully, "I wonder if this man killed Walter and now has come back to the scene of the crime to look for something he couldn't find at the time?"

"Killed Walter?" Florence jumped a little. "Then he's not just a burglar—he's a murderer. Grace, we *must* call the police!"

"Did you ever read a detective story where the police solved the case?"

"Well—"

"Of course not. Therefore it's up to us. We must see justice done for dear Walter, even if he was a crook of some kind. This creature is regaining consciousness. We'll question him."

Tiny Tinker opened one eye and looked up at them blearily.

Florence shuddered. "What makes you think he'll answer our questions?" she asked.

"Surely one thousand mystery novels have taught us the correct procedure as to how to question a gangster! We can't be polite about it. If brutality is called for, we'll have to be brutal."

"You've never hurt a fly in your life," Florence retorted. "How can you start being cruel now?"

Grace ignored the question. "Sssh! He's opening his other eye."

Tiny Tinker blinked painfully up at them.

"What hit me?" he asked.

"We hit you, young man," Grace told him. "We slugged you with the heels of our Dr. Borden's Sensible Shoes. Now we have your hands and feet tied securely so you cannot take it on the lam, or make a getaway."

Tiny Tinker yanked his arms and legs, found the facts as stated, and looked up at them with a tinge of awe on his scrambled features.

"The Usher sisters," he announced. "That's who you dames must be!"

"We find your knowledge of our identity very suspicious," Florence told him, bolder now that she saw the neckties were going to hold.

"Say, you two better untie me," Tiny Tinker said menacingly. "If you know what's good for you. Harry will be looking for me."

"Florence," Grace instructed, "make a note that this person is employed by someone named Harry."

"Certainly." Florence found paper and pencil in the desk and jotted down *Emply by smne nmd Harry*. A trace of alarm appeared on their captive's face.

"I didn't say nothing!" he protested. "What're you two up to, anyway?"

"It's quite simple," Grace said. "You killed our nephew Walter—"

The alarm on Tiny Tinker's face grew astoundingly. "How'd you know that? I mean I didn't neither, you're crazy."

"Aha!" Grace turned a look of triumph on her sister. "We *are* making progress. This man admits he killed poor Walter."

"I don't!" Tiny shouted. "Nothing of the kind. I didn't kill him and I didn't admit nothing. If you know what's good for you, you'll untie me double quick. You're messing in something that's a lot too big for you."

"Aha!" Grace chortled. "Florence, make a note. The prisoner admits he is part of a large criminal conspiracy."

"Yes, Grace." Florence made a note.

Tiny writhed harder. "I didn't! I didn't admit no such thing! What're you two trying to pin on me, anyway?"

"We are simply solving a crime in the accepted manner—just as we have learned it from more than one thousand mystery novels," Grace told him. "Now young man, who's the Big Brain?"

"Who's the what?"

"The Big Brain. Mr. Big . . . Oh, whom do you work for, stupid?"

"I work for Harry Gordon and don't call me stupid. Who can tell what you two dames are talking about?"

"Florence, make a note. Prisoner identifies the master mind of the criminal conspiracy as one Harry Gordon."

"Wait a minute, wait a minute!" Tiny almost wept from sheer frustration. "I didn't never say no such thing."

"*Two* double negatives in one sentence!" Florence exclaimed. "Where did you go to school?"

"Where did I go to school?" Tiny blinked. "What's that got to do with it?" Tiny could hold out against a team of expert detectives for 48 hours, but the methods of the Usher sisters confused him.

"Never mind," Grace said loftily. "Now let us sum up. You have admitted you killed our nephew Walter, that you work for one Harry Gordon, that he is head of a vast criminal enterprise, and presumably you were searching this house for something of Walter's which Harry Gordon wants. Now what is it? Dope? Hot ice? Stolen bonds? Plates for counterfeit money? You might as well tell us, for we'll get it out of you anyway."

Tiny stared up at two pairs of steel-gray eyes giving him the same looks that had made generations of schoolboys quail. He shuddered.

"Yeah," he gulped, "I guess you will. Okay, I'll talk. Because you can't do nothing about it, see. Harry Gordon has this town sewed up. So this is how it was—"

Tiny Tinker started talking, and Florence started taking notes. Tiny had his eye on the clock. If he could talk long enough, Harry would get there eventually. Harry would know how to take care of two sharp old witches like these, in their black taffeta and sweet-little-old-lady bonnets. Harry would probably put 'em on two broomsticks and fly 'em to the moon.

"So there we have the picture!" Grace said when at last Tiny had finished talking. "Walter was a bookkeeper for this Harry Gordon. Walter stole some records of Gordon's criminal activity. But instead of turning them over to the police, Walter hid them and blackmailed Gordon who got tired of paying and sent this—what is your name?"

"Just call me Tiny," Tiny sighed.

"Sent this Mr. Tiny to search the house. Walter came

home too soon and Mr. Tiny shot him. Since then no one
has been able to find the incriminating documents. They're
still somewhere in the house."

"Which must be why Mr. Bingham tried to discourage us
from coming here!" Florence exclaimed. "He's in it too!"

"And now we are on the point of smashing this criminal
ring!" Grace breathed, her eyes shining. "What joy, Florence, what a triumph! Even Nero Wolfe would be proud of
us. All we have to do is find those hidden papers, turn them
over to the special prosecutor whom the governor has ap-
pointed, and Harry Gordon, Mr. Bingham, Mr. Tiny here,
and many other nefarious individuals will be incarcerated."

"Huh?" Tiny wrinkled his brow. But Florence looked a
little doubtful. "How can we hope to find the missing papers if they couldn't?" she asked. "I still say we should call
in the police."

"Florence, you have a negative attitude. First we have to
think the same way as Nephew Walter did. We must put
ourselves in his place. Suppose *we* were blackmailers—
where would *we* hide incriminating documents?"

"Well—" Florence knit her brows.

"How large are these documents?" Grace asked Tiny.

"Size of a ledger page. Walter got away with about
twenty pages."

"Big enough to fill a briefcase," Grace mused. "Now let
me think—if I were Walter—"

"I think—" Florence began, but a voice from the door interrupted her and made both sisters whirl around with little
eeeking sounds.

"Please go right ahead, ladies. But you don't mind if I
come in?"

Harry Gordon advanced into the room, puffing on his
cigar. Mr. Bingham danced nervously behind him. Harry
Gordon came toward Grace and Florence like a truck about

to crush two small gray kittens. He stopped and fixed them with a sardonic glance.

"Well, ladies, you've had a ball with my boy Tiny, haven't you? But the party's over now. This is the end of the line. Sit down in those two chairs until Ed and I get Tiny untied. Then we'll decide what to do with you!"

Tiny Tucker, released from the neckties, sat subdued in a corner. Harry Gordon sat back in one of the easy chairs and pointed his cigar at Grace and Florence, who were huddled on the sofa beyond the desk, subdued but still defiant, like two ruffled hens.

"They made Tiny talk," Gordon rumbled. "I say we ought to put them in cold storage."

"No, no, Harry," Mr. Bingham urged, nervously rubbing his forehead. "Please believe me, what they know would never stand up in court. And as I said before old ladies like these are dynamite. Bump 'em off and the newspapers would jump right off the presses screaming. Every fix you have in would come unstuck. Believe me, Harry, whatever you do, don't ever lay a finger on a sweet little old lady."

"Then what do you suggest?" Harry glared broodingly at the sisters.

"Get them out of town and make sure they never come back."

"My way, they'd be sure never to come back."

"If you think you can intimidate us, you're very much mistaken!" Grace bristled. Florence turned on her furiously.

"He is not mistaken. He *has* intimidated us. Anyway, he's intimidated *me*. And I'm willing to make a bargain with him."

A flicker of interest showed in Harry Gordon's black eyes.

"What kind of a bargain, sister?"

"You want this house because it has certain papers hidden in it. All right, we'll sell you the house, just as it is, and you can find the papers for yourself."

"Go on."

"We'll take a trip around the world, leaving as soon as we have the money."

"Florence, I will not bargain with criminals!" Grace cried.

"Be quiet, Grace. You've been the boss up until now. Well, now I'm in charge. Mr. Gordon, how about it?"

"Pay 'em off and get rid of 'em," Bingham pleaded. "We'll find the papers if we have to tear the house down."

"I dunno." Harry Gordon puffed a cloud of smoke. "It'd be cheaper just to bury them."

"We wouldn't stay buried, do you hear?" Florence told him. "We'd—rise up and haunt you."

"I wouldn't be surprised if you did at that," Harry Gordon said, "All right, I'll give you ten thousand in cash for the house, and you leave town tonight."

"Fifteen!" Florence retorted.

"Why, this house is worth at least twenty thousand dollars!" Grace said in great indignation.

"You're in no position to bargain, lady," Harry Gordon said. "All right, fifteen thousand."

"In cash. And you drive us directly to the station," Florence stipulated.

"A deal. We'll pick up the cash at my office. Tiny!"

"Uh—yes, boss?"

"These old—these ladies didn't find those papers before I got here, did they?"

"No, boss. They haven't touched nothing—nothing but me, that is. They spent the whole time questioning me." Tiny rolled his eyes. "Lucky they ain't on the force."

"All right, let's go. Tiny, stay here. Don't leave this

house until you find what I want. Or I'll call in the wreckers and tear it down to the foundations."

"Right, boss."

"Just one thing." Florence stood up. The set of her chin was determined. "We have nothing to read on the train. We prefer mysteries. We'd like to take two of Walter's books with us."

"Oh, you would, would you?" Harry Gordon's tone was silky. "Which two do you have in mind?"

"Those at the end of the shelf—the two green ones."

"Sure. Hand them over to me, Tiny." Gordon held the books in his hand while his eyes searched Florence's face. "You're smart, sister. You figure Walter microfilmed the papers and hid them in these books, huh? Ed, help me search the—" he looked at the titles—*"The Collected Works of Edgar Allan Poe, Volumes One and Two."*

He and Ed Bingham painstakingly demolished the two old books. They cut open the covers, slit the binding, riffled through the pages. Finally, looking peevish, Harry Gordon handed the wreckage of the two books to Florence. She opened her voluminous purse and dropped them inside.

"Come on, let's get going," Gordon growled. "I'm tired of you two and your ideas. I guess you did just want something to read. But if I thought you were playing games with me—" He glared at them, then led the way to the door. "Come on, there's a midnight train."

A crossing bell clanged. Headlights of waiting automobiles glinted into the coach car. The train began to pick up speed.

"Just midnight," Grace said, her tone discontented. "Florence, do you realize we were in Milwaukee only three hours?"

"But my, they were exciting hours." Florence yawned. "Really, we must go to bed. We need our sleep."

"How can you expect to sleep after having sold out to a gang of thugs and cutthroats? I certainly won't. Why, we've let Walter's murderers go free, and for just a few thousand dollars!"

"Walter was always a rapscallion," Florence answered. "I certainly did not intend to lose my life over him."

"Just the same, nothing like this ever happened in *any* of the books we have read. I feel mortified."

"I don't think you should, Grace. Remember, we have those two books of Walter's, don't we?" Florence drew out the two volumes of Poe's Works and put them on her sister's lap.

"What good are they?" Grace objected. "The criminals searched these books thoroughly. They didn't find the papers or microfilms in them."

"Because they aren't there. Only the clue is there."

"What clue?"

"You said we must think like Walter. Well, we introduced him to Poe as a boy, didn't we? We gave him these two volumes, in fact. That he still kept them showed me he was still fond of Poe, and that gave me the clue to his thinking."

"You're talking in riddles," Grace said fretfully.

"Not at all. In one of these volumes, *The Purloined Letter* comes right after our favorite—and Walter's—*The Fall of the House of Usher.*"

"Oh." Enlightenment began to spread over Grace's face. "The story about hiding the valuable document inside an old envelope that was left out in plain sight!"

"Exactly. So—" Florence reached deeper into her capacious purse and pulled out a framed photograph—the one which showed herself, Grace, and Walter. Less than an hour before it had stood on Walter's desk.

"Walter had as much sentiment as a rattlesnake," she

said. "Why should he keep a picture of himself with us? Only because a picture of yourself and two maiden aunts is about as unsuspicious as anything can be. Nobody gave it a second thought."

"But how did you get it?" Grace asked. "I didn't see you take it."

"In the confusion when Mr. Gordon and Mr. Bingham were bending over to untie Mr. Tiny, I just slipped it into my purse. Now if my analysis is correct, all we have to do is open it up and inside, in back of our picture, we shall find microfilms of the documents which will send Mr. Harry Gordon and all the others to the state penitentiary. Now, Grace, let us look."

The microfilms were there.

"Ellery Queen would be proud of you," Grace said, for she was never one to deny credit where credit was due. "Hercule Poirot would be proud of you. Perry Mason and Lord Peter Wimsey would be proud of you. The Mystery Writers of America would be proud of you, for Edgar Allan Poe is their patron saint."

"Thank you," Florence said, smiling shyly. "In New York we must plan to attend one of their monthly meetings. I feel sure we will be eligible to join as associate members. After that we will take the boat—"

"What boat?" Grace demanded.

Florence looked surprised.

"Why, the boat to London, of course! We have fifteen thousand dollars, so we are going to take a trip around the world—and our first stop will be London.

"London!" Grace sat erect. "The London of Sir Henry Merrivale and Albert Campion! The London of Scotland Yard! Who knows what adventures we may encounter on the foggy London streets? We may be able to help Scotland

Yard bring to justice a criminal who would otherwise evade
its clutches!"

Her eyes focused on a distant unseen spot. Her voice became dreamy. "Perhaps we can even rent a furnished room
on Baker Street!"

THE BLUE GERANIUM

AGATHA CHRISTIE

"When I was down here last year—" said Sir Henry Clithering, and stopped.

His hostess, Mrs. Bantry, looked at him curiously.

The Ex-Commissioner of Scotland Yard was staying with old friends of his, Colonel and Mrs. Bantry, who lived near St. Mary Mead.

Mrs. Bantry, pen in hand, had just asked his advice as to who should be invited to make a sixth guest at dinner that evening.

"Yes," said Mrs. Bantry encouragingly. "When you were here last year?"

"Tell me," said Sir Henry, "do you know a Miss Marple?"

Mrs. Bantry was surprised. It was the last thing she had expected.

"Know Miss Marple? Who doesn't! The typical old maid of fiction. Quite a dear, but hopelessly behind the times. Do you mean you would like me to ask *her* to dinner?"

"You are surprised?"

"A little, I must confess. I should hardly have thought you—but perhaps there's an explanation?"

"The explanation is simple enough. When I was down here last year we got into the habit of discussing unsolved mysteries—there were five or six of us—Raymond West, the novelist, started it. We each supplied a story to which we knew the answer, but nobody else did. It was supposed to be an exercise in the deductive faculties—to see who could get nearest the truth."

"Well?"

"Like in the old story—we hardly realized that Miss Marple was playing; but we were very polite about it—didn't want to hurt the old dear's feelings. And now comes the cream of the jest. The old lady outdid us every time!"

"What?"

"I assure you—straight to the truth like a homing pigeon."

"But how extraordinary! Why, dear old Miss Marple has hardly ever been out of St. Mary Mead."

"Ah! But according to her, that has given her unlimited opportunities of observing human nature—under the microscope, as it were."

"I suppose there's something in that," conceded Mrs. Bantry. "One would at least know the petty side of people. But I don't think we have any really exciting criminals in our midst. I think we must try her with Arthur's ghost story after dinner. I'd be thankful if she'd find a solution to that."

"I didn't know that Arthur believed in ghosts."

"Oh, he doesn't. That's what worries him so. And it happened to a friend of his, George Pritchard—a most prosaic person. It's really rather tragic for poor George. Either this extraordinary story is true—or else—"

"Or else what?"

Mrs. Bantry did not answer. After a minute or two she said irrelevantly, "You know, I like George—everyone does. One can't believe that he—but people do do such extraordinary things."

Sir Henry nodded. He knew, better than Mrs. Bantry, the extraordinary things that people did.

So it came about that evening Mrs. Bantry looked around

her dinner table (shivering a little as she did so, because of the dining-room, like most English dining-rooms, was extremely cold) and fixed her gaze on the very upright old lady sitting on her husband's right. Miss Marple wore black lace mittens; an old lace fichu was draped round her shoulders and another piece of lace surmounted her white hair. She was talking animatedly to the elderly doctor, Dr. Lloyd, about the Workhouse and the suspected shortcomings of the District Nurse.

Mrs. Bantry marveled anew. She even wondered whether Sir Henry had been making an elaborate joke—but there seemed no point in that. Incredible that what he had said could really be true.

Her glance went on and rested affectionately on her red-faced broad-shouldered husband as he sat talking horses to Jane Helier, the beautiful and popular actress. Jane, more beautiful (if that were possible) off the stage than on, opened enormous blue eyes and murmured at discreet intervals: "Really?" "Oh fancy!" "How extraordinary!" She knew nothing whatever about horses and cared less.

"Arthur," said Mrs. Bantry, "you're boring poor Jane to distraction. Leave horses alone and tell her your ghost story instead. You know . . . George Pritchard."

"Eh, Dolly? Oh, but I don't know—"

"Sir Henry wants to hear it too. I was telling him something about it this morning. It would be interesting to hear what everyone has to say about it."

"Oh, do!" said Jane. "I love ghost stories."

"Well—" Colonel Bantry hesitated. "I've never believed much in the supernatural. But this—"

"I don't think any of you know George Pritchard. He's one of the best. His wife—well, she's dead now, poor woman. I'll just say this much: she didn't give George any too easy a time when she was alive. She was one of those semi-invalids—I believe she really had something wrong with her, but whatever it was she played it for all it was worth. She was capricious, exacting, unreasonable. She complained from morning to night. George was expected to wait on her hand and foot, and everything he did was always wrong and he got cursed for it. Most men, I'm fully convinced, would have hit her over the head with a hatchet long ago. Eh, Dolly, isn't that so?"

"She was a dreadful woman," said Mrs. Bantry with conviction. "If George Pritchard had brained her with a hatchet, and there had been any woman on the jury, he would have been triumphantly acquitted."

"I don't quite know how this business started. George was rather vague about it. I gather Mrs. Pritchard had always had a weakness for fortune-tellers, palmists, clairvoyants—anything of that sort. George didn't mind. If she found amusement in it well and good. But he refused to go into rhapsodies himself, and that was another grievance.

"A succession of hospital nurses was always passing through the house, Mrs. Pritchard usually becoming dissatisfied with them after a few weeks. One young nurse had been very keen on this fortune-telling stunt, and for a time Mrs. Pritchard had been extremely fond of her. Then she suddenly fell out with her and insisted on her going. She had back another nurse who had been with her previously—an older woman, experienced and tactful in dealing with a neurotic patient. Nurse Copling, according to George, was a very good sort—a sensible woman to talk to. She put up with Mrs. Pritchard's tantrums and nerve-storms with complete indifference.

"Mrs. Pritchard always lunched upstairs, and it was usual at lunch time for George and the nurse to come to some arrangement for the afternoon. Strictly speaking, the nurse went off from two to four, but 'to oblige,' as the phrase goes, she would sometimes take her time off after tea if George wanted to be free for the afternoon. On this occasion she mentioned that she was going to see a sister at Golders Green and might be a little late returning. George's face fell, for he had arranged to play a round of golf. Nurse Copling, however, reassured him.

"'We'll neither of us be missed, Mr. Pritchard.' A twinkle came into her eye. 'Mrs. Pritchard's going to have more exciting company than ours.'

"'Who's that?'

"'Wait a minute.' Nurse Copling's eye twinkled more than ever. 'Let me get it right, *Zarida, Psychic Reader of the Future.*'

"'Oh, Lord!' groaned George. 'That's a new one, isn't it?'

"'Quite new. I believe my predecessor, Nurse Carstairs, sent her along. Mrs. Pritchard hasn't seen her yet. She made me write, fixing an appointment for this afternoon.'

"'Well, at any rate, I shall get my golf,' said George, and he went off with the kindliest feelings toward Zarida, the Reader of the Future.

"On his return to the house, he found Mrs. Pritchard in a state of great agitation. She was, as usual, lying on her invalid couch, and she had a bottle of smelling salts in her hand which she sniffed at frequent intervals.

"'George,' she exclaimed. 'What did I tell you about this house? The moment I came into it, I *felt* there was something wrong! Didn't I tell you so at the time?'

"Repressing his desire to reply, 'You always do,' George said, 'No, can't say I remember it.'

"'You never do remember anything that has to do with me. Men are all extraordinarily callous—but I really believe that you are even more insensitive than most.'

"'Oh, come now, Mary dear, that's not fair.'

"'Well, as I was telling you, this woman *knew* at once! She—she actually blenched—if you know what I mean—as she came in at that door, and she said, "There is evil here—evil and danger. I feel it."'

"Very unwisely George laughed.

"'Well, you have had your money's worth this afternoon.'

"His wife closed her eyes and took a long sniff from her smelling-bottle.

"'How you hate me! You would jeer and laugh if I were dying.'

"George protested and after a minute or two she went on.

"'You may laugh, but I shall tell you the whole thing. This house is definitely dangerous to me—the woman said so.'

"George's formerly kind feeling toward Zarida underwent a change. He knew his wife was perfectly capable of insisting on moving to a new house if the caprice got hold of her.

"'What else did she say?' he asked.

"'She couldn't tell me very much. She was so upset. One thing she did say. I had some violets in a glass. She pointed at them and cried out. "Take those away. No blue flowers—never have blue flowers. *Blue flowers are fatal to you—remember that.*"'

"'And you know,' added Mrs. Pritchard, 'I always have told you that blue as a color is repellent to me. I feel a natural instinctive sort of warning against it.'

"George was much too wise to remark that he had never heard her say so before. Instead, he asked what the mysterious Zarida was like. Mrs. Pritchard entered with gusto upon a description.

"'Black hair in coiled knobs over her ears—her eyes were half closed—great black rims round them—she had a black veil over her mouth and chin—she spoke in a kind of singing voice with a marked foreign accent—Spanish, I think—'

"'In fact, all the usual stock-in-trade,' said George cheerfully.

"His wife immediately closed her eyes.

"'I feel extremely ill,' she said. 'Ring for nurse. Unkindness upsets me, as you know only too well.'

"It was two days later that Nurse Copling came to George with a grave face.

"'Will you come to Mrs. Pritchard, please. She has had a letter which upsets her greatly.'

"He found his wife with the letter in her hand. She held it out to him.

"'Read it,' she said.

"George read it. It was on heavily scented paper, and the writing was big and black.

"'*I have seen the Future. Be warned before it is too late. Beware of the full moon. The Blue Primrose means Warning; the Blue Hollyhock means Danger; the Blue Geranium means Death. . . .*'

"Just about to burst out laughing George caught Nurse Copling's eye. She made a quick warning gesture. He said rather awkwardly, 'The woman's probably trying to frighten you, Mary. Anyway, there aren't such things as blue primroses and blue geraniums.'

"But Mrs. Pritchard began to cry and say her days were numbered. Nurse Copling came out with George upon the landing.

"'Of all the silly tomfoolery,' he burst out.

"'I suppose it is.'

"Something in the nurse's tone struck him, and he stared at her in amazement.

"'Surely, nurse, you don't believe—'

"'No, no, Mr. Pritchard. I don't believe in reading the future—that's nonsense. What puzzles me is the *meaning* of this. Fortune-tellers are usually out for what they can get. But this woman seems to be frightening Mrs. Pritchard with no advantage to herself. I can't see the point. There's another thing—'

"'Yes?'

"'Mrs. Pritchard says that something about Zarida was faintly familiar to her.'

"'Well?'

"'Well, I don't like it, Mr. Pritchard, that's all.'

"'I didn't know you were so superstitious, nurse.'

"'I'm not superstitious; but I know when a thing is fishy.'

"It was about four days after this that the first incident happened. To explain it to you, I shall have to describe Mrs. Pritchard's room—"

"You'd better let me do that," interrupted Mrs. Bantry. "It was papered with one of these new wallpapers where you apply clumps of flowers to make a kind of herbaceous border. The effect is almost like being in a garden—though, of course, the flowers are all wrong; I mean they simply couldn't be in bloom all at the same time—"

"Don't let a passion for horticultural accuracy run away with you, Dolly," said her husband. "We all know you're an enthusiastic gardener."

"Well, it *is* absurd," protested Mrs. Bantry. "To have bluebells and daffodils and lupins and hollyhocks and Michaelmas daisies all grouped into a tangle together."

"Most unscientific," said Colonel Bantry. "But to proceed with the story . . . Among these massed flowers were primroses—clumps of yellow and pink primroses. Well, one morning Mrs. Pritchard rang her bell violently and the household came running—thought she was in extremis. But not at all. She was terribly excited and pointed to the wall-paper; and there sure enough was *one blue primrose* in the midst of the others . . ."

"Oh," said Miss Helier, "how creepy!"

"The question was: Hadn't the blue primrose always been there? That was George's suggestion and the nurse's. But Mrs. Pritchard wouldn't have it. She had never noticed it till that very morning and the night before had been full moon. She was very upset about it."

"I met George Pritchard that same day and he told me about it," said Mrs. Bantry. "I went to see Mrs. Pritchard and did my best to ridicule the whole thing; but without success. I came away really concerned, and I remember I met Jean Instow and told her about it. Jean is a queer girl. She said, 'So she's really upset about it?' I told her that I thought the woman was perfectly capable of dying of fright, that she was really abnormally superstitious.

"I remember Jean rather startled me with what she said next. She said, 'Well, that might be all for the best, mightn't it?' And she said it so coolly, in so matter-of-fact a tone that I was really—well, shocked. Of course, I know it's done nowadays—to be brutal and outspoken; but I never get used to it. Jean smiled at me rather oddly and said, 'You don't like my saying that—but it's true. What use is Mrs. Pritchard's life to her? None at all; and it's hell for George Pritchard. To have his wife frightened out of ex-istence would be the best thing that could happen to him.' I said, 'George is most awfully good to her always.' And she said, 'Yes, he deserves a reward, poor dear. He's a very at-tractive person, George Pritchard. The last nurse thought so—the pretty one—what has her name? Carstairs. That was the cause of the row between her and Mrs. P.'

"Now I didn't like hearing Jean say that. Of course one had *wondered*—"

"Yes, dear," said Miss Marple placidly. "One always does. Is Miss Instow a pretty girl? I suppose she plays golf?"

"Yes. She's good at all games. And she's attractive-looking, very fair with a healthy skin, and nice steady blue eyes. Of course, we always have felt that she and George Pritchard—I mean if things had been different—they are so well suited to one another."

"And they were friends?" asked Miss Marple.

"Oh, yes. Great friends."

"Do you think, Dolly," said Colonel Bantry plaintively, "that I might be allowed to go on with my story?"

"Arthur," said Mrs. Bantry resignedly, "wants to get back to his ghosts."

"I had the rest of the story from George himself," went on the colonel. "There's no doubt that Mrs. Pritchard got the wind up badly toward the end of the next month. She marked off on a calendar the day when the moon would be full, and on that night she had both the nurse and then George into her room and made them study the wallpaper carefully. There were pink hollyhocks and red ones, but there were no blue ones. Then when George left the room she locked the door—"

"And in the morning there was a large blue hollyhock," said Miss Helier joyfully.

"Quite right," said Colonel Bantry. "Or at any rate, nearly right. One flower of a hollyhock just above her head had turned blue. It staggered George; and of course the more it staggered him the more he refused to take the thing seriously. He insisted that the whole thing was some kind of practical joke. He ignored the evidence of the locked door and the fact that Mrs. Pritchard discovered the change before anyone—even Nurse Copling—was admitted into her bedroom.

"As I say, it staggered George, and it made him unreasonable. His wife wanted to leave the house, and he wouldn't let her. He was inclined to believe in the supernatural for the first time, but he wasn't going to admit it. He usually gave in to his wife, but this time he just wouldn't. Mary was not to make a fool of herself, he said. The whole thing was the most infernal nonsense.

"And so the next month sped away. Mrs. Pritchard made less protest than one would have imagined. I think she was superstitious enough to believe that she couldn't escape her fate. She repeated again and again, 'The blue primrose—warning. The blue hollyhock—danger. The blue geranium—*death*.' And she would lie there looking at the clump of pinky-red geraniums nearest her bed.

"The whole business was pretty nervy. Even the nurse caught the infection. She came to George two days before full moon and begged him to take Mrs. Pritchard away. George was angry.

"'If all the flowers on that damned wall turned into blue devils it couldn't kill anyone!' he shouted.

"'It might. Shock has killed people before.'

"'Nonsense,' said George.

"George has always been a shade pig-headed. You can't drive him. I believe he had a secret idea that his wife worked the changes herself and that it was all some morbid hysterical plan of hers.

"Well, the fatal night came. Mrs. Pritchard locked her door as usual. She was very calm—in almost an exalted state of mind. The nurse was worried by her state and wanted to give her a stimulant—an injection of strychnine—but Mrs. Pritchard refused. In a way, I believe, she was enjoying herself. George said she was."

"I think that's quite possible," said Mrs. Bantry. "There

must have been a strange sort of glamour about the whole thing."

"There was no violent ringing of the bell the next morning. Mrs. Pritchard usually woke about eight. When, at eight thirty, there was no sign from her, nurse rapped loudly on the door. Getting no reply, she fetched George, and insisted on the door being broken open. They did so with the help of a chisel.

"One look at the still figure on the bed was enough for Nurse Copling. She sent George to telephone for the doctor, but it was too late. Mrs. Pritchard, the doctor said, must have been dead at least eight hours. Her smelling salts lay by her hand on the bed, *and on the wall beside her one of the pinky-red geraniums was a bright deep blue.*"

"Horrible," said Miss Helier with a shiver.

Sir Henry was frowning.

"No additional details?"

Colonel Bantry shook his head, but Mrs. Bantry spoke quickly.

"The gas."

"What about the gas?" asked Sir Henry.

"When the doctor arrived there was a slight smell of gas, and sure enough he found the gas ring in the fireplace very slightly turned on; but so little that it couldn't have mattered."

"Did Mr. Pritchard and the nurse not notice it when they first went in?"

"The nurse said she did notice a silent smell. George said he didn't notice gas, but something made him feel queer; but he put that down to shock—and probably it was. At any rate, there was no question of gas poisoning. The smell was scarcely noticeable."

"And that's the end of the story?"

"No, it isn't. One way and another, there was a lot of

talk. The servants, you see, had overheard things—had heard, for instance, Mrs. Pritchard telling her husband that he hated her and would jeer if she were dying. And also more recent remarks. She said one day, apropos of his refusing to leave the house, 'Very well, when I am dead, I hope everyone will realize that you have killed me.' And as ill luck would have it, he had been mixing some weed killer for the garden paths the very day before. One of the younger servants had seen him and had afterward observed him taking up a glass of hot milk to his wife.

"The talk spread and grew. The doctor had given a certificate—I don't know exactly in what terms—shock, syncope, heart failure, probably some medical term meaning nothing much. However, the poor lady had not been a month in her grave before the exhumation order was applied for and granted."

"And the result of the autopsy was *nil*, I remember," said Sir Henry gravely.

"The whole thing is really very curious," said Mrs. Bantry. "That fortune-teller, for instance—Zarida. At the address where she was supposed to be, no one had ever heard of any such person!"

"She appeared once—out of the blue," said her husband, "and then utterly vanished."

"And what is more," continued Mrs. Bantry, "little Nurse Carstairs, who was supposed to have recommended her, had never even heard of her."

"It's a mysterious story," said Dr. Lloyd. "One can make guesses; but to guess—"

He shook his head.

"Has Mr. Pritchard married Miss Instow?" asked Miss Marple in her gentle voice.

"Now why do you ask that?" inquired Sir Henry.

Miss Marple opened gentle blue eyes.

"It seems to me so important," she said. "Have they married?"

Colonel Bantry shook his head.

"We—well, we expected something of the kind—but it's eighteen months now. I don't believe they even see much of each other."

"That is important," said Miss Marple. "Very important."

"Then you think the same as I do," said Mrs. Bantry.

"Now, Dolly," said her husband. "It's unjustifiable—what you're going to say. You can't go about accusing people."

"Don't be so—so manly, Arthur. Men are always afraid to say *anything*. Anyway, this is all between ourselves. It's just a wild fantastic idea of mine that possibly—only *possibly*—Jean Instow disguised herself as a fortune-teller. Mind you, she may have done it for a joke. I don't for a minute think she meant any harm; but if she did do it, and if Mrs. Pritchard was foolish enough to die of fright—well, that's what Miss Marple meant, wasn't it?"

"No, dear, not quite," said Miss Marple. "You see, if I were going to kill anyone—which, of course, I wouldn't dream of doing for a minute, because it would be very wicked, and besides I don't like killing—not even wasps, though I know it has to be, and I'm sure the gardener does it as humanely as possible. Let me see, what was I saying?"

"If you wished to kill anyone," prompted Sir Henry.

"Oh, yes. Well, if I did, I shouldn't be at all satisfied to trust to *fright*. I know one reads of people dying of it, but it seems a very uncertain sort of thing, and the more nervous people are far more brave than one really thinks they are. I should like something definite and certain, and make a thoroughly good plan about it."

"Miss Marple," said Sir Henry, "you frighten me. I hope you will never wish to remove me."

Miss Marple looked at him reproachfully.

"I thought I had made it clear that I would never contemplate such wickedness," she said. "No, I was trying to put myself in the place of—er—a certain person."

"Do you mean George Pritchard?" asked Colonel Bantry. "I'll never believe it of George—though, mind you, even the nurse believes it. I went and saw her about a month afterward, at the time of the exhumation. She didn't know how it was done—in fact, she wouldn't say anything at all—but it was clear enough that she believed George to be in some way responsible for his wife's death."

"Well," said Dr. Lloyd, "perhaps she wasn't so far wrong. And mind you, a nurse often *knows*. She got no proof—but she *knows.*"

Sir Henry leaned forward.

"Come now, Miss Marple," he said persuasively. "You're lost in a daydream. Won't you tell us all about it?"

Miss Marple started and turned pink.

"I beg your pardon," she said. "I was just thinking about our District Nurse. A most difficult problem."

"More difficult than the problem of a blue geranium?"

"It really depends on the primroses," said Miss Marple. "I mean, Mrs. Bantry said they were yellow and pink. If it was a pink primrose that turned blue, of course, that fits in perfectly. But if it happened to be a yellow one—"

"It was a pink one," said Mrs. Bantry.

She stared. They all stared at Miss Marple.

"Then that seems to settle it," said Miss Marple. She shook her head regretfully. "And the wasp season and everything. And of course the gas."

"It reminds you, I suppose, of countless village tragedies?" said Sir Henry.

"Not tragedies," said Miss Marple. "And certainly nothing criminal. But it does remind me a little of the trouble we are having with the District Nurse. After all, nurses are human beings, and what with having to be so correct in the behavior and wearing those uncomfortable collars and being so thrown with the family—well, can you wonder that things happen?"

A glimmer of light broke upon Sir Henry.

"You mean Nurse Carstairs?"

"Oh, no. Not Nurse Carstairs. Nurse *Copling*. You see, she had been there before, and very much thrown with Mr. Pritchard, who you say is an attractive man. I daresay she thought, poor thing—well, we needn't go into that. I don't suppose she knew about Miss Instow, and of course afterward, when she found out, it turned her against him and she tried to do all the harm she could. Of course the letter really gave her away, didn't it?"

"What letter?"

"Well, she wrote to the fortune-teller at Mrs. Pritchard's request, and the fortune-teller came, apparently in answer to the letter. But later it was discovered that there never had been such a person at that address. So that shows that Nurse Copling was in it. She only pretended to write—so what could be more likely than that *she* was the fortune-teller herself?"

"I never saw the point about the letter," said Sir Henry.

"Rather a bold step to take," said Miss Marple, "because Mrs. Pritchard might have recognized her in spite of the disguise—though of course if she had, the nurse could have said it was a joke."

"What did you mean," said Sir Henry, "when you said that if you were a certain person you would not have trusted to fright?"

"One couldn't be *sure* that way," said Miss Marple. "No, I think that the warnings and the blue flowers were, if I

may use a military term," she laughed self-consciously—
"just *camouflage.*"

"And the real thing?"

"I know," said Miss Marple apologetically, "that I've got
wasps on the brain. Poor things, destroyed in the thousands—and usually on such a beautiful summer's day. But
I remember thinking, when I saw the gardener shaking up
the cyanide of potassium in a bottle with water, how like
smelling salts it looked. And if it were put in a smelling-salt
bottle and substituted for the real one—well, the poor lady
was in the habit of using her smelling salts. Indeed, you
said they were found by her hand. Then, of course, while
Mr. Pritchard went to telephone to the doctor, the nurse
would change it for the real bottle, and she'd just turn on
the gas a little bit to mask any smell of almonds and in case
anyone felt queer, and I always have heard that cyanide
leaves no trace if you wait long enough. But, of course I
may be wrong and it may have been something entirely different in the bottle; but that doesn't really matter, does it?"

Jane Helier leaned forward and said, "But the blue geranium, and the other flowers?"

"Nurses always have litmus paper, don't they?" said
Miss Marple, "for—well, for testing. Not a very pleasant
subject. We won't dwell on it. I have done a little nursing
myself." She grew delicately pink. "Blue turns red with
acids, and red turns blue with alkalies. So easy to paste
some red litmus over a ready flower—near the bed, of
course. And then, when the poor lady used her smelling
salts, the strong ammonia fumes would turn it blue. Really
most ingenious. Of course, the geranium wasn't blue when
they first broke into the room—nobody noticed it till afterward. When nurse changed the bottles, she held the Sal
Ammoniac against the wallpaper for a minute, I expect."

"You might have been there, Miss Marple," said Sir Henry.

"What worries me," said Miss Marple, "is poor Mr. Pritchard and that nice girl, Miss Instow. Probably both suspecting each other and keeping apart, and life so very short."

She shook her head.

"You needn't worry," said Sir Henry. "As a matter of fact I have something up my sleeve. A nurse has been arrested on a charge of murdering an elderly patient who had left her a legacy. It was done with cyanide of potassium substituted for smelling salts. Nurse Copling trying the same trick again. Miss Instow and Mr. Pritchard need have no doubts."

"Now isn't that nice?" cried Miss Marple. "I don't mean about the new murder, of course. That's very sad, and shows how much wickedness there is in the world, and that if once you give way—which reminds me I *must* finish my little conversation with Dr. Lloyd about the village nurse."

MISS PHIPPS AND THE INVISIBLE MURDERER

PHYLLIS BENTLEY

"So this is Beckholme. What a lovely landscape! What a beautiful little church!" exclaimed Miss Phipps, walking toward the old wooden lychgate which guarded the entrance. "Seven hundred years old at least! Enfolded in these high hills— Delightful!"

She turned, and discovered she was speaking to empty air. Her niece, Ruth, at whose suburban home on the outskirts of the northern city of Laire she was making a longish visit, was just disembarking her two children from the car. It was Saturday; Ruth's husband, Michael, had gone off to the Laire golf links, so he was not in the party.

Immediately that Pamela, aged four, was set down on the ground she toddled at full speed toward the river, shrieking and waving her little arms aloft in joy. Stephen, her six-year-old brother, ran headlong after her, and Ruth chased them both, for the river banks here were low, and the narrow stream was swift and rocky. Ruth caught a hand of each of her children, and came back across the grass to meet Miss Phipps, not without rebellion from Pamela.

"You'll want to see the church—do you mind going in alone, Aunt Marian? I must keep an eye on these two," said Ruth. Taking her aunt's consent for granted, she turned to the car. "Let's get the food out, shall we, children? It's rather early, but I think we may as well have our picnic now."

With that gleeful pleasure in food characteristic of the young of all species, Stephen and Pam rushed to assist their mother, shouting a good deal and getting in her way, all with the best intentions.

Miss Phipps stood for a moment admiring the landscape again—the towering lonely fells, with cloud shadows moving across their sunlit flanks, the old farmhouses scattered here and there on their lower slopes, the one-arched bridge spanning the silver river, and the gray old church.

She passed through the lychgate and began to move about among the old gravestones, some lying flat in the long grass, some erect, some aslant; she stooped to decipher with interest the worn, half-obliterated names, and entered any inscription which took her fancy in the notebook she always carried.

"Can I help you?" said a courteous voice.

She looked up. A lanky young man, hatless, with thin fair hair, heavy spectacles, and a worried expression, stood at her side. From his dress he was a cleric, from his look he had his troubles.

"If you are searching for some grave in particular, I may be able to help you," he continued.

"Er—no, thank you," said Miss Phipps coldly.

His look of unhappiness deepened, and Miss Phipps felt she had been unkind.

"It's just that I collect names from graveyards," she explained with reluctance. She realized from his look of astonishment that this sounded odd, and went on hurriedly, "I'm a writer, you see. A novelist," she added with distaste—she hated making confidences of this kind to a stranger.

"Oh, really! How interesting!" exclaimed the young

man, cheering up. He hesitated, then went on. "My name is Robert Vesey. I'm the curate-in-charge here. Would it be impertinent to ask—"

"My name is Marian Phipps," said Miss Phipps, scowling and looking down.

"Oh, how delightful! This is indeed a pleasure," said Mr. Vesey, bowing. "I enjoy your detective stories very much indeed. But I mustn't intrude on you while you're at work. You must wish to be alone." He bowed again and turned away toward the gate.

"Thank you!" exclaimed Miss Phipps. Her gratitude was real, for she could never "observe" creatively in company. Few people understood this, she found; Vesey must have a sensitive perception. Pleased, she passed through the church porch, and entered the building.

She knew a reasonable amount about architectural chronology, and prowled about the building with much enjoyment, observing the Latin inscription on the rood screen, the very early arch of the tower, the crude local work in the north arcade. She peeped into the bare little vestry, and craned over the bronze on the tomb in the side chapel.

At length satisfied that she had seen all that was to be seen in the church, she dropped two coins in the box on a table beside the font, labeled "For the Preservation of the Fabric Fund," and turned to write her name in the Visitors' Book which lay beside it. A neat ballpoint pen was, she found, available.

"Not before it was needed," said Miss Phipps aloud, gazing with some distaste at the splashed and untidy page of signatures, which had obviously been written with an old-fashioned and spluttery nibbed pen. An almost empty and very grimy glass inkwell, of the kind used in schools in Miss Phipps's youth—"It has probably been here ever since," thought Miss Phipps irritably—seemed to confirm this view.

"Butterworth," said Miss Phipps, reading the last name inscribed. Below this, at the foot of the page, there were two vacant lines; the upper one of these was defaced by a couple of sizable and irregular black blots. Miss Phipps, who admitted to a certain pride in her own rather dashing signature, wrinkled her nose fastidiously, rejected this messy area, and wrote her name and address on the lower line.

"Do come, Aunt Marian!" called Stephen rather crossly from the door. "Everything's ready—we're waiting for you."

Miss Phipps carefully put down the ballpoint pen—even in the haste necessitated by a child's hunger she could not do violence to a writing instrument—and left the church in a rush. Stephen was already some way down the path. "Oh, I beg your pardon!" she exclaimed as she collided on the porch with a person coming in.

"Granted, I'm sure," said the girl in a scoffing tone.

Miss Phipps disentangled herself with some vexation. She did not like the girl's mockery, and looking at her closely, did not like her appearance either. Basically, reflected Miss Phipps, she is attractive enough: a shapely figure inclining to the plump, abundant dark hair, bright dark eyes, a full mouth, and a wide but not uncomely nose.

But all these good features were distorted, exaggerated, plastered—she boasted (boasted, Miss Phipps felt, was the operative word) false eyelashes and green eye-shadow, heavily tinted cheeks, palely larded lips, and a huge superstructure of hair so elaborate that one wondered if it were taken down and brushed more often than once a week; her pale green slacks and matching sweater were intentionally much too tight, and her green scarf was patterned with huge scarlet squiggles—so that as a sexual display she ruined her effect by overstatement.

The girl's glance was insolent, her smile contemptuous; it was obvious that she despised an "oldie" like Miss Phipps most heartily. Miss Phipps repressed a desire to indicate that the contempt was mutual, and walked on feeling huffed. There was a stir—birds, perhaps—behind a grave as she passed.

The picnic luncheon was agreeably laid out in the shelter of a grassy hollow that Ruth had discovered some 50 yards down the river, and in the eager cries of the children and in the business of supplying their wants and coping with the usual difficulties of picnics—the overturned milk bottle, the fair division of sandwiches, the intrusive wasp—Miss Phipps's irritation was soothed, though not forgotten.

On the following Monday morning, after Michael had gone to work leaving the county newspaper behind him, Stephen, whose summer holiday was not quite over, ran to Miss Phipps with the paper in his hand.

"Look, Aunt Marian!" he said triumphantly, pointing. "That's the lady we saw by the church at the picnic."

"So it is," agreed Miss Phipps, for the portrait, though coarsened in the reproduction, was undoubtedly that of the girl on the porch.

"Miss Eunice Harden," spelled out Stephen.

"That's right," agreed Miss Phipps in a careless tone. She threw the paper aside, for she had already perceived from the picture's caption that Miss Eunice Harden was missing from her aunt's home and was being searched for by the police, and she did not wish to communicate this to Stephen. When he ran off on some ploy of his own, she reopened the newspaper and read the paragraphs accompanying the picture with more attention.

Miss Eunice Harden, it appeared, was an orphan who divided her time between an aunt in Laire, and another aunt and her husband, Mr. and Mrs. Barrett, in Beckholme. She had last been seen in the kitchen of her aunt's farm in Beckholme on Saturday morning, but then had vanished.

At first, no anxiety had been felt, for it was presumed she had returned to her aunt in Laire. There had been a slight tiff, confessed Mrs. Barrett apologetically, between herself and her niece that morning; she had perhaps been a little sharp about Eunice's make-up, which she thought excessive for a sheep farm way out in the fells. Eunice was a hot-tempered girl—spirited, you might say; it was just like her to fling off to Laire; she had, in fact, done it before and taken a job there, but all too soon had given it up and returned to Beckholme.

The day being Saturday, there was a bus from the village a mile or two down the valley to the nearest market town, where there was plenty of transport to Laire.

The next morning, Sunday, Mrs. Barrett had asked the curate-in-charge, whom she saw at church, to telephone to her sister in Laire; but Eunice had not been seen there. Uneasy, Mrs. Barrett went to Eunice's room to see if she had left a farewell note; she had not done so, nor had she taken a suitcase with her. Even her handbag remained on the dressing table. Now alarmed, Mrs. Barrett informed the local policeman. Exhaustive inquiries were being made, round Beckholme and in Laire.

"Oh, dear, oh, dear," mourned Miss Phipps. "Now I shall have to go to the police station. And I'm very much afraid," she added, explaining the affair to Ruth who was at work in the kitchen, "that I shall have to take Stephen with me."

"You can't do that without consulting Michael," said Ruth quickly, raising her head from the stove.

"You're right. But the fact is, Stephen saw the girl—he

must have met her on the pathway when he came to the church to fetch me. He recognized her picture in the newspaper."

"If you saw her on the porch, surely that's enough."

On that day the police seemed to share this view. Miss Phipps having telephoned the Laire police headquarters, a polite young man in civilian clothes turned up at Ruth's house, took down the description of Eunice's dress as furnished by Miss Phipps, and listened carefully but without much interest to Stephen's declaration that he had recognized the lady's picture in the paper, that he had met her on the church pathway, and that she had dark hair and wore "very tight trousers."

But on Wednesday matters took a different turn. While the family was still at breakfast the young detective appeared again, looking grave, with a police car in which he requested Miss Phipps to accompany him to police headquarters. Miss Phipps, however, declined this and took her own. He asked Stephen many searching questions, repeating them once or twice in different forms. What did the lady look like? How was she dressed? Was Stephen going to the church or coming away? Why did he go to the church? Was his aunt inside? Where was she? Was she writing? Did the lady wear a hat? Did he see anybody else near the church? What color was the lady's dress? Who else did he see? All these Stephen answered staunchly, without hesitation or variation, though with a growing impatience.

"She had dark hair—piled up very high," he said.

"But what color was her dress?"

"It wasn't a dress, they were trousers, very tight. I've told you before," said Stephen crossly.

"And what color were they?"

"I don't *know*. A pale color. Green, I think. They were very tight."

"Detective Inspector Dale, from the area which includes Beckholme, asked us to get in touch with you, Miss Phipps," said the Superintendent.

"You told him I had seen Eunice?"

"No. Well, yes; but the point is, your name is in the Visitors' Book at Beckholme Church—and your address. Dale telephoned the appropriate police in London; they tried to find where you were, and eventually phoned Chief-Inspector Tarrant in Brittlesea, whose wife knew you were staying with your niece in Laire. So Dale communicated with us; of course we already knew your whereabouts."

Miss Phipps thought for a moment.

"But why did my name in the Visitors' Book interest Inspector Dale in the first place?" she inquired, perplexed. "How did he come to look at the book, to think it might be relevant?"

"Miss Phipps," said the Superintendent, very grim. "The body of Eunice Harden was discovered in deep grass behind a gravestone in a far corner of the graveyard, towards the river."

"Her *body*!"

"Yes. She had been dead for several days. Strangled. A police dog found her."

"Poor silly girl," said Miss Phipps with compassion. "Was it manual strangulation?"

"No. Her scarf. You mentioned yourself that she was wearing a green red-patterned scarf. Doesn't take much strength, you know."

"She was rather a 'murderee,'" said Miss Phipps sadly.

"What do you mean by that?"

"There's a vulgar word for it which I won't use," said Miss Phipps. "Let's say she enjoyed exciting men."

The Superintendent snorted. "Sexy," he said. "When the body was found in the graveyard, of course the church itself became of prime interest. The dog, in fact, traced her from the Harden farm to the church, and then to the corner where she was found."

"Well—I'm very sorry," said Miss Phipps. "If I can be of any help, Superintendent—"

"Chief-Inspector Tarrant told Dale of the shrewdness of your observation."

"There's nothing to observe in this case as far as I can see."

"Do you see anyone in these that you know?" said the Superintendent, suddenly strewing half a dozen photographs along the table in front of her.

They were of various shapes and sizes and showed different persons, but each portrayed a very young, very fair girl, with large gray eyes. Miss Phipps examined them carefully.

"No," she said.

"Ever seen any of them?"

"No."

"Sure you didn't see any of them at Beckholme on Saturday?"

"Quite sure. Pretty young things. This is the nicest face, I think," said Miss Phipps, pointing.

"That one," said the Superintendent grimly, "happens to be Miss Celia Whitaker."

"And who is she?"

"She is the daughter of a hotel owner in a seaside resort on the far side of the county. At present she is a resident student at Laire University."

"How does she come into this affair?"

"There is talk of an engagement between Miss Celia and the Reverend Robert Vesey."

"And why not? She looks like a thoroughly nice girl," said Miss Phipps. "Oh, Vesey. Curate-in-charge at Beckholme, of course. I saw him there. A very nice young man."

"You saw *him* there? You didn't mention that before! When did you see him?"

"He came out of the church as I was going in."

"Did you actually see him in the act of emerging?"

"Well, no," said Miss Phipps. "I was examining a gravestone. He spoke to me and I looked up and saw him."

"Miss Phipps, this is a very important statement. I am sure you realize its gravity. Robert Vesey could have murdered Eunice, placed her body where it was found, then come round the corner of the church and seen you. It was too risky to try to slip by you unobserved, so he spoke to you."

"I am afraid, Superintendent," said Miss Phipps coldly, "that you are quite on the wrong track. Not only is Robert Vesey a kindly, sensitive young man who wouldn't hurt a fly, much less strangle a robust young woman in his own church grounds in the middle of a sunny morning—"

"Almost any man is capable of murder, if he's entangled with a bad woman and wants to marry a good one."

"—but also, you may perhaps remember that Stephen and I both saw Eunice, alive, *after* Mr. Vesey's departure."

"Stephen didn't see Vesey and therefore doesn't know whether Eunice was alive after he left, or not."

"But I do, Superintendent," said Miss Phipps firmly.

"Vesey could have returned later."

"Anybody could have entered the church later without being seen by our party. We were fifty yards away, in a hollow by the river."

"You saw nobody enter?"

"No."

"Nobody leave?"

"No. But that proves nothing."

"Quite. Miss Phipps, this fresh statement from you opens up an even more unpleasant possibility."

"How so?"

"Are you sure that nobody was in the church when you entered?"

"Quite sure. *Quite* sure. The church is a small one, and I inspected it thoroughly."

"Did you enter the vestry?"

"I didn't enter, but I looked in. There was nobody there."

"She might have been hiding behind the surplices."

"I don't remember seeing any choir surplices," said Miss Phipps thoughtfully. "Ordinary white choir surplices? No. You said that *she* might have been hiding. Who is *she?*"

"You tell me."

"I haven't the least idea. Unless—Butterworth? No, that's not possible, because of the pen used for the Butterworth signature. It wasn't there. And the ink of the signature was black—old."

There was a pause.

"Miss Phipps," said the Superintendent in a tone of vexation, "I'm afraid your observation is not as acute as Chief-Inspector Tarrant claims."

"Superintendent," said Miss Phipps, crimsoning, "will you please make an appointment for me to meet Inspector Dale at Beckholme Church, at half-past eleven this morning."

"Well, it might be useful," mused the Superintendent. "I don't see how it possibly can be useful—but still, this is an uncomfortable case. I won't leave anything untried."

"Thank you," said Miss Phipps icily.

*   *   *

"I hope you had a pleasant drive, Miss Phipps," said Inspector Dale with cold politeness. "About two hours from Laire, I believe."

"Yes," agreed Miss Phipps, who had covered the distance in considerably less time. "This is very beautiful country. But lonely, of course. Remote. Not much for a girl like Eunice to do. Still, I suppose there are a few young men about, even here."

The Inspector looked at her thoughtfully. "Yes," he said. "We get quite a few tourists in the summer, you know. Now if you'll come into the church, Miss Phipps, I will show you—"

"What?"

The Inspector was silent until they had reached the small table by the font. He opened the Visitors' Book at yesterday's entries—there were none for today; the policeman on duty at the lychgate had doubtless kept visitors out. Dale pointed and said, "This."

Miss Phipps bent and read her own signature. On the line above it was now written, with a ballpoint pen and in a large round hand: *Celia Whitaker.*

"No!" exclaimed Miss Phipps, starting back violently. "That signature was not there when I wrote mine. The last signature was *Butterworth*, and I left a line blank—between Butterworth and my name."

"Why?"

"Because of those disgusting blots," explained Miss Phipps.

"You suggest that Miss Whitaker entered the church after you and entered her name above yours to give her, as it were, an alibi?"

"I suggest nothing of the kind!"

"How do you explain this circumstance, then?"

"I don't. Celia must be asked to explain it, surely."

"Either she was here in the church before you—"

"She was not."

"She might have been hiding in the vestry."

"She was not."

"Behind the choir surplices."

"There were no surplices when I looked into the vestry."

"Kindly come with me, Miss Phipps," said Inspector Dale brusquely, striding off up the aisle.

"You don't believe a word I say," said Miss Phipps, panting after him.

The Inspector threw open the vestry doors. A neat row of white surplices depending on hangers from a long coat-stand was revealed—also, the Reverend Robert Vesey, sitting at a table with an open register before him.

"Ah, good morning, Inspector," he said, rising. "Miss Phipps! How nice to see you again."

"These surplices were not here during my visit to the church last Saturday morning," said Miss Phipps.

"No. One of my parishioners launders them each week and returns them on Saturday afternoon, so that they are always clean for Sunday."

"There, you see!" said Miss Phipps to the Inspector.

Dale scowled, then explained. "Miss Phipps has come to see if she can help our investigation into this shocking affair of the murder."

"It's shocking and terrible indeed," said the young man, frowning. "Poor young woman. I have written to the Bishop suggesting that reconsecration of the church is advisable, but I have had no reply as yet."

"You think the murder was committed in the church?" asked the Inspector.

"I've no idea. But just to be on the safe side. Have you made any progress in your investigation, Inspector?"

"We've been looking in your Visitors' Book."

"Oh, really? I brought a new pen last Saturday—I'd just placed it by the book when I saw you, Miss Phipps."

"You were in the church before Miss Phipps?"

"I always come in to say Matins," said Mr. Vesey quietly. "Sometimes I'm a little late, but if it's before noon—"

"Did you see anyone else in the building? No? Will you examine the Visitors' Book with me, sir?"

"Certainly," agreed Mr. Vesey, rising and following the Inspector down the aisle. Miss Phipps trailed after them. "Though I don't see—Celia!" he exclaimed as the book was opened before him. He colored and looked very young. "Miss Whitaker and I are about to become engaged, Inspector," he said with dignity. "You have probably heard that from Beckholme parishioners. But she was not here last Saturday."

"When was she here?" put in Miss Phipps quickly.

"Monday."

"The day Eunice Harden's disappearance was mentioned in the morning newspapers," said the Inspector.

"Yes."

"She knew she could find you here in the church before noon in the morning," pursued the Inspector.

"Yes. But she was not here last Saturday. I don't understand the placing of the signature," said Mr. Vesey.

"Your evidence of changing the pen would prove that Miss Whitaker could not have written her signature before you came in on the Saturday in question," said the Inspector, "and the placing of the signature shows that it was written before that of Miss Phipps."

"No! My evidence contradicts that," said Miss Phipps firmly.

The Inspector scowled again.

"I shall have to question Miss Celia Whitaker," he said.

"Certainly," agreed Miss Phipps. ("And so shall I," she added silently.)

Miss Phipps, having friends in authority in Laire University, knew whom to approach, received prompt attention, and was passed rapidly along the line until she found herself entering the snack canteen in charge of a student in Social Studies who knew Celia Whitaker.

She rather paled at the scene before her. Hundreds—at first sight there appeared to be thousands—of young people of both sexes sat, stood, crouched, or perched around and on small round tables and casual chairs, drinking coffee or orangeade and devouring sandwiches, which they obtained from an intimidating machine by the door. Enormous thick woolen sweaters concealed agreeable figures, long hair dripped into cups, black stockings (unmended) abounded, papers and books were strewn thickly over the floor. There was a loud hum of eager discussion.

Miss Phipps felt daunted by the probable difficulty of discovering one person among so many, but her student guide picked Celia out easily and by energetic signals soon brought her to the door. She looked rather cleaner than many of her companions and her straight fair hair was well brushed. She scowled reluctantly at Miss Phipps until her visitor remarked that she brought a message from Robert Vesey, and then her expression changed.

Miss Phipps's guide took them to a large empty room housing a piano, and left. The silence was welcome.

"Now, my dear child," said Miss Phipps soothingly, "I am on your side and you can trust me. But we must clear all this up, you know. The police will soon be here to question you."

"Yes, they've been trying to do so all morning. But they couldn't find me. I've dodged them," said Celia gleefully.

"You've been to Beckholme this week?"

"Yes. I went up after I read about Eunice Harden being missing. It was in the newspapers on Monday morning. I have a little Mini—father gave it to me on my last birthday, so it was easy."

"But why did you go, my dear?"

"I was worried about Bob—Mr. Vesey. He's too good, that's the trouble with him. He had a terrible time with that awful Eunice; she chased him all over the place; a real nympho. She would even come to the church sometimes in the mornings, knowing she would find him there. From the Harden farm you can see part of the lane to the church."

"I'm afraid that's just what the police guess," said Miss Phipps gravely.

"Yes, Bob had to be awfully careful to keep out of her way," said Celia. "She went after every man in sight, you know."

"Who do you think could have murdered her?" asked Miss Phipps.

"Oh, lots!" said Celia.

"But she had a right to her life."

"Oh, of course," said Celia, looking serious. "But she asked for it, you know."

"Now, my dear Celia," said Miss Phipps soberly, "I am going to ask you a tiresome question, and you must—I repeat, *must*—answer it truthfully. You were at Beckholme on Monday and you put your name in the Visitors' Book above mine, which was written on Saturday morning. Why above mine?"

"Well, it was one of those things which seemed like a good idea at the time," said Celia. "You see, I cut a lot of lectures and things to go to the church, and we're not supposed to leave the University on weekdays. Saturday would be all right. So I had the idea of filling up this vacant line, a page back, to give me a kind of alibi. While I was waiting for Bob, it just popped into my mind, and I did it. It was a silly idea, I suppose."

"It was," agreed Miss Phipps.

"It was silly of me to put my name in the book at all," said Celia. "I don't usually write in his silly old book. But while I was waiting for Bob, you see, it was something to do—to turn over the pages and write my name."

"It was more than silly," said Miss Phipps gravely.

"Really? There was a spot of bother last week about a girl cutting lectures, you know," said Celia. "But I see that it was silly."

"It was a lie," said Miss Phipps.

Celia pouted.

"And it's going to get you and your young man into a lot of trouble."

"Nobody could think Bob would do anything wrong," said Celia quickly.

"The police may well think that both you and Mr. Vesey had cause to hate Eunice because he had been involved in an affair with her."

"Oh, nonsense! He never even called her by her first name. Of course he had to go to the farm sometimes, to see Mrs. Barrett about the surplices."

"The surplices!" exclaimed Miss Phipps.

"Yes, Mrs. Barrett launders them, you know."

"And returns them on Saturday afternoon," said Miss Phipps thoughtfully.

"Well, she wouldn't return them always *herself*," said Celia in a judicial tone. "Bob might call for them, or Mr. Barrett or Eunice might bring them—they have a car, of course; all farmers have a car nowadays, but I don't think Mrs. Barrett drives."

Miss Phipps picked up her bag and gloves. "I must go,"

she said. "Celia, you *must* tell the police at once the reason
for your misplaced signature."

Celia pouted again.

"I shall get into trouble with my Professor or somebody,"
she said fearfully.

"That's your fault for telling, or rather writing, a lie,"
said Miss Phipps sternly. "Can you prove you were in Laire
on Saturday morning?"

"I shouldn't think so," said Celia. "I was working in the
Library."

Miss Phipps groaned.

The door of the farmhouse was opened by a tall, gaunt,
elderly woman, with plain features, untidy gray hair, sallow
skin, large sad dull eyes—and strong hands, noticed Miss
Phipps.

"Mrs. Barrett? My name is Marian Phipps. I'm a friend
of Mr. Vesey and Miss Whitaker, and deeply concerned
about this terrible affair of your niece."

Mrs. Barrett was silent.

"May I come in and have a word with you?"

"I suppose you must," said Mrs. Barrett ungraciously.

The kitchen was large and handsomely furnished, with
fine oak beams, a superb fire, a large ginger cat lying
asleep on the hearth. The cat opened an eye at Miss Phipps
and closed it again, reassured. Mrs. Barrett indicated a
wheelback chair and put the kettle on the fire.

"Mr. Vesey mentioned you," she said in slow country
tones. "Of course we don't do much reading or such out
here."

"Mrs. Barrett," said Miss Phipps in a comfortable,
woman-to-woman voice. "What kind of girl was your
niece?"

"She was a wicked girl, Miss Phipps," said Mrs. Barrett,

fetching a teapot. "She couldn't leave the men alone. Time and again Ethel and I—Ethel's my sister in Laire—have rued the day we took her. But we thought it our duty. Of course Eunice—well, she had a bad start; she was illegitimate, you know."

"Indeed," said Miss Phipps gravely.

"Yes. My brother was always wild, Harden isn't Eunice's legal name, but we thought it best she should be called by her father's name. People know us up here. We didn't want to give her a bad start, you see."

"I take it her parents are dead."

"That's right. Her mother was nothing. My brother was always wild. And then he didn't get on with my husband, you see."

Miss Phipps meditated on the significance of this last statement, and at length remarked, "Your brother worked here, then?"

"Of course. It was his farm," said Mrs. Barrett with a rather sad smile. "And mine and Ethel's, of course. Father left it to the three of us."

"Oh, I see."

"Yes, indeed. Hardens have been here for nigh on two hundred years," said Mrs. Barrett proudly. "People hereabouts still call it Hardens', sometimes."

"How did Eunice get on with your own children, Mrs. Barrett?"

"I have no children," said the woman, turning her head aside.

"Who took the choir surplices to the church last Saturday?" asked Miss Phipps brusquely, changing the subject.

"My husband and I did. Soon after Eunice left," said Mrs. Barrett. She looked Miss Phipps straight in the eye, and her sallow face flushed.

"She's lying," thought Miss Phipps. "But how? And why?"

She paused to reflect. Just then a car suddenly sounded in the yard outside. Mrs. Barrett stood up, and the cat bounded away and curled itself on the window sill behind the curtain.

Somehow this last action shook all that Miss Phipps had heard into a pattern, and she was not surprised by the appearance of the man who entered the room.

Short but stocky, with broad shoulders and strong hands, high-complexioned, with a large loose red mouth, a bold nose, thick eyebrows, bright insolent brown eyes, tumbled dark curly hair; handsome in a coarsely sensual way, and years younger than his wife; many years younger.

Miss Phipps understood immediately why Mrs. Barrett's brother had left home, why Barrett had married a woman so much older and plainer than himself, what he thought of his barren wife, what had happened between him and his sexy niece, why the cat disliked him, why Mrs. Barrett had lied about the surplices for the husband she adored so foolishly.

"Enter a murderer," thought Miss Phipps.

And as usual, Miss Phipps was right.

MRS. NORRIS VISITS THE LIBRARY

DOROTHY SALISBURY DAVIS

If there was anything in the world Mrs. Norris liked as well as a nice cup of tea, it was to dip now and then into what she called "a comfortable novel." She found it no problem getting one when she and Mr. James Jarvis, for whom she kept house, were in the country. The ladies at the Nyack library both knew and approved her tastes, and while they always lamented that such books were not written any more, nonetheless they always managed to find a new one for her.

But the New York Public Library at Fifth Avenue and Forty-second Street was a house of different entrance. How could a person like Mrs. Norris climb those wide marble steps, pass muster with the uniformed guard, and then ask for her particular kind of book?

She had not yet managed it, but sometimes she got as far as the library steps and thought about it. And if the sun were out long enough to have warmed the stone bench, she sometimes sat a few moments and observed the faces of the people going in and coming out. As her friend Mr. Tully, the detective, said of her, she was a marvelous woman for observing. "And you can take that the way you like, love."

It was a pleasant morning, this one, and having time to spare, Mrs. Norris contemplated the stone bench. She also noticed that one of her shoelaces had come untied; you could not find a plain cotton lace these days, even on a blind man's tray. She locked her purse between her bosom and her arm and began to stoop.

"It's mine! I saw it first!"

A bunioned pump thumped down almost on her toe, and the woman who owned it slyly turned it over on her ankle so that she might retrieve whatever it was she had found. Mrs. Norris was of the distinct opinion that there had been nothing there at all.

"I was only about to tie my shoelace," Mrs. Norris said, pulling as much height as she could out of her dumpy shape.

A wizened, rouged face turned up at her. "Aw," the creature said, "you're a lady. I'll tie the lace for you."

As the woman fumbled at her foot, Mrs. Norris took time to observe the shaggy hair beneath a hat of many summers. Then she cried, "Get up from there! I'm perfectly able to tie my own shoelace."

The woman straightened, and she was no taller than Mrs. Norris. "Did I hear in your voice that you're Irish?"

"You did not! I'm Scots-born." Then remembering Mr. Tully, her detective friend, she added, "But I'm sometimes taken for North of Ireland."

"Isn't it strange, the places people will take you to be from! Where would you say I was born? Sit down for a moment. You're not in a hurry?"

Mrs. Norris thought the woman daft, but she spoke well and softly. "I haven't the faintest notion," she said, and allowed herself to be persuaded by a grubby hand.

"I was born right down there on Thirty-seventh Street, and not nearly as many years ago as you would think. But this town—oh, the things that have happened to it!" She sat a bit too close, and folded her hands over a beaded evening purse. "A friend of mine, an actress, gave this to me." She indicated the purse, having seen Mrs. Norris glance at it. "But there isn't much giving left in this city . . ."

Of course, Mrs. Norris thought. How foolish of her not to have realized what was coming. "What a dreadful noise the buses make," she commented by way of changing the subject.

"And they're all driven by Irishmen," the woman said quite venomously. "They've ruined New York, those people!"

"I have a gentleman friend who is Irish," Mrs. Norris said sharply, and wondered why she didn't get up and out of there.

"Oh, my dear," the woman said, pulling a long face of shock. "The actress of whom I just spoke, you know? She used to be with the Abbey Theatre. She was the first Cathleen Ni Houlihan. Or perhaps it was the second. But she sends me two tickets for every opening night—and something to wear." The woman opened her hand on the beaded purse and stroked it lovingly. "She hasn't had a new play in such a long time."

Mrs. Norris was touched in spite of herself: it was a beautiful gesture. "Were you ever in the theater yourself?" she asked.

The old woman looked her full in the face. Tears came to her eyes. Then she said, "No." She tumbled out a whole series of no's as though to bury the matter. She's protesting too much, Mrs. Norris thought. "But I have done many things in my life," she continued in her easy made-up-as-you-go fashion. "I have a good mind for science. I can tell you the square feet of floor space in a building from counting the windows. On Broadway, that naked waterfall, you know . . ." Mrs. Norris nodded, remembering the display. "I have figured out how many times the same water goes over it every night. Oh-h-h, and I've written books—just lovely stories about the world when it was gracious, and people could talk to each other even if one of them wasn't one of those psychiatrists."

What an extraordinary woman!

"But who would read stories like that nowadays?" She cast a sidelong glance at Mrs. Norris.

"I would!" Mrs. Norris said.

"Bless you, my dear, I knew that the moment I looked into your face!" She cocked her head, as a bird does, at a strange sound. "Do you happen to know what time it is?"

Mrs. Norris looked at her wrist watch. The woman leaned close to look also. "A Gruen is a lovely watch," she said. She could see like a mantis.

"It's time I was going," Mrs. Norris said. "It's eleven thirty."

"Oh, and time for me, too. I've been promised a job today."

"Where?" asked Mrs. Norris, which was quite unlike her, but the word had spurted out in her surprise.

"It would degrade me to tell you," the stranger said, and her eyes fluttered.

Mrs. Norris could feel the flush in her face. She almost toppled her new, flowered hat, fanning herself. "I'm sorry," she said. "It was rude of me to ask."

"Would you like to buy me a little lunch?" the woman asked brazenly.

Mrs. Norris got to her feet. "All right," she said, having been caught fairly at a vulnerable moment. "There's a cafeteria across the street. I often go there myself for a bowl of soup. Come along."

The woman had risen with her, but her face had gone awry. Mrs. Norris supposed that at this point she was always bought off—she was not the most appetizing of sights to share a luncheon table with. But Mrs. Norris led the way down the steps at a good pace. She did not begrudge the meal, but she would begrudge the price of it if it were not spent on a meal.

"Wait, madam. I can't keep up with you," the woman wailed.

Mrs. Norris had to stop anyway to tie the blessed shoelace.

Her guest picked at the food, both her taste and her gab dried up in captivity. "It's a bit rich for my stomach," she complained when Mrs. Norris chided her.

Mrs. Norris sipped her tea. Then something strange happened: the cup trembled in her hand. At the same instant there was a clatter of dishes, the crash of glass, the screams of women, and the sense almost, more than the sound, of an explosion. Mrs. Norris's eyes met those of the woman's across from her. They were aglow as a child's with excitement, and she grinned like a quarter moon.

Outside, people began to run across the street toward the Library. Mrs. Norris could hear the blast of police whistles, and she stretched her neck, hoping to see better. "Eat up and we'll go," she urged.

"Oh, I couldn't eat now and with all this commotion."

"Then leave it."

Once in the street Mrs. Norris was instantly the prisoner of the crowd, running with it as if she were treading water, frighteningly, unable to turn aside or stem the tide. And lost at once was her frail companion, cast apart either by weight or wisdom. Mrs. Norris took in enough breath for a scream which she let go with a piper's force. It made room for her where there had been none before and from then on she screamed her way to the fore of the crowd.

"Stand back! There's nobody hurt but there will be!" a policeman shouted.

Sirens wailed the approach of police reinforcements. Meanwhile, two or three patrolmen were joined by a few able-bodied passers-by to make a human cordon across the library steps.

"It blew the stone bench fifty feet in the air," Mrs. Norris heard a man say.

"The stone bench?" she cried out. "Why, I was just sitting on it!"

"Then you've got a hard bottom, lady," a policeman growled. He and a companion were trying to hold on to a young man.

Their prisoner gave a twist and came face to face with Mrs. Norris. "That's the woman," he shouted. "That's the one I'm trying to tell you about. Let go of me and ask *her!*"

A policeman looked at her. "This one with the flowers on her hat?"

"That's the one! She looked at her watch, got up and left the package, then ran down the steps, and the next thing . . ."

"Got up and left what, young man?" Mrs. Norris interrupted.

"The box under the bench," the young man said, but to one of the officers.

"A box under the bench?" Mrs. Norris repeated.

"How come you were watching her?" the officer said.

"I wasn't especially. I was smoking a cigarette . . ."

"Do you work in the library?"

No doubt he answered, but Mrs. Norris's attention was suddenly distracted, and by what seemed like half the police force of New York City.

"I have a friend, Jasper Tully, in the District Attorney's office," she declared sternly.

"That's fine, lady," a big sergeant said. "We'll take a ride down there right now." Then he bellowed at the top of his lungs, "Keep the steps clear till the Bomb Squad gets here."

In Jasper Tully's office, Mrs. Norris tried to tell her interrogators about the strange little woman. But she knew from the start that they were going to pay very little attention to her story. Their long experience with panhandlers had run so true to pattern that they would not admit to any exception.

And yet Mrs. Norris felt sure she had encountered the exception. For example, she had been cleverly diverted by the woman when she might have seen the package. The woman had put her foot down on nothing—Mrs. Norris was sure of that. She remembered having looked down at her shoelace, and she would have seen a coin had there been one at her feet—Mrs. Norris was a woman who knew the color of money. Oh, it was a clever lass, that other one, and there was a fair amount of crazy hate in her. Mrs. Norris was unlikely to forget the venom she had been so ready to spew on the Irish.

She tried to tell them. But nobody had to button Annie Norris's lip twice. It was not long until they wished Jasper Tully a widower's luck with her, and went back themselves to the scene of the blast.

Mr. Tully offered to take her home.

"No, I think I'll walk and cogitate, 'thank you," she said.

"Jimmie gives you too much time off," Tully muttered. He was on close terms with her employer.

"He gives me the time I take."

"Is he in town now?"

"He is, or will be tonight. He'll be going full dress to the theater. It's an opening night."

"Aren't you going yourself?"

Mrs. Norris gave it a second's thought. "I might," she said.

The detective took a card from his pocket and wrote down a telephone number. "You can reach me through this at all hours," he said. "That's in case your cogitating gets you into any more trouble."

When he had taken her to the office door, Mrs. Norris looked up to his melancholy face. "Who was Cathleen Ni Houlihan?"

Tully rubbed his chin. "She wasn't a saint exactly, but I think she was a living person . . . How the hell would I know? I was born in the Bronx!" A second later he added, "There was a play about her, wasn't there?"

"There was," said Mrs. Norris. "I'm glad to see you're not as ignorant as you make yourself out to be."

"Just be sure you're as smart as you think you are," Tully said, "if you're off to tackle a policeman's job again."

He had no faith in her, Mrs. Norris thought, or he wouldn't let her do it.

All afternoon she went over the morning's incidents in her mind. As soon as Mr. Jarvis left the apartment for dinner and the theater, she went downtown herself. The evening papers were full of the bombing, calling it the work of a madman. The mechanism had been made up of clock parts, and the detonating device was something as simple as a pin. It was thought possibly to have been a hatpin.

Well!

And there was not a mention of her in any account. The police were obviously ashamed of themselves.

Mrs. Norris took as her place of departure Forty-sixth Street and Seventh Avenue. Turning her back on the waterfall atop the Broadway building, she walked toward Shubert Alley. Anyone who could even guess at the number of times the same water went over the dam must have looked at it at least as often. And Cathleen Ni Houlihan—no stranger to the theater had plucked that name out of the air.

The beggars were out in droves: the blind, the lame, and the halt. And there were those with tin cups who could read the date in a dead man's eye.

Mrs. Norris was early, and a good thing she was. Sightseers were already congesting the sidewalk in front of the theater. New York might be the biggest city in the world, but to lovers of the stage a few square feet of it was world enough on an opening night.

She watched from across the street for five minutes, then ten, with the crowd swelling and her own hopes dwindling. Then down the street from Eighth Avenue, with a sort of unperturbed haste, came the little beggar-woman. She wore the same hat, the same ragged coat and carried the same beaded purse.

And she also carried a box about six inches by six which she carefully set down on the steps of a fire exit.

Mrs. Norris plunged across the street and paused again, watching the beggar, fascinated in spite of herself. Round and round one woman she walked, looking her up and down, and then she scouted another. The women themselves were well-dressed out-of-towners by their looks, who had come to gape at the celebrated first nighters now beginning to arrive. When the little panhandler had made her choice of victims, she said, and distinctly enough for Mrs. Norris to hear:

"That's Mrs. Vanderhoff arriving now. Lovely, isn't she? Oh, dear, that's not her husband with her. Why, that's Johnson Tree—the oil man! You're not from Texas, are you, dear?"

Mrs. Norris glanced at the arrivals. It was her own Mr. Jarvis and his friend. A Texas oil man indeed! The woman made up her stories to the fit of her victims! She was an artist at it.

Mrs. Norris edged close to the building and bent down to

examine the box. She thought she could hear a rhythmic sound. She could, she realized—her own heartbeat.

"Leave that box alone!"

Mrs. Norris obeyed, but not before she had touched, had actually moved, the box. It was empty, or at least as light as a dream, and the woman had not recognized her. She was too busy spinning a tale. Mrs. Norris waited it out. The woman finally asked for money and got it. She actually got paper money! Then she came for the box.

"Remember me?" Mrs. Norris said.

The woman cocked her head and looked at her. "Should I?"

"This morning on the Public Library steps," Mrs. Norris prompted.

The wizened face brightened. "But of course! Oh, and there's something I wanted to talk to you about. I saw you speaking to my young gentleman friend—you know, in all that excitement?"

"Oh, yes," Mrs. Norris said, remembering the young man who had pointed her out to the police.

"Isn't he a lovely young man? And to have had such misfortune."

"Lovely," Mrs. Norris agreed.

"You know, he had a scholarship to study atomic science and *those* people did him out of it."

"*Those* people?"

"All day long you can see them going in and out, in and out, carting books by the armful. Some of them have beards. False, you know. And those thick glasses—I ask you, who would be fooled by them? Spies! Traitors! And *they* can get as many books as they want."

"Oh, *those* people," Mrs. Norris said understandingly.

"And my poor young friend. They won't even give him a library card, and after I wrote him such a nice reference."

"Do you know where he lives?" Mrs. Norris said as casually as she could.

"No. But I know where he works. He fixes watches for a jeweler on Forty-seventh Street. I walked by there once and saw him working in the window. If you wait here for me, I'll walk over and show you the place tonight. He's not there now, of course, but I'm sure he'll be there in the morning. I hope you can help him."

Considering what he had tried to do for her, Mrs. Norris hoped she could, too. "I'll try," she said.

The warning buzzer sounded within the theater. The lights flickered.

"Excuse me a moment," the woman said and picked up the box. "I've bought some flowers for an actress friend of mine, and I want to give them in before curtain. Wouldn't it be nice if she invited us to see the play? I shan't accept, of course, unless she invites both of us."

Mrs. Norris doubted that she would see the woman again once she got out of sight. She had what might be called a temporary sort of mind. "Tell me before you go," Mrs. Norris asked, "what did you think was in the package under the library bench?"

"What package, dear?" The woman rolled her eyes slyly upward.

"The one you thought I was going to find today when you stomped your foot down on a round nothing."

The old lady clutched at her sleeve with a grubby fist. "That was mine! What do you mean, *you* found it?"

"Then you can tell me what was in it?"

The woman withdrew her hand. Blandly she said, "No, I'll just tell the police if you don't give it back to me."

"I'll tell them myself," Mrs. Norris thought. She said,

"You'll be late with your flowers. Hand them in and we'll take a nice walk, you and I, and settle everything."

"I'll be right along," the woman said, and moistened her lips in greedy anticipation.

DON'T HANG A
DEAD AUNT

INGRAM MEYER

They had parked the car on Main Street and were walking down the long, uneven walkway towards the old mansion. Pixy's feet hurt, and he had sharp little pebbles in his shoes.

"Shouldn't wear those fancy things on a job," said Grandma.

Pixy just grunted. He looked distastefully down at her sneakers. It was embarrassing to walk in public with her. Pixy had resigned himself years ago to her little idiosyncrasies, but the footwear would always be a sore point. They had, in fact, lost business over those scruffy, smelly things, and goodness knows, there wasn't much doing in the private eye profession these days. So he tried once more.

"Nice hairdo you've got there, Gran." It really was nice. All done up and coiled around, held with a large, glittering, mother-of-pearl clip. Her silver hair glistened in the spring morning sun.

"Thanks," answered Grandma.

"Nice suit, too. Pretty blouse. Earrings are new?"

"Thanks. And—yeah." Her two-piece greenish tweed suit was huge, but it was well cut, hiding her ample rolls and bulges. The truth was, from the top of her head to the bottom of her skirt, Grandma was some smart-looking lady.

From the hem of her skirt to the toes of her shoes she was a mess. Thick crinkly beige cotton stockings, shabby faded tennis shoes with knots in the laces—and holes! There was a frizzy hole on the outside of the left shoe, and one toe was almost coming out the right one. It was disgusting. Passersby would stare, fascinated.

"About the shoes, Gran—"

She sniffed, looking nastily up and down Pixy's spare, five foot two frame. Her eyes rested on his elevator shoes, and one of her eyebrows shot up. Pixy shut up.

She wasn't actually his real grandmother. Then again, wasn't she the whole town's granny? For she had been the marrying kind in her younger years—and man, had she been married! Left and right. Grandma had changed surnames like other women changed their linen. MacDonald, Kinski, Rossilini, Morgan, Zachow, and Lieberman had been names one could remember—and spell. At the end she had changed it back to her maiden name, Smith.

When Grandma became single once more, she had decided to become something other than a housewife for a change. And what she had really wanted to be was a movie star or something in that line. But she hadn't known anybody in this town who had connections or influence anywhere important. The only person who led a fairly exciting life here was her next door neighbor Pixy. So in the end she had bought herself a partnership in his business. That had been almost ten years ago.

"Watch out for that bramble stuff," warned Pixy. But Grandma's sneakers had already ground the thorny entanglement into the earth.

They had arrived at the Giles house.

"Funny place," muttered Grandma. "Five hundred yards off Main Street, and you'd think you were at the end of the world."

"Yeah. And it's creepy. Was an unpleasant place when old Horace was still alive. But now it's dead. A dead house." Pixy shivered. He was a darn good detective and had solved over the years quite a few so-called unsolvable crimes. But they had been bright-light downtown things. You put him into an old deserted house, and Pixy became jelly. Pixy believed in ghosts, if the truth must be known. And the only person who knew this truth was Grandma.

"You are not going to do a disappearance act, are you?" She looked suspiciously at her partner. He didn't answer, for his stomach felt funny. He looked at the brown, two story clapboard building, with its double row of rectangular windows in heavy wooden frames. Some windows had tattered curtains in them, some were cracked, and all were filthy and cobwebby. There were ghosts here—definitely!

They walked up the half dozen wooden steps to the front door, and Grandma took out the key.

"Think we'll find anything in there, Gran?"

"We had better! No results, no money."

"We *are* getting a bit short on that."

"Nobody spends money on private dicks any more. And why should they? Cops will do the jobs for free. Some cases even get solved." She sighed.

"They didn't get any results here, though. Probably got the willies and ran off." Pixy chuckled.

"See who's talking." She opened the door and got hold of Pixy's arm. Together they walked into the old house.

The house was in surprisingly good shape on the inside. Only a thin layer of dust had accumulated on top of the heavy oak furniture and ceramic lamps. The air was stuffy, though, and the windows looked even filthier from the inside than they had from out—if that was at all possible. Pixy noticed a fat grey spider hanging from a string of frayed curtain, and he could have sworn it looked him straight in the eyes.

"It has black eyes," he said aloud.

"Who?"

Pixy didn't bother to answer. He felt jumpy and could have kicked himself for it. Grandma walked around the living room.

"Kind of cozy in here, isn't it?" she said. "Guess old Horace wanted to discourage unwanted visitors, so he kept the outside messy and uninviting."

They went back into the hallway, and Pixy looked up the steep, unlit stairway.

"Stairs look waggly," he said. Grandma stopped beside him.

"What d'you mean—waggly? Carpet is a bit threadbare, railing needs a little paint, but that doesn't make the stairs unsafe." She started slowly up, her sneakers going flip flop. Pixy stayed behind until she turned at the landing. Then he took the steps two by two, until she turned at the landing. Then he took the steps two by two.

"Scared by yourself down there?" snarled Grandma.

"'Course not." Pixy walked bravely down the long, narrow hallway, opening doors at random. His heart beat furiously, but he wasn't going to let *her* know. Even she wouldn't understand that he knew, was absolutely sure, that they weren't alone.

"Come here and have a look. This seems to be some sort of den," Grandma called.

Pixy hurried back and, standing on his toes, looked over her shoulder. Well, well. Downstairs had been a bit sinister, with all the chunky furniture crowded everywhere, and with the ugly portraits on the walls. The stairway, the upstairs hall, and the bedrooms he'd peeked into had been decidedly odd—all plum-color, purplish and brown. But this now, this den or whatever, made Pixy's skin crawl. For here, on the walls, hung shrunken heads. That's right! He closed his eyes and shook his head. When he looked again, sure enough, they were still there. Eight heads, all kind of rust-colored and shrivelled up, with long black hair tied into ponytails.

"Who are they?" whispered Pixy.

"How the hell should I know! Souvenirs?"

"I mean, *they* aren't why we are here, are they?"

"Not likely," answered Grandma. "You read Horace's posthumous letter to us. It stated clearly that somebody only had to find his Aunt Adabelle's remains and give them a decent burial. The house can't be sold until she's outa here."

"What he really meant, her ghost has to get out of here before—"

"Stop that nonsense, Pixy. Ghosts and spirits, my foot! You really are weird sometimes, you know."

"Well, I feel a presence in this place."

"You give me the creeps. I should have come alone." She was getting mad, so Pixy kept quiet.

"Horace and his aunt were anthropologists. Were said to have been shipwrecked for a couple of years somewhere in New Guinea around the time the Second World War broke out," said Grandma. She felt a little sorry for snapping at her younger partner. But he could drive her absolutely crazy. Why she had ever gone into business with this little chicken was a mystery in itself to her. She must have been daft. Or maybe he had brought out some deeply buried, motherly feelings in her. Grandma had no children of her own.

The two detectives walked all around the large room, opening desk drawers, lifting sofa cushions. Grandma even took out a long bunch of dried pampas grass and looked inside a tall, skinny, golden and black jug.

"Any bones in there?" mocked Pixy. Grandma didn't bother to answer.

"*Are* we looking for bones?" asked Pixy. He had paused by the window. "Because if we are, how do we know they aren't out in the garden? It looks awfully untidy out there. Weeds and junk all over the place."

"Not according to the letter. Says only to remove Aunt Adabelle's remains from the house before selling it and dividing the money among those funny relatives." Grandma looked suspiciously at the jug again, but there was nothing in it except the pampas grass. She gave it a slight kick with a tennis shoe.

Grandma and Pixy took off their jackets and rolled up their sleeves. Then they went seriously to work. They looked into cupboards, emptied storage boxes, looked into the freezer and the oven, took out air vents and furnace filters—in short, they turned the house upside down. But they found neither bones nor ashes nor anything that could remotely be Aunt Adabelle.

Exhausted, they went back to the kitchen where Grandma perked a pot of coffee.

"I wish we'd never heard of old Horace," grumbled Pixy.

"Well, we need the money, don't we?" Grandma sighed.

They sat for a while in silence and drank their coffee. Pixy's stomach growled, but he wasn't going to eat anything in this house. He hoped he would be home early enough. He had asked What's-Her-Name from down at the end of his street out for dinner.

They went next up to the attic. There wasn't much there, though, just a few boxes with books and old clothes. There were empty suitcases and a couple of broken chairs. In the corner stood a headless dress dummy with a faded velvet ballgown on it. Grandma lifted the skirt, but there was only wire and cheesecloth underneath.

"Too bad this thing hasn't got a head," joked Pixy. "We could have put it into a coffin and—"

"You want to be a stand-up comedian, Pixy, you go to Las Vegas." Grandma was on her way downstairs again.

They took another look at the living room, but to no avail. Very tired, both dropped into overstuffed, plum-colored armchairs. Pixy wished he could turn on the television, but he didn't quite dare with Grandma around.

They both heard it. First there came a faint clunk from above, then a sound like something sliding across the floor. Pixy's heart missed a beat, and Grandma jumped up.

"There's someone up there," she whispered.

"I told you so! Ever since we came here, I tried to tell you, there's someone else in the house. I felt eyes."

"Pixy, one more word of ghosts out of you, and I'll murder you with my bare hands!"

They both walked quietly out into the hallway.

"Should have brought a gun. Why didn't we bring guns?" hissed Pixy. Fear made him mean. Could one shoot a ghost?

"Because we never carry guns," whispered Grandma. "We aren't fiction toughies! And stop clicking your teeth! Damn it, Pixy, you make me nervous."

"*I* make you nervous? What about that upstairs? *Do* we go up?" Oh man, he hoped not. "Or do we go somewhere and call the cops?"

Grandma just looked pityingly at her partner, then started to tiptoe up the stairs. Pixy was right behind her.

"Sounded like the noise came from the den, what?" he whispered.

They paused outside the door and put their ears against it. No sound came from within.

"Maybe something just toppled over from a draft or something," said Grandma. "Let's go inside."

Pixy grabbed the door handle, and both detectives burst into the room. There was no one there. Pixy walked slowly towards the desk, and Grandma went to look behind the sofa. Her sneaker hit something hidden under the ruffles. She yelled. Pixy spun around and watched with fascinated horror as one of the shrunken heads came rolling towards him, like a billiard ball. The hair was wrapped all around it, with the eye sockets peeking through. It crashed against the desk leg and came to a halt.

Grandma recovered from the shock and walked slowly over.

"Heck, I kicked it with my practically bare toe." She looked shaken. "I mean, it is pretty horrible to kick a poor shrunken head with one's toe." She stooped and picked up the head, turning it this way and that.

"How can you touch that thing?" Pixy was disgusted.

But Grandma took it over to the window where the light was better.

"Come here a minute, Pixy. Have a good look at this thing. Does anything strike you as odd?"

"Does anything strike me as odd!" cried Pixy. "How odd can something get? Here I'm in the same room with a nice old lady—a lady who's mucking about with a human head. And I'm being asked if anything is—"

"Calm down. That's not what I meant. Have a look at this hair, and then compare it with those ponytails over on the wall. See any difference?"

They both turned to the display wall, and Grandma held the head against the other ones.

"See," she said. "These all have coarse, straight, blue-black hair. And now feel this here. It's soft and dull. I shouldn't wonder if this has been dyed."

"I'll be damned!" exclaimed Pixy. "You're right, it is different. You think we found Aunt Adabelle? That's great! Now we can collect our money."

"Not so quick! Slow down, Pixy. We've only got the head."

"Oh, for Pete's sake, Gran! Do we now look for a shrunken body? Listen, I can't stand this house another moment. Let's get out of here!"

"Hmm." Grandma sat down on the sofa, putting the head in her lap. "You know, Pixy, what I don't understand is, why did this particular head fall off the wall?"

"She wants a decent burial, that's why. If they don't get put in the earth by a clergyman, some of them walk, you know."

"Walk?"

"Sure. At nights."

"Pixy! I warn you, don't give me that ghost garbage."

"But it's true."

"Then why don't the other seven on the wall . . . walk? Tell me that, Pixy."

"Because they are probably New Guinea natives. They are used to having their heads shrunk and hung up for decoration. Anyhow, seems old Horace learned a few tricks from the natives about—er—ornaments while being ship-wrecked, huh?"

Grandma just shook her head. "Yeah, I guess he must have." She turned the shrunken head so it looked straight at her.

"She doesn't look too unhappy, really, do you think, Pixy?"

Pixy felt his spine tingle. "Doesn't look especially happy, neither," he grumbled. All he wanted was to get out of this creepy house. If only they hadn't been so desperate for money, he'd never have agreed to take on this silly job.

"You think we'll get paid for only—that?" he asked. "Maybe that's all there is here."

"It probably is. I'm not so morbid as to think for one moment that old Horace did her in right here. No, Pixy, what I think is that this poor thing died in New Guinea—maybe of some tropical disease—and this was the only way her poor, grief-befallen nephew could manage to take her home with him. Remember, those were bad times, with a worldwide war on, when Horace and Adabelle were shipwrecked. You couldn't just throw a body onto some fast jet and fly home within a couple of hours."

"No, I suppose not, Gran."

Grandma got up from the sofa, putting the shrunken head into her pocket. Then she said, "Listen, Pixy. Remember what you joked about up in the attic? About the dress dummy?"

"About using it for a body?"

"That's right." Grandma looked slyly at her partner. "We do need some cash—and soon. Would take a long time, maybe months, or even years, to convince certain people about the missing body."

Pixy looked at Grandma and grinned.

"Want me to order the coffin right away?"

A WEB OF BOOKS

LOREN D. ESTLEMAN

The visitor stepped inside the bookshop and blinked. The muted light and cool, dank air seemed otherworldly after the bright heat of the New Mexico street. As he closed the door, feathers of dust clinging to the spines of the decaying volumes on the shelves crawled and twitched in the current of air. The place smelled of must.

"Can I help you?" bleated the old man seated behind the dented desk. He was thin and angular, his shoulders falling away under a fraying sweater. Dull black hair spilled untidily over his collar. His face was narrow and puckered and dominated by spectacles so thick he seemed to be peering from the other side of a fish tank.

"Are you the owner?"

The old man nodded. "My name is Sharecross."

"Jed Kirby. I'm an investigator with Southwestern Life and Property." He didn't offer to shake hands. The missing finger on his right hand, a souvenir of Korea, provoked questions he was tired of answering. "I tried to call you yesterday."

"The lines are down east of town. A Santa Ana blew through over the weekend."

Kirby dismissed it with a wave of his good hand. "I'm looking for a man named Murchison, Alan Murchison. We think he has information about an item of missing property insured by us."

"I don't know the name. Is it a book that's missing?"

"A very rare volume entitled *The Midnight Sky*, by James Edward Long, published in Edinburgh in 1758. About ten inches by seven, four hundred and fifty pages, bound in brown morocco with gold leaf on the page ends. It was stolen from a private library in Albuquerque last month. We think Murchison is the thief."

"Ah, that one," Sharecross said. "Only two copies are known to exist. Each is worth as much as some whole collections. What makes you think he'd come here?"

"He's on the run. He was nearly apprehended in Silver City, but he managed to elude the police. He'll probably try to unload the book for whatever he can get and use the money to skip to South America. Our information has him heading this way."

"Dear me, that seems like a lot of trouble over one book, even *The Midnight Sky*."

"The book's just part of it, although it's the part that most directly concerns us. The law would dearly love to have him. He murdered the owner in order to gain possession."

"Dear me," repeated the bookseller.

"It pieces together like this." Kirby caught himself gesturing with the incomplete hand and switched. "Murchison, a dealer who supplies rare curiosities to collectors who don't ask questions, went to this man Scullock with an offer to buy the book. When Scullock refused to sell, Murchison lost control and split the fellow's cranium with a bronze bust of Homer the police found near the body. Then he grabbed the book and left. When his customer got suspicious and backed out of the deal, he took off."

Sharecross looked thoughtful. "Your company must be

particularly anxious to recover the item, since you beat the police here."

"It's insured for two hundred thousand dollars, payable to Scullock's heirs if we fail to get it back. My employers aren't in business for their health."

"Who is?" The old man stretched a scrawny arm and lifted a book the size and thickness of a bathroom tile from a stack at his feet. "Two hundred thousand is far outside my budget, Mr. Kirby. This is more my speed." He handed it to the visitor.

It was bound in burgundy leather, heavier than it looked. Kirby ran fingers over the hand-tooling, opened it carefully, and glanced at the publisher's ads bound into the back of the book. "First edition?"

"Third. Browning's *Ring and the Book*, the one with the erratum on page sixty-seven. I paid seven hundred and fifty dollars for it in Las Cruces two years ago. That's more than I can afford to pay for any book, but I couldn't resist it. The pension I get from the Santa Fe police department won't stand that kind of strain often."

Kirby looked up, startled. "You were a policeman?"

"Detective. Many years ago, I'm afraid."

Too many, thought the other. He returned the book. "Old books don't really interest me. You'd know Murchison if you saw him. He's small, kind of fragile-looking, with prematurely white hair. Wears tweed jackets and smokes a pipe."

A fresh furrow appeared in Sharecross's forehead.

"He's been in, hasn't he?"

"Just once." The old man fondled the Browning. "To buy a book, not sell one. A badly dilapidated copy of Shakespeare's tragedies for ten dollars. That was yesterday. He said his name was Thacker. I think he's staying at the hotel."

"Where's that?"

"Across the street, next to the old town well."

Kirby hurried out. As the door closed behind him he glimpsed Sharecross easing a thick volume down from a high shelf.

Twenty minutes later the visitor was back. Behind the desk Sharecross lifted his eyebrows inquisitively over the big book. It was a current edition of *Who's Who in Book Collecting*.

"What kind of law you got around here?" Kirby demanded.

"Sheriff McCreedy," came the reply, after a moment. "But he's at the county seat. There's no way to reach him with the telephone lines down, short of going there. What's wrong?"

"Murchison's dead. Someone shot him."

"Shot him! Are you sure?"

"Bullets make holes. The blood's still fresh." Kirby paused. "The book isn't in his room. I searched."

Sharecross dragged over the old-fashioned upright telephone on his desk.

"You said the lines were down," Kirby reminded him.

"Not in town. Hello, Birdie?" He spoke into the mouthpiece. "Birdie, get hold of Uncle Ned and ask him to fetch the sheriff. It's urgent." He rang off. To Kirby:

"Ned Scoffield's ninety-seven, but he can make that old Indian motorcycle of his sing. He'll have the law here by sundown."

"Whoever killed Murchison was after the book. Now that he has it, there's no way he'll be within fifty miles of here by sundown."

"Maybe he doesn't have it. Did you search Murchison's car?"

"Car!" Kirby cuffed his forehead. "Stupid! He didn't walk here. Where would I find it?"

"Behind the hotel would be my guess. That's where all the guests park. Maybe you should wait for the sheriff." But the old man was talking to the visitor's back. He was already out the door.

Kirby got the dead man's license number from an upset clerk at the front desk. The plate belonged to a late-model sedan under a skin of desert dust. The inside was an oven. He stripped off his jacket and got to work. After half an hour he climbed out, empty-handed and gasping, and leaned back against a fender to mop his face with a soaked handkerchief. Sharecross approached through shimmering waves of heat, *Who's Who* under one arm.

"Nothing?"

Kirby, too overheated to talk, shook his head.

"I see you checked out the trunk and engine compartment," observed the bookseller, nodding at the open lid and dislodged hood. "I just came from Murchison's room. He was shot twice at close range. Whoever did it must have used a silencer or he'd have alerted everyone in the hotel."

"What were you doing there?" Kirby was cooling off slowly. Dusk was gathering.

"I conducted a search of my own. Once a cop, always a cop. There's something missing besides *The Midnight Sky*."

"A towel?"

"The Shakespeare I sold him. You didn't happen to find it?"

"No, but why should you care? You got your ten bucks."

"It seems to me a thief who'd kill for Long's *magnum opus* couldn't be bothered with such a common item. Also, I asked some of the other merchants what they could tell me about Thacker, or Murchison, or whatever he was calling himself. Carl Lathrop at the dry goods said he sold Thacker a thirty foot extension cord last night just before closing."

The other contemplated his handkerchief. "What could he have wanted with that?"

"That's one mystery. Another is why was he wasting time here when he knew the law and your company were on his heels? Why stop here at all, for that matter? Why not head straight for Mexico and peddle the book in one of the major tourist centers? He seems to have made a lot of mistakes for an experienced criminal."

"He'd never been chased before. Maybe he panicked."

"Maybe," agreed Sharecross. "Or maybe he came here to meet a partner. Maybe it was his partner who killed him. Well, we can stand here spinning theories all night and freeze to death. The desert cools off fast when the sun goes down. Why don't we go back to the shop and wait for the sheriff?"

On the way they passed the town well. It was partially boarded over and the ancient peaked roof leaned ten degrees off plumb.

"If it's dry it should be torn down and the hole filled in," Kirby observed. "It's a safety hazard. Someone could fall in."

"You're probably right, but I'll be sorry to see it go. When it does I'll be the second oldest thing in town after Uncle Ned Scoffield."

The bookshop seemed even gloomier by electric light. Pacing up and down, glancing at the titles on the shelves, Kirby asked his host why he had quit the police. "Job get too tough?"

"It got too easy. The pattern never varies. Someone commits a crime and attempts to confuse the issue, but the more he tries the simpler it grows. He spins a web and ends up catching himself." He wiped his glasses. His eyes were sardine-colored. "I find tracing a book's provenance far more challenging."

Sirens shattered the desert peace. Two blue and white prowl cars ground to a halt in front of the shop, their lights throbbing and splashing red and blue all over the street. A middle-aged man whose tanned face matched the color of his uniform shirt strode in, towing three deputies in similar attire. They all wore Stetsons and high boots.

"What's going on, Avery?" demanded the man in front.

"Murder, sheriff." Sharecross put on his spectacles. "The victim is registered at the hotel under the name Thacker, though he's known elsewhere as Alan Murchison. You'll find him in Room 14 with two bullets in his chest." He indicated Kirby. "I think a paraffin test on this gentleman's hands will show within a reasonable margin of certainty that he fired the gun that put them there."

Before Kirby could react, one of the deputies seized him and hurled him up against a wall full of books. He was commanded to brace himself on his arms and spread his feet. "The old man's crazy!" he protested. "What motive would I have to—" Rough hands frisked him.

Sharecross said, "You won't find the gun on him. My guess is he chucked it into the well. As things stood he barely had time to kill Murchison, search his room for the book, ditch the murder weapon, and come back here to report the crime."

Sheriff McCreedy directed his deputies to watch the prisoner and accompanied Sharecross outside. The sun was almost gone.

"I've something else to show you before we look at the body." The old man filled him in on the way to the abandoned well.

"Kirby was the dead man's partner," he explained, when

the sheriff had been brought up to date. "Or perhaps I should refer to him as Jed Carlisle instead of Kirby. That's the name he's listed under in *Who's Who in Book Collecting*. Carlisle was the customer who commissioned Murchison to find *The Midnight Sky*. The way I read things, Murchison tried to shake him down for more money by threatening to pin the owner's murder on his customer. Carlisle agreed to his terms, said he'd meet him here. It's an out-of-the-way place, perfect for what he had in mind. Then he came here, posing as an insurance investigator to throw off the authorities, and shot Murchison to death. He made two mistakes. The first was failing to find out where the book was hidden before he silenced his victim.

"I don't think Kirby, or Carlisle, has much respect for rural law officers, sheriff. When a search of Murchison's hotel room and car didn't yield his prize he was content to sit back and let you comb the town for it, confident that when it was found he could step forward and claim it for his 'company.' But then he was more bold than smart or he wouldn't have planned this whole thing the way he did."

The sheriff pulled at his lower lip. "What made you suspect him in the first place?"

"He seemed to have more than an employee's knowledge of that book. I tested him by handing him a rare Browning. He claimed that kind of thing didn't interest him; if that were so he would simply have glanced at it to be polite and handed it back. Instead he stroked the binding, lifted open the cover as if it were made of glass, looked closely at the advertisements bound in at the back. After that I consulted *Who's Who*, going through it entry by entry until I found one that fit the man I knew as Jed Kirby. There aren't very many wealthy bibliophiles who are missing the third finger from their right hand. It's a Carlisle trademark, like J. Pierpont Morgan's swollen nose."

"You said he made two mistakes. What was the second?"

"Look in the well."

Shadows filled the ancient excavation. McCreedy produced his flashlight and switched it on. Sharecross directed him to train the beam up under the dilapidated roof. Near the apex, secured by a black cord to the rod that had once supported the bucket, dangled a thick volume with a worn cover beginning to split along the hinge.

"Is that *The Midnight Sky*?" asked the sheriff.

"Hardly." The bookseller untied the second knot that held the book in place. It dropped into the well, pulling its cord. As it descended, a paper-wrapped parcel roughly the same size rose from the depths. Sharecross freed it from the cord and unwrapped it. The sheriff's flashlight gleamed off handsome leather and gold leaf. "Carlisle's second mistake was being in too much of a hurry when he disposed of the gun. He should have looked at the well more closely. The Shakespeare made the perfect counterweight. Note what Murchison tied them with."

McCreedy examined it. "Looks like an extension cord."

"Thirty feet long, I should judge. It was Murchison's last trick. If he'd purchased that much rope and Carlisle found out, the well would have seemed the logical next step. Extension cord was just offbeat enough to keep everyone guessing."

"Except you."

The old man ignored the reluctant compliment. "I told Carlisle earlier that the criminal often catches himself in his own web. This one was spun out of leather and buckram and gold and paper. A web of books. Murchison used a book to help conceal the book he had committed murder to obtain. That book, and Carlisle's obsession to have it, drove him to murder the murderer. A book made me suspect him, and another book led to his identification and apprehension.

And now, sheriff—" he paused uncomfortably and adjusted his spectacles on his thin nose—"I imagine it's your intention to, er, throw the book at him."

Sheriff McCreedy stared at him in mute accusation.

"Yes. Well," said Sharecross, and turned back in the direction of his shop.

PIERRE CHAMBRUN'S DILEMMA

HUGH PENTECOST

After ten years as public-relations director for the Beaumont, New York's top luxury hotel, I tell myself that I have come to know Pierre Chambrun, the Beaumont's legendary manager, better than anyone else on the staff. There is, of course, Betsy Ruysdale, his fabulous secretary, who appears able to read his mind in advance, but there are some of us who think she may be much closer to him than just a member of his efficient crew. That is another story, a secret that only Chambrun and Betsy could reveal.

Chambrun is king of his world. The Beaumont is like a city within a city, with its own security force, hospital, shops, restaurants, bars, and living quarters for a thousand people. Chambrun knows everything there is to know about its operation—exactly what is happening in every nook and cranny of his elegant establishment almost moment to moment. The difference between the Beaumont and an ordinary town is that except for a few people who own cooperative apartments on the upper floors, the residents are transient, coming and going from all over the world. It is a home-away-from-home of many diplomats involved in the work of the United Nations. Movie stars, social luminaries from London, Paris, or Monaco pass in and out.

In addition, Chambrun knows all there is to know about every guest—their credit ratings, their love lives, their po-

litical affiliation, their habits, good and bad. It might have
embarrassed some of them to know how much intimate information we had about them. The information wasn't difficult to collect with an efficient front office, with a
security service and housekeeping staff, with Maitre d's,
bartenders, and sharp and observant bellmen.

It might have surprised the staff even more to know how
much Chambrun knew about those who worked for him,
their home lives, their children, their special problems. This
was in no way a method of checking up on employees for
security reasons. It was his way of being a friend. It
equipped him to offer help before anyone had to ask him
for it. These people, hundreds of them, were his family. It
was his concern for one of his "family" that projected
Chambrun, one summer day, into a terrorist plot to commit
a murder that threatened to shake the power centers of the
world.

General Achmed Hassan, the Mid-Eastern diplomat, had
come to New York for negotiations at the United Nations.
He came from an area dominated by terror and confusion.
His goal was some kind of peaceful solution of the problems of oil and Western economy. His enemies—fanatics
for the most part—were as numerous as his friends and
supporters. Every moment of his life was threatened by terrorists who would gladly assassinate him given an inch in
which to maneuver.

I can't tell you much about the outside forces set up to
protect General Hassan. I suppose the FBI, the CIA, and
certainly the New York Police, covered every move he
made in the city and at the UN. They had in the past protected Sadat, a friend, and Castro, an enemy, with calm efficiency. Protecting the General in the Beaumont without
turning the place into an armed fortress that would frighten
its regular guests was Chambrun's job, and Jerry Dodd's,

our security chief, and mine, and every other employee of the hotel.

The General had four personal bodyguards who shared his suite on the 21st floor. Jerry Dodd's men patrolled the hallways. I, Mark Haskell, kept the press away. When times came for the General to leave the building, an elevator was reserved for his private use which took him to the basement garage where a car, surrounded by police, waited to take him to the UN.

The General had all his meals in 21A. The food was prepared by the General's own special chef, watched over by an FBI man. The meals were served by a waiter, chosen by Chambrun, who had been with the Beaumont for more than twenty years. "I would trust my own life to Luigi Cantora," I heard Chambrun say when he selected the waiter to serve the General. "And I care quite a bit more for myself than I do for our guest."

On the summer day in question Luigi Cantora did not report for work. It was the first time in twenty years he didn't report for work. He didn't call in sick. He just didn't show. Chambrun replaced him, but that wasn't good enough for him. There was something wrong with a member of his "family." He could have sent me, or one of Dodd's men, or Betsy Ruysdale, to check. He went himself. Luigi was his friend.

Not long ago a movie company was considering making a film out of one of the stories I've written about Pierre Chambrun. I was asked if I could suggest an actor who would be right for the role. Unfortunately the actor who would have been perfect was not available, the late Claude Rains. Short and stocky, like Chambrun, but moving with the grace of a dancer. Pouches under eyes that could be bright with humor, dark with anger, or cold as a hanging judge's. A touch of vanity shows in his expensive and impeccable taste in clothes. When he goes out on the streets of the city he carries a blackthorn walking stick. Walking sticks have gone out of style until recently, when men have started to think again about self-protection in a violent city. Chambrun is, I suppose, in his late fifties, but I wouldn't recommend tangling with him, not when he is armed with his blackthorn. In what he calls "the dark days," the time of the occupation of Paris by the Nazis, he had, in his late teens, learned all the arts of head-on confrontation.

That summer day Chambrun walked east toward a small building near the river where Luigi Cantora lived. Occasionally people would turn to look at him, his hat worn at a rakish angle, and swinging his stick. He was actually headed for a friend in trouble.

Chambrun knew things that morning about Luigi Cantora that I didn't know. Luigi was a dark Italian in his early sixties, with a deeply lined face; he was stooped a little with the years. His wife, Serafina, was twenty years his junior. Their only son had been killed in Vietnam. They were close, Luigi and Serafina, dependent on each other to survive their grief. If Luigi was too ill to go to work, Serafina would have called Chambrun, knowing that Luigi had a special job serving General Hassan. The only explanation Chambrun could think of for Luigi's not calling was that something had happened to Serafina—an accident, a sudden severe illness. Luigi would not act responsibly if something had happened to his beloved wife.

Chambrun knocked on the door of the Cantora apartment. There was no answer.

He rapped sharply with the knob of his blackthorn stick. Still no answer. Then he called out.

"Luigi! It's Pierre Chambrun!"

After a moment there was a sound from inside, the turning of the lock, and Luigi opened the door. He looked ravaged.

"Oh, my God, Mr. Chambrun," he said.

He stood aside and Chambrun walked into the neat little living room, so perfectly cared for by Serafina.

"What has happened to Serafina, Luigi?" Chambrun asked. "I know something has happened to her or you would have called in."

"Oh, my God, Mr. Chambrun!"

"Tell me, Luigi. I'm your friend. I want to help you if I can."

The old Italian turned away and his body convulsed with sobs. "You cannot help! There is no way to help me."

"*Tell me what has happened, Luigi!*"

"The terrorists have her!"

"What terrorists? What are you talking about?"

"The enemies of General Hassan," Luigi said. "They have taken her to be a hostage."

"Stop blubbering and tell me! How can I help you if I don't know what has happened?"

Luigi turned back. "I must help them commit a murder or they will kill Serafina."

"How on earth are you supposed to help them commit a murder?"

Luigi was silent.

"You must tell me," Chambrun said. "I am your friend. I am Serafina's friend. You know that."

"I have been warned not to go to the police, not to go to the FBI, not to go to you."

"You haven't come to me, I have come to you," Chambrun said.

"They will know you are here, Mr. Chambrun. They are watching. They will think I've sent for you to help me. They may already have—have dealt with Serafina. You couldn't know, but your coming here may have cost her her life!"

I can imagine how that jolted Chambrun, but I doubt he showed it in any way.

"If you had to commit a murder to save her, why are you sitting here doing nothing?" he asked Luigi.

"I couldn't! I couldn't move! I was unable, like a man who has suffered a stroke. But it must be tomorrow morning or—or else. They have been in touch with me again. I—I have a last chance."

"To kill General Hassan?"

"To make certain he dies."

"How?"

"If I tell you, and you prevent it—"

"I promise you, Luigi, I will do nothing to risk Serafina's life. How are you supposed to make certain the General dies?"

Luigi turned away, his face working. "They cannot get to the General directly," he said. "There are his bodyguards, there are Jerry Dodd's men, there are FBI agents in the hotel. He is thoroughly protected from all ordinary violence. But I—I take him his food and drink."

"Poison?" Chambrun asked.

Luigi nodded.

"Impossible," Chambrun said. "He has his own trusted chef. The chef is watched, in all stages of his preparations, by an FBI agent."

"They know that," Luigi said. "There is one weak link in all the protection they've set up, Mr. Chambrun. I take the food wagon up from the kitchens, on the service elevator, to the rear door of the General's suite. I am not watched because you selected me, I am to be trusted. Tomorrow morning, when I take up the breakfast wagon on the service elevator, I will be intercepted somewhere between the kitchens and the twenty-first floor. Someone will poison the food and I will go on with it—and serve it."

"And if you sound an alarm?"

"For God's sake, Mr. Chambrun, they have Serafina! If a dozen generals have to die I would save her first. Before you came I made up my mind. I will go through with it. Now you will try to stop me!"

I can visualize Chambrun taking a flat Egyptian cigarette from his silver case, his eyes narrowed against the smoke as he lit it.

"I will not try to stop you, Luigi," he said. "You will do exactly what the assassins have ordered you to do. What I do—well, that is something else again."

"It is a very neat dilemma," Chambrun said. He was sitting behind the carved Florentine desk in his plush office on the Beaumont's second floor. The blue-period Picasso looked down at him from the opposite wall with triangular eyes. Jerry Dodd and Betsy Ruysdale and I were with him, the three people I think he trusts implicitly. "We prevent Luigi from delivering the poisoned breakfast to the General and Serafina dies. We don't prevent him and the General dies."

"You haven't any choice," Jerry Dodd said. He is a dark, wiry little man, intense, expert at his security job. "You have to protect the General."

"I have to protect Serafina," Chambrun said. "She is my friend's wife. I've promised him not to endanger her."

"You have to make a choice, Pierre," Miss Ruysdale said.

Chambrun smiled at Miss Ruysdale, a sly, almost mischievous smile. "I know, and I have made a choice," he said. "I plan to save them both."

"You have no idea where Serafina Cantora is being held," Jerry Dodd objected. "You have no way to find her."

"So I will have to find a way, won't I?" Chambrun replied.

"Do I notify my people and the FBI that we are expecting trouble?"

Chambrun's smile vanished. "You don't mention any of this to a single living soul," he said.

"You're playing some kind of fancy game with human lives," Jerry said. He always has the guts to stand up to Chambrun.

"Only a fancy game can save them both," Chambrun said. "What I want from you, Jerry, is to tighten your protection of the General, don't let anyone become complacent. But I don't want you to change the routine by a hair—no sudden surveillance of the service elevator, no watchful eye on Luigi. What I have told you is as sacred and secret as if you were priests in the confessional."

"Just don't blame me if we mess up on the General in some way," Jerry said. "Is that all, boss?"

"That's all," Chambrun said. "The zero hour isn't until tomorrow's breakfast."

Jerry took off, obviously not convinced that Chambrun was making sense. There was, however, no doubt he would carry out his orders to the letter. When the day comes that we can't follow The Man, blindly, our world will have collapsed.

"You have appointments," Betsy Ruysdale reminded Chambrun when Jerry was gone.

"I'll keep them," Chambrun said. "Remember, Ruysdale"—he never calls her by her first name, just "Ruysdale"—"nothing is to change. All routines as usual—until tomorrow's breakfast."

Ruysdale nodded and took off for her private office.

"What can I do to be useful?" I asked Chambrun.

He sat very still for a moment, staring down at a blank pad on his desk top. Then he looked up at me. "If I muff this, Mark, there won't be much flavor to living."

I didn't say anything.

"The General's breakfast is served at eight thirty," he said. "I want you here with me at eight o'clock."

"Right."

"I may need you very urgently then, Mark. Meanwhile, today, don't let the press and media people develop any kind of special or sudden interest in the General. Invent something, if necessary, to keep them looking somewhere else. The Queen of England may be coming to stay with us; Greta Garbo is planning a party to announce her return to the screen. Anything to keep them looking away from the General."

"Count on it."

"You think I'm out of my mind, Mark?"

"No, but I don't know what's going on in it—in your mind."

"It's quite simple," he said. "I hope to save two lives."

If it had been anyone but Chambrun, I might have protested, loud and long. No individual has the right to play games with life and death. The General, forewarned, could be kept perfectly safe. He was surrounded by an army of trained people. Serafina Cantora was an unfortunate victim of fanatical evil. All hostages are such victims. Someone playing games with the situation was running intolerable risks.

But not Chambrun. If any man could assess the odds for success and against failure, that man was Chambrun. He had lived and succeeded all his life by taking calculated risks.

I have to tell you that I went through the next hours—the rest of that morning, the afternoon, and a long evening—under a kind of tension I wouldn't have believed. The Beaumont seemed to operate with its usual Swiss-watch efficiency, but for me violence seemed to be waiting around every corner. We all live with violence but for me, that day, it was pinpointed, focused on the Beaumont.

The big trouble was expected tomorrow morning, but somehow I expected it might erupt long before that. I had an ear to the ground. I knew when the General left for the UN about ten in the morning. I knew when he returned about six in the afternoon. I knew when the changing of the guard took place, when a new group of FBI agents took over, when Jerry Dodd's crew changed.

The General lived through the day without incident. The newspaper and other media people had shown no interest in him. I was exhausted when I went to my apartment on the second floor and fell into bed, alerting the switchboard to call me at six thirty in the morning. I wouldn't have believed it possible, but I slept as though I'd been slugged.

I must have jumped three feet clear of the bed when the phone rang. It was only the operator telling me it was time to get moving. The sun was streaming through my windows. This was the day when one of two people was scheduled to die, and both of them might.

Chambrun was already in his office when I got there at a quarter to eight, fifteen minutes ahead of the time I'd been ordered to report. He was wearing a light gray tropical worsted suit with a little white flower in the buttonhole. He looked as if he'd slept like a baby; he was refreshed, ready for anything. I knew from my shaving mirror that I looked as if I'd been on an all-night binge.

"We are sharing the breakfast hour with the General," Chambrun informed me.

With murder scheduled for eight thirty, I told myself.

We went to the 21st floor and Chambrun rang the bell to the General's suite. The door was promptly opened by one of the dark-faced bodyguards.

We were led into the luxurious living room where General Hassan was already at work at his desk. He got up from his chair to greet us, a handsome man with the brilliant smile of a professional public figure, a neatly trimmed beard and mustache, and dark eyes, bright with pleasure.

"It is a delight to see you, Mr. Chambrun," he said.

The General wasn't alone. The guard who had admitted us stood by the door to the vestibule. Another was at the opening of the corridor that led to the bedrooms. A third, I guessed, was at the rear of the suite waiting for Luigi Cantora to arrive with the breakfast wagon.

"It's rather early in the day, General, but there seemed to be no other time to fit myself into your busy schedule," Chambrun said. "Have you met Mark Haskell, our public-relations director?"

The General's handshake was firm and friendly. "Like everything else in this establishment, Mr. Chambrun, the machinery turns soundlessly. Mr. Haskell has kept me well protected from the press. Please sit down. You will share coffee with me when it comes. It should be here any moment. And now, what can I do for you, Mr. Chambrun?"

"I just wanted to make certain everything is as you wish it to be," Chambrun said. "That you are satisfied with the routines, that the service is satisfactory."

"My own people in my own palace could not be more perfect," the General said. "Ah, here is Luigi with the breakfast."

Luigi Cantora looked like a man about to face a firing

squad as he wheeled in the breakfast wagon, followed by a guard. When Luigi saw Chambrun, his eyes bulged like marbles.

"We missed you yesterday, Luigi," the General said.

"My—my wife was ill, sir," Luigi muttered.

"I trust she is feeling much better today," the General said.

"Thank you, sir."

Luigi wheeled the breakfast wagon into place in front of the General. Luigi's hands were obviously shaking as he shifted some of the silver-covered plates and moved the silver coffee pot into position. I felt the inside of my mouth go painfully dry. Almost certainly, from Luigi's panicked appearance, death was lurking there for the General.

The General was evidently in high good humor.

"I think you will find extra coffee cups in the pantry, Luigi," he said. "Please fetch two for Mr. Chambrun and Mr. Haskell."

Luigi seemed frozen where he stood.

"Luigi—" Chambrun said, very quietly.

The coffee! It had to be the coffee! The old waiter made a despairing sound, turned, and stumbled out of the room. The General filled the one coffee cup on the wagon with a flourish, picked up the cup, and held it out toward Chambrun.

"For you, my friend," he said.

Chambrun's face looked carved out of stone. He didn't move in his chair. One of the guards took a quick step forward, apparently to pass the cup. He stumbled as he reached the breakfast wagon, reached out to prevent himself from falling, sent the coffee cup flying, spilling most of the contents on the front of Chambrun's immaculate summer suit. The guard's other hand overturned the coffee pot on the wagon.

Both Chambrun and the General were suddenly standing.

"How could you be so clumsy, Abdul?" the General said sharply.

The guard muttered something apologetic in a language I didn't understand. He was blotting at Chambrun's stained suit with a napkin. Then he turned to the breakfast wagon to work on the coffee spill there. I glanced past him and saw Luigi in the entrance to the pantry, clinging to the door jamb like a man whose legs had turned to gelatin. Chambrun spoke quietly to the old waiter.

"Help clean up the mess, Luigi, and bring General Hassan fresh cloth and napkins—and a fresh pot of coffee," Chambrun said.

Luigi nodded and began puttering, almost aimlessly.

"I'm deeply sorry for Abdul's awkwardness, Mr. Chambrun," the General said. "I trust you will wait for fresh coffee."

"I'm afraid not, General," Chambrun said. "I have a rather busy schedule this morning, and I'll have to change into a more presentable suit of clothes."

"Another time," the General suggested.

"It will be a pleasure, General."

Out in the hall I grabbed Chambrun's arm. "That was no accident," I said. "You'd forewarned them!"

He gave me an odd, cold look. "I agree with you, Mark. It was not an accident. But I assure you, I've talked to no one about this but Luigi, you, Jerry Dodd, and Ruysdale."

"Then why—"

"If I had taken a swallow of that coffee and dropped dead on the spot," Chambrun said, "it would have closed off the only avenue they have for getting at the General. As it is, tomorrow is another day."

"And you won't be there for breakfast tomorrow."

"If I have to be," Chambrun said, "it's 'goodbye, Sera-fina.'"

It was pretty hard to concentrate on the routines of the day. Chambrun, I knew, would never tell me anything but the truth. He hadn't warned the General or his guards about a planned assassination by poison. That meant there was treachery within the ranks of the General's close and personal protectors—specifically, the man called Abdul. One rotten apple in the barrel. If the plan to use Luigi, forced to cooperate out of fear for his wife, was to be tried again it would have to be delayed until tomorrow's break-fast.

The General would have his lunch at the UN, and who could know where he might dine. Our unexpected pres-ence this morning had aborted the plan, but Abdul—he must have thought very cleverly—had saved them a sec-ond chance. Serafina Cantora was still a hostage, and the terrified Luigi would continue to cooperate. Abdul and his co-conspirators must have felt certain of that. We, on our side, had a day and a night, but what could we do with that time?

A little after ten o'clock that morning I was in my office, down the hall from Chambrun's, when I got a call from The Man.

"I need your help, Mark," he said.

"Anything you say."

"Meet me at the elevator. We're going places."

Two or three minutes later we met. He was wearing his rakish hat and carrying his blackthorn walking stick. Ap-parently we were going somewhere outside the hotel.

Chambrun pressed the down button and we descended to the garage in the basement of the hotel. He didn't explain anything until we reached his own private Mercedes which was waiting for us with Jerry Dodd at the wheel. Chambrun got in up front with Jerry. He turned to me in the back seat as the car started up the ramp.

"I figured Abdul would have to report to his pals," he said. "So I alerted Jerry. Abdul wouldn't, I thought, make an outside call through the hotel switchboard. The General's guards change when he leaves the hotel for the UN."

"The boss was right," Jerry said, as he maneuvered the car out into the city traffic. "The first place Abdul went when he was relieved was to a pay phone in the lobby. I was on his heels. I could see him dial a number. He spoke, excited, in a language I couldn't understand. But I checked with a chum at the phone company and got an address for the number he'd called. About ten blocks away on the Upper East Side."

"That's where we're going," Chambrun said.

"To do what?" I asked.

"Not to whistle Dixie!" Jerry said.

Our target turned out to be a dilapidated brownstone not far from the river. Jerry parked the Mercedes about a block from the house he indicated.

"Let me case the joint," he said, and took off.

We waited for what seemed an interminable length of time. Then Chambrun sat up straight. On the front steps of the house down the block we saw Jerry. He'd removed his suit coat and he was, of all things, industriously sweeping the front steps of the house.

We left the car and walked briskly down the block to the house. The front door stood open behind the sweeping Jerry.

"The janitor was a sucker for a ten spot," he said. "Foreigners have rented the rear apartment on the first floor." He grinned at Chambrun. "I have the passkey."

We went into the dark hallway and down the corridor to

the rear. Jerry signaled us for silence. He slipped a key noiselessly into the lock, again indicating we should stay behind him. He turned the key and was instantly three steps into the room beyond.

"A leak in the bathroom," we heard him say. "I thought you guys were out."

Chambrun pushed forward, I right behind him. Two dark-skinned men faced us, startled by our sudden appearance.

"Chambrun!" one of them said. They knew The Man by sight. They had probably scouted the Beaumont thoroughly before they'd put their murder scheme into action.

"I assume Mrs. Cantora is in the back bedroom," Chambrun said, coldly. "Will you be good enough to bring her out here, Mark?"

I must have looked like a sleepwalker as I started for the far door. One of the terrorists recovered and took a quick step to block the way. There was a gun pointed straight at my chest.

Chambrun's heavy blackthorn stick moved in a short arc. There was a sound like splintering kindling, the gun went hurtling across the room, and the terrorist screamed and went down to his knees, cradling his shattered arm. The second man was down, with Jerry Dodd sitting on his chest, a gun pressed against the terrorist's forehead.

As if he were taking a stroll in the park, Chambrun stepped over the man he'd struck and went into the back room. A moment later I heard a woman's voice, frightened but relieved. She had been tied to a chair, a gag in her mouth, Chambrun told us later.

He reappeared, his arm around Luigi Cantora's beloved Serafina. "It's all right, Serafina," Chambrun said gently. "It's all over. I'll take you to Luigi. He'll be overjoyed to see you." He turned to me. "You can call the police to take care of these scum, Mark," he said. And then to Jerry, "Get in touch with General Hassan at the United Nations. He may want to disinfect his private army." He gave Serafina a little hug. "We must be going, my dear. I have a hotel to run."

THE FIVE SENSES
OF MRS. CRAGGS

H. R. F. KEATING

I: *Seeing*

Of all the various cleaning jobs that Mrs. Craggs had had in the course of a long work life, the one at the place they called Murray's House was the one she liked best. Yet she was the person most responsible, when you came down to it, for bringing that job to an end.

Murray's House was a funny old place. It had belonged back in the Eighteenth Century to old Peter Murray, the inventor and discoverer and gatherer of curiosities, and eventually it had been left to the Borough, who kept it as nearly the way it had been as they could and charged the public to see it. Not that many of the public were willing to pay, but there it was.

Certainly Mrs. Craggs got to like the old place very much. It used to please her to think, when she toiled up the stairs, that she was seeing exactly the same twirls and curls in the banisters that old Peter Murray had seen all those years before. And though she didn't particularly understand many of the curious wooden machines and other things the house was filled with, she liked them all the same. Old Peter Murray had worked on them and put his skill and care into them, and you could tell.

So it was all the more awful when Mrs. Craggs arrived

for work one morning, with her friend Mrs. Milhorne, and found that the night porter, old Mr. Berbottle, had been murdered, an event which was to result before long in the final closing of the old house. Thanks to Mrs. Craggs.

Of course everybody said at once that there could be no doubt who had killed Mr. Berbottle: the skinheads—the neighborhood gang of young hooligans. They were always breaking into places and this time poor crotchety, persnickety old Mr. Berbottle must have disturbed them and for that had his head laid open with a piece of lead piping. And all the previous day's receipts, such as they were, had disappeared.

The worst of it was, though, that this had been the first time the money had been left on the premises overnight. Generally, after the manager, Mr. Fingles, had checked it, the money was taken and put in the night safe of the bank by Mr. Tanker, the day porter, a rippling-muscled former bosun of a sail-training ship, who stood for no nonsense from skinheads or anyone else. But Mr. Tanker had been taken ill at lunchtime, and the manager had said there would be no harm in leaving the money in the house for just one night. He and Mr. Berbottle between them were quite capable of looking after it. Only, when it had come to it, Mr. Fingles, who was notorious for liking his half bottle of wine with his dinner, had been so soundly asleep in his comfortable little private flat at the top of the house that he had not heard a thing.

So there the police were all over the place and there was little Mr. Fingles, who had discovered the body when he had come down to collect the mail, in more of a state of agitation than usual, rushing up and down on his little clickety heels and getting in everybody's way. "Like a regular old clockwork doll," Mrs. Craggs had murmured to Mrs. Milhorne, her fellow worker, as they waited for the fingerprint men and the police photographer to finish.

They had a long wait of it too, with nothing more exciting to see for most of the time than the Detective-Superintendent in charge prowling about and looking important, though, as Mrs. Milhorne said, "It isn't as if it's exactly what you'd call a mystery killing, is it?" But at last the Superintendent himself came up to the two of them.

"Very well, ladies," he said, "I shall be here for some time to come, I expect, but there's nothing to stop you two going ahead with your work now. My lads have got everything they want."

And then he paused and became a bit uneasy.

"There is one thing, though," he added. "The porter's room there, where it happened."

"Yes?" said Mrs. Craggs, glancing along to the little room with the ticket window.

"Well," said the Superintendent, still looking uncomfortable, "the fact of the matter is there's—well, there's what you might call traces on the floor in there, and I don't know whether you'd object to—er—dealing with them."

"I couldn't," declared Mrs. Milhorne, with great promptness. "I'm afraid to say I'd come all over queer. I'd be bound to. I've got nerves, you see."

"You don't have to do it," Mrs. Craggs broke in. "The porter's room has linoleum on the floor, and lino polishing's my department, always has been."

She turned to the Superintendent and jerked her head at Mrs. Milhorne.

"She's dusting," she said.

And so off to her dusting went Mrs. Milhorne, though not without putting a hand to her skinny chest and declaring she could "feels the heartbeats something terrible," and Mrs. Craggs matter-of-factly fetched herself a pail of hot water and a scrubbing brush and tackled the porter's room, thinking all the while how old Mr. Berbottle had been so nosey and persnickety and interfering, and how now none of it was doing him any good.

It was only later, when she was on her knees polishing the thin strip of brown linoleum that edged the entrance hall, that she came across something that made her stop suddenly and rise to her feet with a decidedly grim expression on her battered old nutbrown face.

"Mrs. Milhorne, dear," she called to her friend, who was halfway up the stairs, busy doing some fancywork with her duster on the twirls and twiddles of the old banisters.

"Yes, dear?"

"I think I'm just going to have a word with that Superintendent," Mrs. Craggs said. "I want to tell him about this footprint on the lino."

"Footprint on the lino?"

Mrs. Milhorne abandoned her dusting and came down to look. She found her friend standing with sturdy legs wide apart over a footprint, or to be accurate, half a footprint, just on the edge of the lino where it met the broad, but very threadbare, central carpet.

"It's a bare foot," Mrs. Milhorne pronounced after a long inspection. "Looking as if it was on its way to go out by the front door."

"Yes, dear," said Mrs. Craggs.

"And you're going to the Superintendent about it? Well, I know you don't like to have your polish trod on when you've just got it looking all nice, but to go to Scotland Yard about that—well, it beats all."

And Mrs. Milhorne indulged in her favorite trilling laugh.

"He's not Scotland Yard, he's local," said Mrs. Craggs, and off she stumped.

Mrs. Milhorne decided to have a rest from her dusting and stay where she was by the footprint. To her immense surprise, scarcely ten minutes later Mrs. Craggs came back with the Superintendent. And the great man himself actually squatted down and closely examined the half footprint. Then he pushed himself to his feet and set off up the stairs, looking extremely thoughtful.

At the turn, however, he encountered the manager, coming click-clacking excitedly down. And it was then that Mrs. Milhorne got her biggest surprise of all.

"Mr. Fingles," the Superintendent said to the manager in a voice doom-laden with formality. "I should like you to accompany me to the station, where I have a number of questions I wish to put to you."

It wasn't until the news was in the paper that Mr. Fingles had been charged with the murder that Mrs. Craggs agreed to answer a single one of the many questions Mrs. Milhorne had plagued her with. Then she did explain.

"Clear as the nose on me face really, dear, when you come to think," she said. "Why would a naked footprint be right there on the lino at the edge of the hall?"

"I'm sure I don't know," Mrs. Milhorne replied. "Unless someone just happened to be creeping along there."

"Of course they were creeping, dear. And who would have to creep so as to get right up close to old Mr. Berbottle if it wasn't someone he knew and would wonder what they were doing carrying a piece of lead piping? Especially if it was someone who can't walk about anywhere without making a noise like a little old tip-tapping clockwork doll?"

Mrs. Milhorne pondered over this at length.

"I suppose you're right, dear," she said at last. "But I would've thought a bare footprint like that meant our Mr. Tanker, not Mr. Fingles. Mr. Tanker was always saying how he wore no shoes when he went climbing up all those masts on that ship of his."

"And why would Mr. Tanker want to murder Mr. Berbottle?" Mrs. Craggs demanded.

"I'm sure I don't know, dear. But, come to that, why *did* Mr. Fingles want to murder him?"

"Because of the money, of course," Mrs. Craggs answered. "And Mr. Fingles with his bottles of wine to buy and his nice comfortable flat up there to keep going."

"The money?" Mrs. Milhorne asked.

"Yes. Wasn't this the first time the money had been left here overnight? And wasn't Mr. Berbottle, rest him, just the sort of interfering old fool who would go and check the money against the tickets issued, even though he knew that was Mr. Fingles' job?"

It took Mrs. Milhorne a little time to sort it all out, but she got there in the end.

"You mean Mr. Fingles had been pinching a bit of the takings all along, to help him out, like?" she said. "Now, why couldn't I have seen that?"

Mrs. Craggs gave her a slow smile.

"Because you ain't very keen to get down on your hands and knees, dear," she said, "and see what's in front of your face."

II: *Smelling*

When Mrs. Craggs had the washing-up job at a select residential hotel, she used to allow herself a little treat in the summertime. Between finishing the lunch dishes and beginning on the tea things she took a cup for herself and sat with it in the storeroom. It was not exactly comfortable.

Mrs. Craggs had to perch herself on a packing case and there was precious little light.

But it had one distinct advantage as far as Mrs. Craggs was concerned: a row of frosted-glass louver windows high up in one wall that formed the back of the hotel's delightful rose garden. So, in consequence, Mrs. Craggs, sitting on that packing case in the gloom of the storeroom amid a strong smell of soap, was often able to hear the most fascinating conversations.

She was quite unashamed of this. As she said to her friend and coworker, Mrs. Milhorne, to whom she occasionally retailed certain, but not all, of the things she heard, "If they don't know it, then it don't do them no harm. And I think it's interesting." And so, day by day, she contrived to get a notion of almost all the hotel's regular guests, and even visitors who came only for tea often could be added to her bag.

So when, one day, sitting on her accustomed uncomfortable seat, she heard old Mr. Danchflower refer to the elderly visitor with whom he was taking tea as "Lady Etherege," Mrs. Craggs pricked up her ears. Mrs. Craggs enjoyed feeling she was getting a worm's-eye view of the aristocracy and it did no harm to have a tidbit to feed to Mrs. Milhorne from time to time.

Not that, it soon developed, Lady Etherege was any great shakes when you came down to it. She was blue-blooded all right—you could tell that just by listening to her delicate, tired old voice—but she was far from being rich. Of course, she didn't come right out with that. Not at what was probably the first time she met old Mr. Danchflower who, though he might not be particularly aristocratic, was certainly well off, as you had to be to stay in one of the hotel's best rooms summer and winter alike.

Yet bit by bit, as Mrs. Craggs savored her good, big,

strong cup of tea and listened to the two elderly voices floating in through the louver above her, it became quite plain that old Lady Etherege lived like a church mouse.

Mrs. Craggs began to feel really sorry for her. It was all right being poor when you were used to it, but to end your days like that when you'd begun grand as grand, that was hard. Not that Lady Etherege didn't have compensations, it seemed. She even had, so her conversation revealed little by little, an admirer.

Admittedly he was an admirer at a distance. Over in France. And the form his admiration took was no more than sending her for each birthday a bottle of perfume. But what perfume! Mrs. Craggs gathered that the latest bottle had actually been taken, with great reverence, out of Lady Etherege's handbag and that now its stopper was being gently removed and Mr. Danchflower was being permitted a discreet inhalation.

"Oh, excellent," Mrs. Craggs heard him say. "Really, madam, a most delicate scent. What shall I say it reminds me of? Not these roses even. It's far more subtle than that."

"Yes, yes," came Lady Etherege's voice. "It comes from a past age. An age I once knew, let me admit it."

Mrs. Craggs could have sworn she even heard the sigh through the narrow slits of the frosted-glass louver.

"Ah," Lady Etherege added, "there was a time, my dear sir, when I myself had no hesitation in entering a boutique in the Rue St. Honoré and buying perfume at twenty-five pounds a tiny bottle."

"Twenty-five pounds," said old Mr. Danchflower. "I can well believe this cost that much, madam. A most remarkably fine and delicate scent."

"Oh, well," Lady Etherege answered, her simper, too, almost floating through the narrow window, "since we are friends I can tell you that this tiny bottle actually cost even more than that. My dear, dear old admirer accidentally left the bill in the package last year and before I crumpled it up I could not help noticing that the sum mentioned was the equivalent—you'll hardly believe this, but everything is so very, *very* expensive nowadays—was the equivalent of no less than forty pounds."

"Indeed, indeed, madam. But I do believe it I assure—"

And then through the open louver came what could only be described as a feminine shriek of utter horror, followed an instant later by the small but unmistakable sound of breaking glass.

"Madam, how could I? I—I don't know what I did. I could have sworn the bottle was safe on the arm of the bench, but—"

Old Mr. Danchflower's voice faded into utterly over-whelmed silence. But, rooted on her packing case, Mrs. Craggs could hear all too clearly Lady Etherege's choked sobs, though it was plain she was doing all in her power to restrain them.

And then, seconds later, she heard her own name being loudly called out in the kitchen.

"Mrs. Craggs, Mrs. Craggs! Where is the woman?"

It was Mr. Browne, the under-manager, in even more of a tizzy than usual. Mrs. Craggs slipped down off the packing case, put her teacup where it wouldn't be noticed, and emerged.

"Ah, there you are. There you are. Quick, quick, Mrs. Craggs, out into the rose garden with a bucket and cloth. As fast as you can, as fast as you can. There has been the most terrible disaster."

Mrs. Craggs, without saying she well knew what the disaster was, rapidly filled a bucket with water, seized a floor cloth, and went scuttling round after Mr. Browne.

"It's perfume," Mr. Browne explained, quite unnecessarily since the whole of the garden was now smelling to high heaven of a scent that certainly wasn't that of roses. "A most unfortunate accident. But we must sweep it all away on the instant. On the instant. It must be as if it had never been."

So Mrs. Craggs scarcely looked at the two sad spectators of the tragic scene, Mr. Danchflower standing erect and still deeply blushing and little Lady Etherege beside him, dabbing the daintiest of handkerchiefs to her old tired eyes. Instead Mrs. Craggs swooshed most of the contents of her bucket over the thick oily stain on a large flagstone and then began to mop up as fast as she was able till the pail itself smelled like an oversize bouquet of every flower you could think of.

And, as she worked, Mrs. Craggs heard the two old people talk.

"Madam, may I say again that I cannot think how I could have been so abominably careless. I didn't see the bottle, but I suppose my sleeve must have just caught it."

"It's perfectly all right."

"No. No, madam, it is not all right. You have lost something extremely valuable to you, not only financially but sentimentally. It is not all right, madam."

"It—it was of some sentimental value, yes."

"Madam, that I can never repair. But at least—please be so good as to let me write you a check for forty pounds."

"Oh, no. No, really. Really I could not."

But old Mr. Danchflower had sat down on the bench, taken his check book from his pocket, and was already writing. Lady Etherege sat down beside him.

"No, really, sir," she said. "From an acquaintance of such short standing I could not possibly—"

"Nonsense, madam, nonsense. There, take it!"

"Well. Well, if you insist . . . And there I do believe I see the stopper. I think I will just keep it. You know, a—a souvenir."

Her frail old hand reached down to somewhere near where Mrs. Craggs's floor cloth was at work and the fingers closed round the ornate glass. And then Mrs. Craggs's fingers closed round Lady Etherege's.

"Oh, no, you don't," Mrs. Craggs said loudly.

"Don't? Don't? I do not understand."

Beneath Mrs. Craggs's grasp the thin fingers wriggled hard.

"Oh, yes, you do," said Mrs. Craggs. "You understand quite well that this stopper's got a false compartment in its top. A compartment filled with the delicate scent Mr. Danchflower liked so much, and not with this nasty cheap muck ponging to high heaven."

And then old Lady Etherege dropped the stopper, slid her hand from Mrs. Craggs's grasp, rose in an instant, seized the half-full bucket, emptied its contents all over Mrs. Craggs, and was out of the garden, into the street, and had hopped onto a passing bus before anybody else had time to realize what Lady Etherege had done.

And, as Mrs. Craggs said, "For days and days afterwards you could tell I was coming round the corner yards before I got there. What a niff!"

III: *Touching*

One of the places where Mrs. Craggs once worked as a charwoman was the Borough Museum, and she was there at the time that the celebrated Golden Venus was on a week's loan exhibition. Indeed, she had the honor, obtained not without difficulty, of being allowed to dust this small but extremely ancient and valuable object.

At first, of course, no one had seen the necessity for carrying out such an everyday task. But when the Venus had been on its special display stand surrounded by its own rope barrier for some 48 hours, it became evident that even something as precious as this needed the attentions of the duster. Mr. Slythe, the museum's assistant curator, had not been in favor of delegating this task to Mrs. Craggs.

"But the Venus, but a charlady," he had twittered. "What if she did some damage? My mother's dailies are always breaking things. Always."

Mrs. Craggs stood there impassively, waiting to know whether or not she was going to be allowed to get on with it. And it was Mr. Tovey, the curator himself, who gave the final go-ahead.

"Nonsense, man," he said to Mr. Slythe. "The statue's solid metal, unharmed for over two thousand years, and you know how firmly it's fixed to the plinth. We both of us saw to that."

"Ah, well, yes, I suppose so, I suppose so," Mr. Slythe agreed. And then he approached the statue for about the fiftieth time since it had been installed and started once more what Mrs. Craggs called "his cooing act."

"Ah," he said, "the patina, the patina, the inimitable patina of age."

If he'd said that once he'd said it twenty times, Mrs. Craggs thought irritably.

And then Mr. Tovey, not to be outdone, approached the sacred work of art in his turn. And repeated what he had said some twenty times since the piece had been installed.

"The hand of genius, the unmistakable hand of genius. Marvelous, magnificent, absolutely wonderful."

"Shall I do it now, sir?" asked Mrs. Craggs.

"Oh, very well, carry on then. Carry on."

And both Mr. Tovey and Mr. Slythe turned away so as not to see Mrs. Craggs's common yellow duster touch the product of "the unmistakable hand of genius" or "the patina of age." And then they both slewed round again to make sure that, in spite of everything, Mrs. Craggs was not wreaking havoc on the great work.

Indeed, the week of its exhibition was one of considerable strain for both the curator and his assistant. There was not only the public, which would keep coming and looking, attracted in numbers such as the museum had never seen before by stories in the papers about the immense value of the little golden statue, but there was the question of security at night. Of course, a firm of guards had been hired and a pair of them made hourly patrols past the Golden Venus on its plinth while others were on duty at both the front and back doors. But Mr. Tovey had decided this was not enough and had arranged with Mr. Slythe that they should each spend half of every night of the exhibition week on the premises.

Both of them took every chance to point out to anybody who would listen, even to Mrs. Craggs if no one better offered, what sacrifices of time they were making, and of saying simultaneously in their different ways that, of course, it was really no sacrifice at all to be able to spend hours in private contemplation either of "the unmistakable hand of genius, coming down to us through the centuries" or of "the patina, the wonderful patina of age, so fine, yet so very, very enduring."

So it could hardly be expected that either of them would react with calm when, on the last morning of the Venus' stay in the museum, Mrs. Craggs told them one after the other that the object over which she had just used her common yellow duster was not the genuine Golden Venus but a substitute.

She lay in wait first for Mr. Tovey.

"I'm very sorry to have to tell you, sir," she said when he re-entered the museum, "that is not the same statue as what I dusted yesterday."

"What—what do you mean, woman? Not the same statue?"

"I can tell, sir. I can tell by the touch. I've dusted that five times in all since it's been here and I know the feel of it as well as I know the back of me own hand."

"We'll have a look at this," Mr. Tovey declared.

And he took the steps two at a time up to the landing where the Golden Venus stood. He drew a long breath and glared hard at the statue, then rounded on Mrs. Craggs.

"Piffle, my good woman," he said. "Sheer and utter piffle! Why, you've only to look to see the hand of genius there, the unmistakable hand of genius."

"And you've only got to lay a duster on it to know it's not the same as what it was yesterday," Mrs. Craggs declared, with equal firmness.

Mr. Tovey drew himself up. But he did not pour forth the torrent of words Mrs. Craggs had braced herself for. Instead he suddenly thrust his big round face close to hers and spoke in a low whisper.

"Now, listen to me, my good woman, you are wrong. You cannot be anything else. I have a lifetime of knowledge behind me when I tell you that statue *is* the Golden Venus. But I know what the press is and what reporters are capable of. So, understand this, you are not to breathe one word of even the possibility of a theft. Not one word."

Mrs. Craggs looked doubtful. But Mr. Tovey was a persuasive employer and at last she mumbled agreement. Yet, thinking the matter over, she came to the conclusion that his prohibition ought not to include his fellow art expert, Mr. Slythe. So she waited her chance and at last managed to corner him at a spot not far from the Golden Venus, during a slack period in the museum's unaccustomedly busy life.

"Can I have a word?" she asked.

"Yes, yes. What is it? What is it now? Always something. Always some pettifogging detail preventing one from concentrating on one's true work."

"Well, if you say that someone putting a dummy in place of that Golden Venus is a detail," Mrs. Craggs answered, "then that's your privilege. But I think it ought to be gone into."

Mr. Slythe was even more upset than Mr. Tovey. He scooted over the stone floor toward the statue as if he had been unexpectedly put on roller skates and he peered at it with such fearful intensity that he might almost have melted it. And then he returned, white-faced, to Mrs. Craggs. But not with dismay. With anger.

"You wretched, wretched person," he said. "How dare you? How dare you say a thing like that to me? It's enough to give me a nervous breakdown. Yes, a nervous breakdown."

"Then you don't think it has been changed?" Mrs. Craggs said.

"I do not. Why, anyone with a grain of sensibility could see that *piece* has the patina of age on every inch of it. The unmistakable patina of age. And you tell me that it is a substitute!"

And Mr. Slythe wheeled round and marched away to the sanctuary of his private office.

Mrs. Craggs ought to have been convinced. But, if she was, then why was it that she came to the museum the evening after the immensely successful Golden Venus exhibition had been triumphantly concluded and put in a good many hours of overtime, unpaid? She got out her dustcloths and worked away, rubbing and polishing stairs and corridors, showcases and display rooms. The museum had never gleamed so in all its days.

And at last her prowling duster encountered what she had hoped it would. In next to no time she was out on the steps of the building looking up and down the street, and before long she saw what she was looking for—the local police constable passing on his beat. She beckoned to him.

"I want to report a theft," she said.

The constable hurried in and Mrs. Craggs led him to the place where, dusting and polishing, she had come across a loose tile in the wall decoration of one of the rooms.

"Look," she said.

And she prised out the tile and the one next to it, to reveal a long cavity in which, reposing on a layer of cotton-wool, was nothing less than the real Golden Venus.

"It was changed over during one of the gaps between the security patrols," Mrs. Craggs declared.

The constable, who had been aware of the precautions taken over so valuable a piece of property on his beat, saw at once what the situation was.

"It must have been one of them two," he said. "The whatsit—curator, Mr. Tovey, or his Number Two, Mr. Slythe. One of them must have hidden it here till he could slip it out. But—but which? They were each on guard alone half the night. Which could it be?"

"That's simple enough," Mrs. Craggs replied. "They both of them told me I was an old fool for saying it had been changed over. But only one of them made a fuss about not telling anyone else. It's the 'unmistakable hand of genius' you've got to go for, not 'the patina of age.' "

IV: *Hearing*

When Mrs. Craggs first went to work for old Mrs. Proost she rather liked listening to the old lady's music boxes. They were her most cherished possession, left to her by her husband who had died years before and who had devoted his life to the collection. But, as time passed and Mrs. Proost insisted on playing one box or another the whole of the time Mrs. Craggs was cleaning in the house, the charwoman began, as she said to her friend Mrs. Milhorne, "To really hate the blessed things."

"I like a good tune," she said, "same as anyone else. But to hear that tinkle, tinkle, tinkle all day and every, why, it's more than human ears can stand." Mrs. Milhorne wondered how the old lady herself could put up with it. "I'll tell you," said Mrs. Craggs. "It's because she doesn't hear a single note."

Why ever not, Mrs. Milhorne wanted to know. It wasn't as if the old lady was deaf, because she'd seen her herself, out doing a bit of shopping and talking with the best "and never a sign of them little things behind your ear."

Mrs. Craggs had smiled at that. "Oh," she said, "she wouldn't let on. Go to any lengths she would to pretend she's heard every word. Nod and smile like an old teetotum. But I know. I can go into that sitting room of hers and so long as I take good care to stand where she can't see me lips, I can say 'Wotcher, me old mate, how's all the little tinkle boxes then?' and she don't take one blind bit of notice."

But Mrs. Craggs put up with the tinkle-tinkling because

Mrs. Proost was a nice old thing, even if she was too proud to admit how little she could hear. And all went well. Till the day the old lady asked Mrs. Craggs if, as a special favor, she could come back the next afternoon and serve tea.

"It's my nephew," she said. "My husband's brother's boy. Tony. Such a dear little fellow he used to be, though I'm afraid his parents, poor dear souls, spoiled him dreadfully."

Mrs. Craggs replied that certainly she would come the next day at three and she asked how it was that the young man had never visited his aunt in all the years Mrs. Craggs had been working for her.

"Oh, but you see," said Mrs. Proost, "he's been dreadfully busy. Yes, in the North. He's been away in the North for—oh, for quite eight years now. A most important post."

"What's that then?" asked Mrs. Craggs, opening her lips wide.

"Oh, dear. Well, you will think me silly, but I can't quite recall. It was something to do with aeroplanes, I think. Or was it aerodromes? But it *was* important. I can tell you that."

Mrs. Craggs had been in the kitchen, slicing bread nice and thin for some twenty minutes when the visitor arrived. She answered his ring at the door and showed him into the sitting room. But she was not impressed. Nephew Tony was a good deal older than Mrs. Proost had led her to expect, and he had too travel-worn a look for someone with an important job to do with airplanes, or even airfields. As he walked ahead of her across the hall, she thought she could hear one of the soles of his shoes flapping slightly.

So, instead of retiring discreetly until four o'clock, when it had been agreed she should bring in tea, Mrs. Craggs contrived to stand by the door of the room, as if she was, despite her flowered apron and best hat worn in honor of the event, a sort of footman.

Nephew Tony was very breezy and bold and Mrs. Craggs could see old Mrs. Proost looking at his face carefully as he sat opposite her and so succeeding in answering his hearty remarks about thinking he "wouldn't bother with a taxi from the station, just gave myself a tuppenny bus ride, you know." More like it he walked, thought Mrs. Craggs, even though it was three miles.

But just then Mrs. Proost realized that the charwoman was still hovering over the proceedings.

"Mrs. Craggs," she said, "you may serve tea."

"Bit early, ain't it?" Mrs. Craggs asked, after advancing to where her lips could be read.

"Never mind," Mrs. Proost replied, with a dignity recalling the days when she'd had a real parlormaid in black dress and lace cap. "Master Tony and I will take tea now."

"Very good," said Mrs. Craggs. And so impressed was she with the high tone that her employer had achieved, she added, though rather belatedly, "Madam."

But nevertheless out in the kitchen she got the rest of the tea things onto the tray in record time and made the tea itself—in the silver teapot, appearing especially for the occasion—without actually waiting for the pot to warm. And when she entered the sitting room again, she thought she had arrived only just in time.

Nephew Tony was talking about Mrs. Proost's music boxes. And what he was saying sent columns of red anger marching through Mrs. Craggs's head.

"You see, Aunt," he was arguing, "these boxes may be quite valuable and since the truth of it is that, though you play them often enough, you can't really—"

With a fierce jerk of the tea tray between her outstretched arms Mrs. Craggs sent a stream of hot liquid from the spout of the silver pot plummeting straight down onto Nephew Tony's lap.

"Oh, lor, sir, lor," Mrs. Craggs said in instant apology. "What must have come over me? Oh, sir. Sir, you are a mess. Come out to the kitchen right away and I'll sponge you down. We gotter save that nice suit."

And though the suit in fact was of a cut and color that indicated years of service that had begun a long time ago, Nephew Tony did hurry out to the kitchen.

There Mrs. Craggs did nothing at all about sponging the broad spatter of tea. Instead she faced the not so young man with her arms akimbo.

"Now you just listen to me," she said. "I know what you were just going to tell her. And you're not to do it."

"What—what do you mean?" Nephew Tony asked.

"I mean you were going to tell her she's so deaf she can't hear them musical boxes. And I daresay you were going to offer to sell 'em for her. And with a big difference between the price you get and the money you'll give her."

"I don't know what you're talking about," Nephew Tony said. "If I was offering my aunt some good business advice, it's hardly any affair of yours. The money she gets for those boxes would probably be enough to keep her in comfort for the rest of her days."

"She's happy enough as she is, and don't you think nothing else," Mrs. Craggs answered. "She may not hear a single tinkle those blessed boxes make, but she thinks we all believe she does and that's what keeps her going. So don't you try putting your oar in."

Nephew Tony, dabbing for himself at his trousers with a snatched dishcloth, darted the charwoman a glance of fury.

"I'll thank you to keep your interfering nose out of our family business," he said. "I'm going straight back in there and tell my aunt it's plain common sense to sell those boxes, and that I know where I can get a fair price for them."

Mrs. Craggs folded her hands and stood with them in front of her, leaving the way to the kitchen door clear. But there was a look in her eyes that stopped Nephew Tony dead in his tracks.

"What are you looking like that for?" he demanded.

"Because," said Mrs. Craggs, "if you go in there I shall come after you and tell your dear aunt that her nephew's just finished a good spell in quod."

"Prison? How did you know—what do you mean 'prison'?"

"I mean just what I say. That someone who's been out of the way so long he thinks you can still get anywhere on a bus for tuppence hasn't been up in no North of England. He's been inside. I got ears in me head and unless you want me to tell her what I heard, out you go."

"Well," Mrs. Craggs said to Mrs. Proost a few minutes later, taking care to stand where the old lady could see her lips. "Well, I'm sure I don't know where he's gone. Upped and off he did, just like that. 'Spect he remembered an aeroplane he'd got to build or something."

"Yes, yes. I expect that was it," the old lady said. "Young men like him have so much on their minds, you know."

"Yes, dear—yes, madam," said Mrs. Craggs. "That's true enough. And now shall I turn one of your musical boxes on for you? I expect you'd like to hear a nice cheerful tune."

V: *Tasting*

One of the things Mrs. Craggs had to do when she was
Mrs. Fitzblaney's daily help was to stay late every Thursday evening and take up supper to Mrs. Fitzblaney's husband, the old Colonel, who was bedridden. "Thirty years
between them two if there's a day," Mrs. Craggs used to
say to her friend, Mrs. Milhorne. But she got well paid for
this extra work, time and a half always. She had been quite
firm about that the moment she was first asked, since she
well knew there was money and to spare in that household.
The Colonel always had the best and liked the best, there
was no doubt about that. Though there was doubt about the
Colonel himself. The doctor had said years before that he
might go any day, and every time that Mrs. Craggs came to
the house she half expected to hear the worst.

But every Thursday evening Mrs. Fitzblaney went off to
her art class. "And holding hands with the art master, if all I
hear's true," said Mrs. Craggs. "Still, that's no business of
mine. A little of what you fancy don't do you no harm,
that's my motto."

And every week Mrs. Fitzblaney left behind her two
ounces of Patna rice to be boiled for ten minutes by the
clock and no more and a saucepan of ready-prepared curry
to be heated up.

"Fair fussy he is about his curry, the old boy," Mrs.
Craggs would say. It had to be cooked in the afternoon by
Mrs. Fitzblaney in exactly the way the Colonel liked it, and
all Mrs. Craggs had to do was to see that she knocked on
the bedroom door, with the tray in her hands, at eight
o'clock to the second.

She had been late once, but only once. At half a minute
past eight the Colonel's voice, despite his illness, had come
roaring down the stairs. "Bearer! Bearer! Where's that

blasted bearer! Fellow's late on parade. I won't have it. D'ye hear, damn and blast you? I will not have it." Very much on her dignity Mrs. Craggs had been when she went in with the tray that night.

But being on the dot was not all. That curry had to be hot as well. Not spicy hot. The Colonel liked it that way, but there the doctor had put his foot down. But as near boiling-hot as dammit that curry had to be. There had been trouble about that once too.

"Bearer, what the hell's this? Bloody *ice* pudding? Eh, man? Eh?"

"I do my best," Mrs. Craggs had replied. "And what's more, if I may make so bold as to mention, I am not a man, nor yet a bearer neither, whatever that may be."

But all the same ever afterward she took the precaution of dipping a finger into the saucepan and having a taste, when she thought the curry was ready, to make sure it had reached a really hot heat. The stuff was nasty enough, she thought, but she was not going to be called names at her age.

And then one Thursday came and, as Mrs. Craggs said later to Mrs. Milhorne, "I will not forget, not so long as I has breath in my body to remember by."

At the start it did not seem to be different from any other Thursday evening. Mrs. Craggs, who came to the house to do the cleaning in the afternoon, got through her work as usual. It was the sitting room on Thursdays, and the hall. And at just the usual time Mrs. Fitzblaney came down the stairs dressed as usual in her painting things— "Pair of jeans that should've been in the dustbin years ago," said Mrs. Craggs. "And too tight for her by a long chalk where I won't mention"—and as usual Mrs. Fitzblaney fussed over telling Mrs. Craggs what she knew perfectly well already.

"You won't forget to be on the dot of eight with his supper, will you, Mrs. Er—?" "Never did have the common decency to get me name right, but that was Mrs. Fitzblaney all over," said Mrs. Craggs—and no sooner had Mrs. Craggs assured her that she had no need to worry about that than it was "Oh, and Mrs. Er—, I forgot to say. You will make quite, quite sure the curry's hot, won't you? The Colonel gets so cross if it isn't just to his liking, you know, and it's terribly bad for him to—to— Well, you know, lose his temper."

"There won't be no cause for complaint from me," said Mrs. Craggs.

And there was not. At 7:30 to the second—she had the radio on "dead quiet" to make sure—onto the stove went the water for the rice and on too went the curry over a nice low heat. And at 7:45 precisely Mrs. Craggs had the rice dished and waiting and was making doubly sure the curry was really hot. She put her finger in, winced at the heat, but nevertheless lifted a yellow-brown gob to her lips and bravely tasted it.

"Hot as hot," she said to herself. "Old Blood-and-Guts'll have no complaints tonight." Then she poured the curry with care onto the center of the hollowed-out mound of rice, put the plate on the tray, and carried it upstairs. The Colonel never ate a dessert. "Blasted sweet stuff. Nobody wants to put that in their mouth," he used to say.

Mrs. Craggs knocked at the door of the bedroom just as she heard the church clock strike eight, and "Come in, come in," the Colonel shouted. Mrs. Craggs entered, carried the food over to the bed tray which was already on parade over the Colonel's knees, and set it down.

"Hm," grunted the Colonel. And then he had the grace to add, "Hah. Thank you." Mrs. Craggs knew her services were not required any longer and down she went to the kitchen.

She ought really at this point to have put on her hat and coat and left. The Colonel always pushed aside his tray when he had finished and Mrs. Fitzblaney brought it downstairs when she got back from the art class. That was the regular routine. The Colonel objected to "blasted women always coming in and out of the room like a set of damn railway trains."

But tonight something stopped Mrs. Craggs as she went to take her hat off the peg on the back of the kitchen door. It was not anything particular, just a feeling—a feeling that something was not quite as it ought to be.

For perhaps a full half minute she stood there, nose up against her coat as it hung on the peg, the hat held high in her hand. And then she got it.

"Hot," she said. "It was too hot. Spicy hot as can be." And then she dropped her hat on the floor just where she stood, wheeled round and was out of the kitchen and thumping off up the stairs in as little time as it takes to tell. She got to the top of the stairs. She made for the Colonel's door. She thrust it open without so much as a knock or a word of apology and said, "Stop!"

"Stop? Stop? What the hell d'you mean by 'stop'?"

Afterward Mrs. Craggs said to Mrs. Milhorne that she had never seen a man look so astonished. "You'd have thought it was the Angel Gabriel come in," she said. "You would have, honest."

But at the time Mrs. Craggs failed to answer the Colonel's question. Instead she fired one of her own. "That curry," she said, "have you tasted any of it?"

"Of course I've tasted my bloody curry, woman," the Colonel thundered back. "What's the infernal stuff for if it isn't to be tasted?"

"Then don't you eat one bit more," said Mrs. Craggs.

"What blasted nonsense is this? The first decent hot curry I've had in the last five years and you have the abominable impertinence to come in here and tell me to stop eating it. I'll do no such thing."

And the Colonel plunged his fork deep into the browny-yellow concoction and lifted a gigantic quantity, all dripping, toward his mouth.

It was then that Mrs. Craggs did an unforgivable thing. She launched herself across the room toward the bed and knocked the Colonel's full fork flying.

"What the—"

Words failed the Colonel.

"Oh, sir," said Mrs. Craggs, "I'm sorry. I really am. I don't know how I even dared to do it, sir."

"And nor do I, you infernal harridan. You're dismissed, d'you hear? Get out, do y'hear me, get out!"

But it was at that moment that the Colonel began to be seriously ill. Mrs. Craggs rolled up her sleeves and set to, and the doctor said afterward that it was solely owing to the sensible way she went about it that the Colonel came out of it as well as he did. But, as she said to Mrs. Milhorne, "I wasn't exactly as calm as a tuppenny cucumber at the time."

In fact, she had gabbled and babbled and said a lot of things that hardly made sense, all of which had had the effect of calming down the old Colonel and probably saving him to live out the rest of his life as the happy resident of a nursing home for ex-officers with proper batmen in attendance.

"It was it being so hot, sir," Mrs. Craggs had babbled that evening. "I mean I know it has to be hot. But not hot like that. And I know Mrs. Fitzblaney knows it mustn't be, 'cos she's always telling me so. And then, when I realized that it was too hot, spicy hot I mean, all of a sudden it come over me why it was. And only why. Poison, I thought. It's to hide the taste of poison. She's done it. She's aiming to be off with that artist fellow and live in comfort on the proceeds. Well, a little of what you fancy does yer good, but there's some things goes too far. And murder's one."

THE DEATH OF
THE BAG MAN

STEPHEN WASYLYK

In spite of the cheery rays of the rising sun slanting through the windows, a pall seemed to hang over the first-to-breakfast residents in the dining room of the Golden Age Retirement Center, Inc., destroying their appetites and causing them to pick at their food despondently.

Even Morley and Bakov were affected. Morley's newspaper lay untouched alongside his plate, his eggs and toast growing cold as Morley sipped at his coffee unhappily; and Bakov spooned up his oatmeal slowly, without his usual complaint about his diet.

Bakov put down his spoon with a sigh. "It is a terrible thing, Morley," he said. "What are we to do?"

"I do not know, Bakov," said Morley, his face sober. "When they raised the rates last time, we captured the bank robber and the bank gave us a reward, but I do not think we can go out and capture a criminal this time, even though the city has many criminals who should be captured. We must think, Bakov. Surely there must be a way for each of us to earn the few dollars that are necessary. Although we are seventy-five, we must be good for something."

Bakov passed a chubby hand over his bald head carefully, as if not to disarrange the hair that was no longer there. "That is true. We are not senile or stupid. But I do not see how poor Miss McIlhenny will manage. She stayed awake in the recreation room all night watching the old movies on the TV as usual because she is afraid to go to sleep because she thinks she will die, but this time she cried and she is still crying. Where can she go and what can she do? She is eighty-two and not well."

Morley rose, his gaily patterned Hawaiian shirt hanging loosely from his bony shoulders, his bushy gray hair haloed by the slanting rays of the morning sun. "There are others also, Bakov, but it is as the Director says. The Center must pay the bills or it will go bankrupt and then there will be no Center at all for anyone. But what the Director does not understand is why no one will give him the money. He has been everywhere and seen everyone. They will not help, even though it is really not a large amount."

Morley tucked his newspaper under his arm. "But . . . " He shrugged. "We have yet a week, Bakov. We will sit in our deck chairs and think as we watch the men destroying the apartment building across the street. Perhaps I will get a brilliant idea. I am good at getting brilliant ideas."

For more than a week workmen had been gutting the gracious old building across the street, sending debris down long wooden chutes to waiting dump trucks. Now that phase was over. A shell of marble and brick was all that remained, and rows of black rectangles that had once been windows stared at Morley and Bakov like vacant eyes that presaged death.

"It is a terrible thing to destroy such a fine building," said Bakov.

"Nothing lasts forever," said Morley pompously.

"Some things," said Bakov. "Just the other night on the television I saw the things in the Egypt that they call the Pyramids. They have lasted for a long time."

"It is simple, Bakov. In Egypt there is not enough progress

because there are not yet many cars. Some day the Egypts will all own cars like people in America and they will tear down the Pyramids to make a shopping center with a big parking lot."

The demolition crew had erected a plywood wall well out from the base of the building, closing off the sidewalk and part of the street to protect passersby, leaving only an opening at each end so that the trucks could pull in and out. Now one of the men appeared in the near opening, shouting and waving his hard hat, and the other men ran toward him, all disappearing inside.

"Aha," said Morley. "Something is wrong."

One of the men reappeared in the opening and ran into the street, looking one way and then another. He spotted a police car that had parked to one side, either because the two officers had been assigned to the demolition or they were as interested as everyone else in seeing the building come crashing down. The man darted toward the police car, spoke to the driver, and in a few minutes all three ran into the building.

Morley leaped to his feet, his hair bristling, his shirt flapping. "Something has happened, Bakov. Let us go see."

"No," said Bakov. "Always when you go see, we get into trouble."

"What trouble can there be in an empty building?"

"Wherever the police go, there is trouble."

"Then stay, Bakov. I will go alone." Morley started down the broad lawn toward the gate in the wrought-iron fence.

Bakov watched, sighed, then heaved his bulk from his deck chair and followed, muttering to himself, "If I do not go, he will get into trouble. If I go, he will still get into trouble, and I also. So why do I go?" He lumbered across the lawn after Morley, both of them moving rapidly in spite of their age, and they crossed the street together.

They stopped at the opening in the plywood wall, peered inside, and saw nothing except a debris-littered sidewalk.

"Come on," said Morley.

Bakov nervously peered upward. "A brick will fall on my poor head."

Morley cocked his head, listening to the approach of police sirens, blue eyes sparkling with excitement. "Listen," he said. "More police are coming."

"Then I am going," said Bakov.

Morley took his arm and pulled him with him as he crossed the sidewalk. "They can only tell us to leave," he said. "By that time we will have seen what is wrong."

They went through the doorless opening that once had been the main entrance. The lobby was now a gloomy cavity illuminated only by daylight filtering through the entrance. The demolition men were gathered around the two policemen, one of whom was taking notes. Beyond the group lay what appeared to be a large bundle of rags.

Morley identified it first, clutching Bakov's arm fiercely. "It is a man, Bakov!" he whispered.

He sidled forward almost to the body when one of the policemen yelled, "Hey! Get away from there!"

Morley stepped back, his eyes still on the body, his brow furrowed.

Bakov moved aside quickly as several men came through the door, led by a heavyset man with close-cropped hair who stopped when he saw Morley, lifted an arm with index finger pointing at the doorway, and said, "Get out!"

Morley drew himself up, his shoulders squared. "Do not speak so to a private citizen who has committed no crime."

Arm still extended, finger pointed, the man repeated, "*Out!*"

"You will be sorry," said Morley. He motioned to
Bakov. "Come," he said. "When Lieutenant Hook cannot
find the murderer, as usual, perhaps he will speak to us
nicely and then we will decide to help."

An internal pressure seemed to make Hook swell a little.
"*OUT*!" he said.

Morley moved toward the door, stopping the moment
Hook's attention left him.

"All right," said Hook to the policeman. "Let's have it."

"One of the demolition men was giving the building a
final check," said the policeman. "He found the body and
called us. No one has been near it except me. I could see
someone shot the man in the chest and he was dead, so I
kept everyone away."

Hook motioned to one of his men.

The detective went through the dead man's pockets. "No
identification," he said, rising to his feet. "The last time that
coat was pressed was during the Lyndon Johnson administration. The shirt and pants are two sizes too big and came
out of a ragbag somewhere. He doesn't have any socks and
I don't know what holds the shoes together."

"How old?" asked Hook.

"Hard to say. Late fifties, early sixties."

"Some old bum or wino, I guess," said Hook.

The detective shook his head. "I think not. Looks more
like an old guy down on his luck."

Hook raised his voice. "Does anyone know this man?"

Morley stepped out of the shadows. "He is the Bag
Man," he said.

Hook whirled. "I thought I told you to get out."

Morley's eyebrows arched. "And if I had gone, who
would answer your question? I tell you, he is the Bag
Man."

"The what?"

Morley spoke as if Hook were a child. "The Bag Man. He walks the streets with a big brown cloth bag over his shoulder and sometimes he asks the people who pass if they will give him a quarter. Bakov and I watched him many times and we were curious, so one day we crossed the street and talked to him because no one else paid attention. They just pushed him aside and we felt sorry for him. I asked him what he was doing and he smiled and said he was looking for help and did I have a quarter. I explained I did not have a quarter and neither did Bakov, but if he was hungry he could come into the Center and be our guest at the mid-morning tea time, which he did."

"He was not hungry," said Bakov. "He gave me his little sandwiches."

"You took a bum into the Center?" asked Hook.

"What bum? He was a poor old man asking for quarters, so we gave him tea instead."

"What did he carry in the bag?" asked Hook.

"I do not pry," said Morley loftily.

"I do not think it was money," said Bakov, "or it would not be necessary for him to ask for quarters."

Hook looked from one to the other. "Tell me," he said carefully, "did it occur to either of you to ask his name?"

"Of course," said Morley. "Were we to call him Mr. Bag Man? He said his name was Chaucer Galinsoga."

Hook blinked. "He must have made it up. No one could be named Chaucer Galinsoga."

"It is indeed a strange name," said Bakov, "but a policeman once told me your name is Ironhead Hook, which is also a strange name although not as strange as Chaucer Galinsoga."

Hook glared at him. "Did he tell you where he lived?"

"No," said Morley. "He said only that the Center was a fine place and we were lucky, which we already knew."

"What else did he say?"

"He did not say much," said Bakov. "He was too busy writing in his little book."

Hook almost yelled. "What little book?"

"The little book he kept in his coat pocket," said Morley.

Hook turned to the detective who had gone through the dead man's pockets. The detective shrugged. "No book," he said.

Hook folded his arms. "Tell me something," he said to Morley and Bakov. "You take an old bum in off the street because you feel sorry for him, you give him tea and sandwiches which he doesn't eat because he isn't hungry although he is asking people for quarters, he asks you questions and he writes the answers in a little notebook while he tells you very little of himself. Did it occur to either of you that this was a little unusual?"

"Of course," said Morley. "Because we are old, we are not stupid. He said he was writing a book."

Hook's voice rose. "An old bum with no socks was writing a book?"

"I am not a writer but I know one does not require socks to write a book," said Morley patiently. "Perhaps he did not like to wear socks, but that is not important. I have told you that he carried a brown cloth bag always, but there is no bag here." His eyes scanned the dark recesses of the lobby. "Where can the bag be?"

"The bag won't be here," said Hook. "The man was killed elsewhere and his body brought here." He pointed. "You can see where it was dragged across the floor through the brick and plaster dust."

"It is very clever of you to puzzle that out," said Morley admiringly. He stiffened suddenly, his eyes bright,. "The car! It was the car!"

"What car?" asked Hunt.

"The car I saw last night," said Morley.

Hook's eyes narrowed. He thought for a moment, then took Morley and Bakov by the arms. "There is too much confusion here," he said. "Let's go across the street and talk about this."

At an outdoor table on the quiet patio Hook produced his notebook and held his pen expectantly. "Now tell me about the car."

Morley cleared his throat. "We were all upset at the Center yesterday. Many found difficulty in sleeping, I among them, so I looked out the window and thought about our problem. From the window it is possible to see the front of the building across the street. Naturally I saw no person because only fools, criminals, and policemen walk on the street at that hour.

"Then a car came. It stopped and the driver made it go backward to the wooden fence the building wreckers put up so that the innocent people would not be hit on the head by a falling brick. Then the headlights went out. I could see nothing more because it is dark there. After a few minutes the car drove away again and I went to sleep because I did not consider the car important."

"What kind of car was it?" asked Hook.

Morley shrugged. "Who can tell? Do they not all look alike these days?"

"Could you at least see the color?" asked Hook. "Was it light or dark?"

"In the dark it was dark and in the light it was light," said Morley testily. "It was no color." He scratched his nose gently and his eyes twinkled as he glanced at Bakov. "It does not matter. I have already solved the crime for you."

Hook leaned back. "Tell me," he said tightly.

"The Bag Man was writing a book," said Morley. "Obviously it was a book about the graft and the corruption in the city of which everyone already knows but can prove nothing, but the Bag Man had the proof in his book that the Mayor does not work for the people but for the greedy gangsters, so it is necessary that the greedy gangsters steal his book and destroy him, for which they hire an evil hit person who shoots the Bag Man and takes his body to the empty building because he thinks they will knock the building down on top of the poor Bag Man and destroy the evidence of the crime. You see? It is necessary only for you to go to the Mayor and demand that he confess and then crime will be solved because the Mayor will tell the names of his greedy friends."

Bakov nodded. "That is true. All the famous detectives on the television have solved this crime many times. The only thing that is different is how the evil hit person pays for his crime. Sometimes the evil hit person's car goes over a big cliff and explodes."

His face solemn, Morley nodded at Hook. "So you see, you have only to go demand that the Mayor tell you who is responsible."

Hook's face seemed to have swelled and acquired a tinge of purple.

Morley looked at him closely. "I think perhaps you have the high blood pressure like Bakov."

Hook slammed his notebook closed and put it in his pocket.

Morley's voice held laughter. "Do not be so angry. Bakov and I were only making a joke. We know that such a crime is only for the television." He shook his head. "I do not know who killed the Bag Man."

Hook made an effort to smile. He took a deep breath. "At least I am pleased to hear you will not interfere this time."

"I will not interfere," said Morley. "Bakov and I have other problems and we cannot help you."

Hook's eyes rolled up. He mumbled a few words gratefully and left.

"Come, Bakov," said Morley. "It has occurred to me that I have not yet read my morning newspaper and there are many jobs advertised there for people who would like to work. We will look at them. Perhaps we will find something."

"I do not think anyone would advertise a job for two seventy-five-year-old men," said Bakov.

"We will lie about our age," said Morley. "We will tell them we are only sixty."

Across the street the demolition proceedings had been suspended for the day to preserve the scene of the crime and Morley occupied himself in reading each little ad in the Help Wanted section. Finished, he sighed.

"There is nothing, Bakov. Perhaps there will be others tomorrow."

He began turning the pages, scanning the headlines, when he stopped, adjusted his glasses, and bent forward.

"That is strange, Bakov," he said, pointing. "Here on the page that tells of the parties of the rich people, I see the name Mrs. Galinsoga. I wonder if she could be a relation of Chaucer Galinsoga, the Bag Man."

"The Bag Man was poor," said Bakov. "How could he be the relation of someone rich?"

Morley folded the paper slowly. "But he was strange, Bakov. He was writing a book even if he had no socks. Perhaps he was a rich man in disguise."

"Rich men do not write books," said Bakov. "They are too busy being rich."

"It is a strange coincidence," said Morley. "Perhaps we should go talk to this Mrs. Galinsoga."

"We do not know where she lives," Bakov pointed out.

"The phone book will give us the address," said Morley. He stood up and dropped the paper into the deck chair. "I am interested in this, Bakov. Let us go investigate."

"Let Lieutenant Hook investigate."

"Hook is not too bright a person, Bakov. Already we have found it necessary three times to help him catch a murderer. Let us go."

"I do not wish to go."

"The paper calls her the beautiful Mrs. Galinsoga."

"Rich ladies are always beautiful," said Bakov. "Never once have I seen the newspapers call a rich woman ugly, even though there are just as many ugly rich people as there are poor ones and I have met many beautiful women. What is one more?"

Morley pointed at him. "You are truly getting old, Bakov."

Without a word Bakov stood up, tried to pull in his bulging stomach, patted his nonexistent hair, and brushed off his sleeves. "For what do you wait, Morley?" he asked.

They located the address and reached it by a combination of free rides for senior citizens on bus routes that took them across the city to the suburbs, where they found the numbers and the name *Galinsoga* on a brass plate fastened to a head-high stone wall pierced by a driveway. They followed the driveway through a stand of trees until they saw the house itself, a handsome combination of dark-brown brick and peaked roofs surrounded by tailored shrubbery.

To one side of the house the driveway flared out into an apron before a garage. Three cars were parked there; a foreign-made light-green station wagon, a two-seater off-white sports car, and a metallic gray Mercedes sedan.

A small thin man, no bigger than Morley, his gray hair

cut short and his clothes protected by white coveralls, was industriously running a cloth over the hood of the Mercedes.

"The tradesmen's entrance is in the rear," he said.

"We are not members of a union," said Morley. "We are here to see Mrs. Galinsoga." He peered into the windows of the sedan. "Is this the car of Mrs. Galinsoga?"

The man pointed at the two-seater. "That is Mrs. Galinsoga's. This one belongs to Mr. Galinsoga."

"Her husband?"

"No. Her brother-in-law." The man placed his hands on his hips. "What do you want, anyway?"

"Do not be rude," said Morley, "or I will tell Mr. Galinsoga you have missed a big spot on his car and he might wish to hire a younger man whose eyes are better."

They left the man polishing carefully and went up to the front door where Morley pushed the bell.

A pretty, dark-haired young woman in a black uniform with a white apron opened the door and frowned. "You two can't be selling subscriptions."

"We wish only to speak to Mrs. Galinsoga about Mr. Chaucer Galinsoga," said Morley.

She held the door wide. "Come in."

The room in which the young woman asked them to wait was low-ceilinged, the walls were lined with books, the furniture was leather-covered, soft, and grouped around a huge fireplace.

A tall slim woman about 40, with brown wavy hair framing a delicate, aristocratic face, entered the room, concern in her eyes. The fingers of one hand pulled nervously at the neck of her soft pullover as she looked from one to the other. "I am Mrs. Galinsoga," she said. "You have news of my husband?"

Morley's eyes were puzzled. "Perhaps there are two

Chaucer Galinsogas. I speak of the one who does not shave and wears old clothes and shoes but no socks and carried a brown cloth bag, which is hard to believe of a man married to such a beautiful rich woman."

"That is true," said Bakov. "He would at least have socks if he was *your* Mr. Chaucer Galinsoga."

"Then you have seen him," said Mrs. Galinsoga excitedly. "You see, Chaucer is a professor of sociology at the university but he is writing a book on the socio-economic difficulties of our senior citizens, so he dresses in old clothing every few days and goes into the city to experience the problems from a personal viewpoint. He feels it is necessary to study the subject first-hand." She waved at the room. "Obviously, he could get no feeling for the matter here."

"What did she say, Morley?" whispered Bakov.

"I think the Bag Man was writing a book about old people who have no money," said Morley.

"That would indeed be a very thick book," said Bakov.

Morley shifted uncomfortably. "I do not know why the police have not already told you. I am very sorry but Mr. Chaucer Galinsoga of the old clothes and no socks has been murdered."

Mrs. Galinsoga gave a little scream and covered her face with her hands.

A middle-aged man with full iron-gray hair and a square face came into the room.

Mrs. Galinsoga wailed. "Oh, Jeffrey," and collapsed on his chest, her tears wetting the lapel of his tweed jacket.

The man looked over her head at Morley. "What is this?"

The woman looked up. "They say that Chaucer has been murdered."

"Nonsense," snapped the man. "I just reported him missing to the police. They would have told me."

"The police have many departments," said Morley. "Who are you?"

"Jeffrey Galinsoga. Chaucer is my brother."

"And are you also a professor?"

"We are both professors of sociology. Suppose you tell me what this is all about."

Morley explained.

Mrs. Galinsoga wailed, "I told him it was dangerous to walk around the city like that, but he insisted."

The doorbell rang. Morley heard the door open and then the maid led Hook and a detective into the room. Hook stopped short and glared at Morley and Bakov.

"Why are you so late?" demanded Morley. "It was necessary for me to tell Mrs. Galinsoga and the Bag Man's brother everything. It remains only for you to question them."

Hook pointed at the door. "Get out!"

"We will go," said Morley. He turned to Mrs. Galinsoga. "I am sorry about your poor husband. He was a nice man."

The pretty young maid stood in the entrance hall, obviously eavesdropping. Her chin lifted and she looked at Morley defiantly. "I want to hear what the policeman says."

"Do not worry about the policeman," said Morley. "I will tell you all about the crime. Let us go into the kitchen."

Bakov brightened. "I like kitchens."

"Are you hungry?" asked the young woman.

"He is always hungry because the diet person at the Center will not allow him to eat what he wants to eat," explained Morley. "Your kitchen is for talking, not eating."

They sat at a small table while Morley told the maid what he knew.

"What is your name?" asked Morley.

"Sue Ann," said the young woman.

"You live here?"

"Of course. So does the cook, but she is off today."

Bakov sighed. "That is just my luck."

Sue Ann went to a sideboard and came back with a bowl of fruit. "Take your choice," she said. "It is good for you and will not hurt your diet." She patted Bakov's bald head. "My grandfather has the same problem."

Bakov beamed. "You are a fine young person." He selected three bananas, placing one in each shirt pocket and peeling the third.

"Was last night the first time Mr. Galinsoga did not come home?" asked Morley

"Oh, he was home," she said. "He came in about eight when Mrs. Galinsoga was upstairs dressing for the party. He went directly to the den. I brought him a sandwich and a cup of coffee. Then his brother came in to pick up Mrs. Galinsoga and take her to the party, which he often does because Mr. Galinsoga has been busy with his book for months. The two men talked until Mrs. Galinsoga came down. She and the brother left about nine, shortly before I did." She smiled. "I had a date."

"Was Mr. Chaucer Galinsoga wearing his old clothes?"

She nodded.

Morley frowned. "That is indeed strange. If Mr. Chaucer Galinsoga was working in his den at nine, how then did he end up murdered in the empty apartment building?"

Bakov peeled his second banana. "That is a good question, Morley, but as you told Lieutenant Hook, there was the car."

"That is true," said Morley thoughtfully. He rose to his feet and paced the kitchen slowly. He stopped. "Aha," he said. He resumed pacing, stopping once again. "*Aha*," he said, more loudly this time. He went back to his pacing, coming to a sudden halt with his arm thrust into the air. "*AHA*!" he said.

"What is this *Aha*?" asked Bakov.

"Come, Bakov," said Morley.

"I have not finished my banana," said Bakov.

"Eat while you walk," said Morley.

He led them back to the library where Lieutenant Hook and the detective were still questioning Mrs. Galinsoga and the murdered man's brother, the four of them standing in front of the fireplace.

"I thought I told you to leave," snapped Hook.

Morley held up a hand. "I would like only to ask a few questions, which will not bother anyone."

"Let him ask," said Mr. Galinsoga. "He was nice enough to come here and tell me about poor Chaucer."

"When you and Mr. Jeffrey Galinsoga came home from the party, was Mr. Chaucer Galinsoga in his den?" asked Morley.

She shook her head. "The den was dark. I assumed he had gone to bed."

"Would you not know this when you also went to bed?"

"We had separate bedrooms," she said. "Naturally, I would not disturb him and I didn't know he was gone until this morning."

Morley scratched his nose reflectively and then pointed at the couple. "Arrest them!" he said to Hook.

"What for?" asked Hook.

"Together they killed Mr. Chaucer Galinsoga."

"That's ridiculous!" said Mrs. Galinsoga.

"No," said Morley. "I will explain. It is called the love triangle. Mr. Jeffrey Galinsoga and Mrs. Galinsoga were lovers and they wished to get rid of Mr. Chaucer Galinsoga, so they came home from the party and murdered the poor man and took his body to the empty building so the building would fall on top of him and conceal the crime."

Mrs. Galinsoga's eyes were wide. "Jeffrey and I?"

"Of course," said Morley. "Did you not go out often with Jeffrey Galinsoga to parties? Did you and your husband not have separate bedrooms? Is it to be believed that Jeffrey Galinsoga could associate with such a beautiful rich woman and not have romantic feelings? Is it to be believed that because your husband was always busy that you would not turn to Jeffrey Galinsoga in your loneliness?"

"You are a ludicrous old man," said Jeffrey Galinsoga. "The wild fantasies emanating from your senile brain are hardly amusing. There is not one single fact to justify your conjecture."

"There is the car," said Morley. "Your car—the metallic gray one. A car of such a color is dark in the dark and light in the light and of no color at all. Lieutenant Hook has only to take it to the building when it gets dark while I look out my window as I did last night and I will identify it as the same car, which means that you took the body of your poor brother to the building."

Jeffrey Galinsoga's face paled. With one quick movement he threw Mrs. Galinsoga into Hook and the detective, all three collapsing, whirled, and sprinted for the front door.

Only Bakov was in the way, his partly consumed banana halfway to his lips. Galinsoga thrust Bakov aside, the banana arching gracefully through the air, and, in one of those freak accidents that can never be duplicated deliberately, the banana landed on the floor a split second before Galinsoga's heel came down on the same spot, and Jeffrey Galinsoga gave an excellent imitation of an overweight Peter Pan before crashing to the floor.

Bakov looked down at him ruefully. "He has ruined my good banana," he said.

*   *   *

Morley and Bakov settled into their deck chairs after dinner for a breath of fresh air before joining the other residents in front of the big color TV in the recreation room.

"I wonder if Lieutenant Hook is still angry," said Bakov.

"I do not understand Lieutenant Hook," said Morley. "Did I not solve the crime as usual and did you not capture the criminal with your banana?"

"He said you almost blew it," said Bakov. "I do not know what that means."

"It means only that I was wrong about the love triangle," said Morley. "Mrs. Galinsoga loved her husband dearly, even if he did not wear socks. Does it matter instead that Jeffrey Galinsoga killed his brother because he said his brother stole his idea of a book about old people with no money? For many months Jeffrey had been making notes but it was his brother who had the idea of pretending to be an old person with no money to see what it was really like, so he became the Bag Man, walking the streets and talking to old people as if he was one of them, and Jeffrey Galinsoga knew that such a book would be better than his.

"Could I know that while Mrs. Galinsoga was upstairs, Jeffrey demanded that his brother stop because the book about old people was really his idea, but his brother refused? Also, could I know that Jeffrey took Mrs. Galinsoga to the party but sneaked out and came back and murdered his brother because he was angry and jealous, and that he then placed the Bag Man in the trunk of his car and went back to the party to bring Mrs. Galinsoga home?"

"It was not very nice of him to drive around with Mrs. Galinsoga while her poor husband's body was in the trunk."

"Jeffrey Galinsoga was not a nice person or he would not have murdered his brother over a book about old people with no money because there are enough old people with no money for everybody. But it was obvious that only he could drive into the city to dispose of the body. I did not see how he could do this without Mrs. Galinsoga's knowing, so I thought she also was guilty. When Jeffrey Galinsoga saw the empty building he thought that would be an excellent place, but he could not know I was looking out the window, and even Lieutenant Hook said that if I had not seen the car it would have been very difficult to prove that Jeffrey Galinsoga was guilty."

He shook his head. "Lieutenant Hook has only a little imagination for a homicide person. He sent his men to check the records of the Social Security and the Welfare to find where Chaucer Galinsoga lived instead of looking in the phone book as any sensible person would do, which was why you and I had to tell Mrs. Galinsoga her husband had been murdered."

"Mrs. Galinsoga is not only rich and beautiful, but a nice person," said Bakov. "She forgave you for saying she killed her husband."

"Her husband told her so many stories of old people with no money he had met, she feels she must now take the pages he had written and his notes and finish his book."

"I do not see how she can do this," said Bakov. "She is not a professor of the sociology with no socks."

"It is simple, Bakov. Did I not say that we were good for something? I explained to her she requires the assistance of two intelligent old people such as us, because who knows better what should be in such a book? So she said we will be her consultants and she will pay generously for our valuable experience. We will then give the money to the Director and no one will have to leave the Center, including Miss McIlhenny." Morley smiled. "The dead Mr. Galinsoga would be very happy to know of this."

Bakov sat upright. "Is this true, Morley?"

"Of course. I would not lie about such a thing."

"I did not hear her say this. Where was I?"

Morley sighed. "In the kitchen with Sue Ann, eating a banana."

THE UPSTAIRS ROOM

PATRICIA MOORHEAD

They say when you are in imminent danger of death your whole life passes in front of you. Funny, I can only bring the last three days into focus.

My name is Rachel Rose. I live alone in the little green and cream Victorian on the corner of Church Street and Second, Mr. Rose having passed on a year and a half ago. Our only daughter, Miriam, lives one town away, which is close enough for both of us. She has a new house, a nice job, and a good husband. She thinks I'm nosy, with not enough to do, so she suggested this bird identification class at the college. Mondays. I enrolled to please her.

Our professor is a very nice young man. His assignment for us this semester is to chronicle a nesting pair or to document a tree colony for at least one month. He said he plans to grade heavily on our journals. I chose that big oak in our front lawn for bird-watching for obvious reasons, the first one being that the upstairs bedroom puts me very near the birds in the higher branches and they can't see me at all. Not to mention weather. And bugs. After the initial class on Monday morning, I took my new bird book and notepads upstairs to turn the bedroom into an observation tower.

Daddy built this house for Mama the year they were married. I have lived in it all my life except for a brief whirl at college just before World War II. Upstairs has just the one bedroom, which was mine during my childhood. There is something about this room few people know. Some stray spark of whimsy led Daddy to construct a hidden door to the attic built into a bookcase. I never liked going into the attic when I was little. Cobwebs. The romance of a hidden passage was lost on me, unfortunately. Our daughter Miriam showed a similar lack of interest in the secret doorway when it was her turn to occupy the bedroom. This room has two windows; one faces south, one east. They both look onto our front lawn, the oak, and the whole street corner. I seldom come up here. Climbing stairs is harder than it used to be. Anyway, my company is mostly daytime company, since no grandchildren have yet come along to discover Daddy's secret.

Nothing much is stored in the attic except a box of Mr. Rose's belongings that I can neither use nor part with. However, I now have need of his fine binoculars.

We live right downtown in the older part. There aren't many neighbors any more. To the east, directly across Church Street, is a little steepled church, one of several for which the street was named. No longer consecrated, it has been a repertory theater, a luncheonette, and an art gallery over the years, all now defunct. It remains unoccupied. North on Church Street, less than two blocks away, is our new City Hall and the police station. Catercorner from me, on the southeast corner, is a sorry motel that I never give so much as a glance. Ever. Past that, going south on Church Street, is the parking lot for Coleman's Mortuary, which faces on Main Street. The southwest corner, shades of the past, is a vacant lot. I look at the corner of Church and Second all day long, but at eye level. From the upstairs windows the perspective changes. Here, you are looking down on the world unseen, like an Old Testament angel.

I pulled the platform rocker in front of the window facing east and put Miriam's white wicker desk and chair in front of the window facing south. That way I can look and write at the same time. I put the journal and the bird book and pencils on Miriam's desk and sat in the rocker with Mr. Rose's binocs for a few minutes to get the feel of my role as a wildlife observer.

As I explained, this corner isn't heavily populated but it leads to a lot of places, so there is a fair amount of traffic, both cars and people. There is usually plenty of parking and, of course, no time limit. I raised the binocs and looked down at a man standing on the corner in front of the church. For a breathless moment I felt I was face to face with him. Through the glasses he looked near enough to touch. It was unsettling because it seemed as if I should be just as visible to him. I viewed him both with and without the glasses several times, marveling at their power. I watched pedestrians walking, chatting, bent on their own affairs, little knowing how well I could see their actions. I felt like a voyeur, guilty and fascinated at the same time. I also realized it was nearly one o'clock, so I left everything for tomorow and went downstairs. My programs.

Yesterday, Tuesday, I dressed early, armed myself with the clock radio and a thermos of coffee, and climbed adventurously to my observation tower. I sighted several birds in the oak. I also discovered that finding their shapes and descriptions among the little bitty pictures in a bird book is not too easy. However, I was eager to begin my journal.

7:30 A.M. *Tuesday* Seven quail run single-file across Second into a bramble on the vacant lot while I hold my breath for their safety. Quickening traffic pattern.

7:42 A.M. Mourning call of a dove, but not from our tree. I can't see it anywhere.

7:50 A.M. Several police patrol cars coming and going. The day shift makes its staggered changes from now until nine o'clock. Seeing the boys in force every morning always gives me a nice feeling of security for the rest of the day, alone as I am.

7:52 A.M. Cat in the vacant lot is stalking something. I fear it is our seven little Order, Gallinaceous: Family, Cracidae: Subfamily, Phasianinae. A dusty gray car half a block long pulls up and parks on Second Street in front of the vacant lot directly in my line of vision. I feel a flush of annoyance. Driver remains in the car. Quail fly off. Cat sits in the tall grass and sulks.

7:53 A.M. Red Volkswagen bug parks in front of the church. Two young girls leave the car and walk north. Secretaries, surely.

7:55 A.M. Man and dog walking eastward on Second on our side of the street.

7:57 A.M. Jogger rounds the corner of Church Street and jogs west. Automobile traffic heavy. Birds quiet.

7:58 A.M. Station wagon parks in front of the gray car. I recognize the driver, a young woman whom I know by sight but not by name. Works somewhere in City Hall. She climbs out of the car, skirt pulled up, arms loaded with binders and dripping with papers, hedonistic hairdo. She walks back to speak to the person in the gray car. I raise the binocs and thrill to the nearness of them. I feel certain they can hear me breathing, but really I know better.

7:59 A.M. The young woman is wobbling off up Church Street, butt flying, hair to the wind.

8:10 A.M. Can hear a bird singing explosively. Look where I will, he is not visible to me.

8:45 A.M. Dark green van stops short of the intersection beside the old gray car. The man opens his door quickly and scoots around to the driver's side of the van. He looks up the street and down the street all the while they are talking. It is the same man I saw standing in front of the church yesterday. Their conversation ends abruptly, the van drives away, the man returns to his car.

9:20 A.M. Sight birds in the topmost branches. Two. Look like miniature peregrines. Order, Falconiforms: Family, Falconidae. American kestrel. *Falco sparverius.*

10:10 A.M. The man in the old gray car sits close to the window. I can see his face quite well. Seems agitated, checks his watch often.

10:14 A.M. He leaves the car carrying something folded, like cleaning, in a plastic bag. Crosses the street to that awful motel and enters unit 1.

10:23 A.M. Hammering noises from the church steeple. Sight a woodpecker. Order, Piciformes: Family, Picidaei: *Melanerpes formicivorus.* That man from the gray car is rummaging through a big public trash bin in the shadow of the steeple. Furthermore, he is taking a brown grocery bag *from* the garbage and returning to the motel room with it. Oh dear.

10:28 A.M. A couple knock at #1 and they are admitted.

10:30 A.M. Same couple leave, disappearing quietly down Church Street walking south.

10:45 A.M. A business type in a suit comes from Second Street, knocks, and is admitted.

10:46 A.M. Same man leaves motel walking north on Church Street.

10:59 A.M. A white car parks in front of unit 1. Two people get out, rap on the door, and are admitted.

11:02 A.M. Same people come out and drive off.

12:02 P.M. The man leaves the motel room wearing a windbreaker despite a warm afternoon. It is large and loosefitting, with ample pockets.

12:04 P.M. He turns east on Second Street at a brisk walk. I can no longer follow his movements even with the glasses.

12:45 P.M. I notice the man is back. Somehow I missed his return. He is standing in front of the church, just where he was yesterday. I watch him for a while. It is, of course, legal to stand on a street corner and greet people so long as you're fully clothed and all, and to shake the hand of whom you please. What real proof have I of wrongdoing?

12:48 P.M. I put away the binocs and close shop. I forgot to eat lunch. Besides. My programs.

7:30 A.M. *Wednesday* At my post in the rocker. This morning's weather is much like yesterday's.

7:35 A.M. Eight quail run across Second Street; I am happy to note the addition. Good omen. Traffic thickening.

7:37 A.M. Watch cars and drivers through the binocs. I don't feel as self-conscious about watching people today, nor do I have that skittery feeling about being seen.

7:45 A.M. City police are beginning their shift changes. I am comforted by their presence, for I may have need of them today.

7:51 A.M. The man in the old gray car drives up and parks in the same spot as yesterday. It's a two-door Chevrolet Impala. Driver in his late forties, dark blond hair poorly trimmed, sunglasses, wash-and-wear chinos, yellow T-shirt, navy blue and white windbreaker, soiled athletic shoes.

7:57 A.M. Station wagon sighted. Brown and gold fairly late model Pontiac. The same hurried young woman I saw yesterday parks behind the gray Chevrolet. I am watching carefully this time. As she walks past him, she leans over to speak. A folded white packet drops neatly into her mess of books and papers, and away she goes with innocent nonchalance. The man remains in his car and continues his watch checking.

8:45 A.M. Dark green van pulls up and stops in the street as before. The man leaves his car, walks to the driver's side of the van the same way he did yesterday. Feelings of déjà vu. They engage in animated conversation. There is no mistaking this time; I'm watching for the "drop." I take a special look at the fresh-faced driver of the van so I can identify him should I be called to do so.

8:46 A.M. Van drives off up Second Street. The man returns to his auto.

8:47 A.M. I pour myself a cup of coffee and sit in the rocker for a while to manufacture additional courage for my next step.

While gazing through the binocs at this man who so repulses me, I am struck by the pathos of his life: standing on street corners, living in a trash-filled has-been of a car or in a sordid motel room, but mainly going through the drudgery of hours of empty waiting. Is this the fast-paced, glamour-filled drug scene we see nightly on TV? Well, whoopy. Even so, it can't go on. I lay aside the binocs, and walk slowly downstairs. To the telephone.

Whom do I call? I've never been faced with this kind of situation before. This is one of the times I sorely miss Mr. Rose. I hate having to call any government office. No matter which one I ask for, it's never the right one. I always have to explain what I need to three or four uninterested voices in turn.

9:20 A.M. I call the city police. The girl on the line doesn't switch me to anyone else. She listens with great patience and wants to hear all the details. I am so happy to have gained a responsive ear that I pour my heart out to her. I tell her everything I have seen from my window these last three days. She is very reassuring. She thanks me profusely and cautions me not to tell anyone at all about this, to keep it "confidential." She tells me to stay exactly where I am and someone will be right over.

9:45 A.M. I return to my observation point upstairs just in time to see a patrol car pull up in front, and I am greatly relieved. A quick look through the binocs at the redheaded policeman turns my knees to ice. It is the fresh-faced youngster who drives the green van. He glances up at my window and strides toward the front door. He beckons imperceptibly to Mr. Gray Car standing across the street, who walks rapidly toward my back door. There is no time to run downstairs and bolt the doors. I lock the bedroom door, but the flimsy latch is made for privacy, not protection. I push the bookcase door open, crawl through, and shove it closed behind me.

I check through Mr. Rose's things for something to help me. His .22 target pistol, carefully wrapped in burgundy flannelette, leaps to hand. It feels cold and very heavy. Mr. Rose showed me how to load it once, and had me shoot at the target a few times. I should know which end to point, he said.

It is only a matter of time before that redheaded cop realizes that, even accounting for the tall ceilings in this little house, there is still room for an attic and that somewhere there has to be an access to it.

So here I sit crouched in a corner of my own attic in my own house while two murderous strangers range downstairs from room to room through my beautiful things, hunting for me. I can hear their footsteps on the stairs heading for the bedroom, where they will find the binocs and the journal.

My eyes are accustomed to the darkness now. I can see quite well in the dim light of the attic. Mr. Rose's .22, warming to the touch of my hand, is aimed in the immediate vicinity of the secret doorway, waiting for it to open.

So much for Miriam's bright ideas and her damn bird-watching class.

THE HEADMASTER HELPS ONE OF HIS BOYS

RICHARD FORREST

If the fight hadn't occurred directly in front of the Administration Building, the headmaster might not have found out about it for at least an hour. As it happened, the noise produced by the group surrounding the participants was enough to cause him to trundle from his desk out to the stone steps where he stood blinking in the mellow autumn sun.

Bright red and yellow leaves waffled in the air as they floated toward the ground. A shaft of light glinted off the blade of the weapon held by the smaller of the two combatants.

"He's got a knife!" a smallish fourth former's voice cracked.

"Unfair, unfair!" was the raised chant.

It was an incongruous confrontation. The larger of the boys was obviously older and had a reach that exceeded the other's by several inches. He looked puzzled as he warily crouched. A lock of sandy hair fell over his forehead.

The boy holding the knife was slight and wiry. His narrow face was pinched in concentration as he circled the knife before him in slow lethal sweeps.

"I am appalled," the headmaster said as he approached the group. "This is unforgivable."

The crowd around the fighters parted and fell silent. The

headmaster's cane tapped impatiently on the walk by his side. "Look at this. Just look at this," he said. "And just what is going on here?"

"We are fighting, sir," the larger of the boys said quietly.

"That is obvious and no excuse for the insult to a book."

The crowd's gaze fell to the sidewalk near the tapping cane. A library book lay splayed face down on the concrete.

"It fell from my hands, sir," the boy said as he hastily retrieved the volume and smoothed the pages flat.

"A book is a precious thing and should be treated with reverence," the headmaster said. "What's your name?" His cane pointed to the boy holding the knife.

"Braxton, sir."

"Come to my office, Braxton." He turned and scurried back toward the Administration Building.

Braxton shrugged. He flipped the knife blade closed, shoved it into his pocket, and slowly followed the headmaster.

Many years ago, when the Administration Building neared completion, the headmaster had expropriated a spot in the main hall for his desk and phone. He had never seen fit to occupy his more luxurious office on the second floor, which for reasons unknown, now contained old football helmets. Since the building housed several classrooms and the library, in addition to the academy's administrators, his central location gave the headmaster the opportunity to observe each boy at least once during the day as they entered and left the building.

Braxton stood stiffly before the desk. "I guess I'll be shipped."

"Shipped? We don't ship anyone at Greenfield. Ah, yes, you're Braxton. New boy, heh? As I recall, you've been at Choate, Kent, and Andover."

"They all shipped me."

"Is that a fact? A veritable Baedecker of New England preparatory schools, you are. Fighting, I would suppose?"

"Cheating, sir."

"Cheating? Really? A difficult thing, cheating. Tried it once myself. Spanish, first level, as I recall. It created terrible problems. They promoted me to Spanish II, which made cheating twice as hard. Goodness knows what would have happened if I had gone on to Spanish III . . . Mother and I would like you to dine with us tonight, Mr. Braxton. We serve at eight."

The boy's shoulders slumped forward. His skin seemed to tighten even further over his drawn face. "I don't think I would really be welcome if you knew about me, sir."

The headmaster leaned forward slightly. "Is that a fact? Knew what, Mr. Braxton?"

The headmaster's wife was not an austere cook, but a believer in no-nonsense fare. Her meals, when they were not eating at the great hall with the students, consisted of an unadorned roast, potatoes, and a green vegetable. There was always more than enough.

The headmaster mumbled an inaudible grace, looked up to smile at his white-haired wife at the far end of the table, and then over at Braxton by his side. Dishes were passed.

"Mr. Braxton cheats, Mother," the headmaster said as the student flushed.

"I do hope you do it well, Mr. Braxton," she said. "It's terribly embarrassing to me when I find the boys doing it in the usual ways." She smiled at her husband at the head of the table.

"Mr. Braxton is in my geometry class."

She held the platter of lamb slices in one hand as she tilted her head to the side.

"I could never understand why one cheats in geometry.

By the time you write down all those theorems in those little tiny places, you practically have them memorized anyway."

"It seems that Mr. Braxton has another problem, Mother," the headmaster said as he served himself a mound of mashed potatoes.

"What is that?"

The plate of lamb was passed to the head of the table. "His mother has been indicted for murder."

"How unpleasant," she said. "The headmaster will have to do something about that."

"That would be in order," the headmaster said as his fork speared three slices of lamb.

James L. Lambert slammed from his limousine and strode toward the construction trailer. On his way he hastily glanced up at the partially completed high-rise. It vaulted upward 29 stories with one more to go. He grimaced at the sight and threw open the trailer's metal door.

"Any messages?" he barked at the wispy blonde hovering over a desk piled with invoices and time cards.

She groaned and handed him a stack of two dozen pink message slips. "A thousand. The mayor's is on top. They want to put the tax abatement motion before the City Council tonight."

Lambert thumbed quickly through the messages. "About time," he mumbled. "Call Ajax Iron. I want another half-dozen iron men on high steel by tomorrow morning. If we don't top out by Friday, I won't get my next construction advance."

"Yes, sir." She pushed back a strand of hair and reached for the phone. Lambert began to walk toward his office in the rear of the trailer. "There was one odd call, Mr. Lambert. A funny-sounding old man. Said he wanted you to call at once."

"Everyone wants me to call at once," Lambert snapped over his shoulder.

"Said he was the headmaster," she mumbled and continued dialing Ajax Iron.

Lambert stopped and slowly turned. "The headmaster?"

"Uh, yes, something like that."

"Well, damn it! Don't just sit there. Get him on the phone. Never mind, I'll do it." He hurried toward the phone in his office. He knew the telephone number and dialed Greenfield Academy.

"Headmaster, sir. James Lambert, class of '50."

"Yes, Mr. Lambert. How nice of you to return my call. One of our boys up here is in difficulty and I need your help."

"Of course, sir."

"It seems that he comes from your city, Middleburg, and his mother is involved in some unpleasantness."

"What's his name, headmaster?"

"Braxton, but his mother's new married name is Lovelace."

"It's in all the newspapers down here, sir, and evidently quite a case. Mrs. Lovelace killed her husband after they had only been married a few months."

"I'd like the details, Lambert. Get everything all together. You know what I need—police reports, autopsy findings, all the things like that. I don't need to tell you what to do—as I recall, you did a fine job on a term paper back in '48. 'Mao and the Supremacy of the Red Revolution,' I believe it was called."

Lambert gulped. "I wish you wouldn't mention that paper, sir. I'm on the Republican State Committee now."

"Are you really, Lambert? Excellent. We shall put that in

the next alumni news. Can you get that information for me
and ship it up here by messenger on Saturday?"

"Saturday?" Lambert's mind went into overdrive calcu-
lations. He had the necessary clout to obtain the needed information but it would require a dozen personal visits to
half a dozen city and state agencies and the calling in of
two dozen past favors. It could be done, but it would be a
full-time job.

"Did you hear me, Mr. Lambert?" the headmaster continued. "Remember. One of our boys is in trouble."

"I heard you, sir." His voice dropped. "I'll get the information to you by Saturday."

"Good fellow, Lambert."

The Lambert Construction Company pickup truck arrived at Greenfield Academy at noon on Saturday. The driver
braked to a halt by the entrance to the Administration
Building and leaned out the window to hail a passing student. "Where's a guy called the headmaster?"

The fifth former pointed down a curving walk now half-
covered with bright autumn leaves. "See those two men
walking down there?"

"The good-lookin' guy with the blond hair?"

"No, that's Mr. Galton of maintenance. The little old guy
who walks kinda funny. That's the headmaster."

"I got a delivery for him," the driver said and slowly
drove toward the walking couple.

The headmster had the carton containing the murder-
investigation material placed on his desk in the hallway. He
noticed that the container was a liquor carton that had once
held a case of Chivas Regal. He was glad that James Lambert '50 had good taste. He began to unpack the documents,
depositions, and reports and organize them in a manner that
followed the thread of the murder investigation.

Helen Braxton Lovelace married William Lovelace, 20 years her senior, on April 4th of this year. On August 11, Mr. Lovelace was dead. On August 12 a warrant was served on Mrs. Lovelace and she was arrested on a charge of felony murder in the first degree. She was presently out on $100,000 bail pending the commencement of her trial.

The headmaster picked up a group of 8-by-10 glossy photographs. He shuffled them into sequence and began to examine each one carefully. The first was an exterior shot of the Lovelace mansion. It was a large English Tudor house with a circular drive bracketed by well-tended box hedges. A white magic-marker cricle had been drawn around two second-floor windows. An inscription on the back of the picture stated that the windows were located in the master bedroom where the body of Mr. Lovelace had been discovered.

The headmaster took a magnifying glass from his center drawer and examined the area immediately above, below, and to the side of the murder-scene windows. There was a sheer drop of at least thirty feet to the ground, no windows were located above the bedroom, and there were no cornices, overhangs, or crevices that would have afforded a hand- or foothold for an intruder.

A detective report taken from the carton revealed there were no footprints or ladder marks in the soft moist soil immediately below the murder-scene windows.

A second group of photographs consisted of interior shots taken inside the murder room. The headmaster wrinkled his nose as he hastily flipped through them. It was not a pleasant task, but then again, it had to be done. He reshuffled the pictures and began again, this time carefully examining each detail.

The corpse lay supine on the twin bed nearer to the door. A blanket and sheet were half drawn off the pajama-clad body and the handle of a large kitchen knife protruded from the center of the chest. There were several shots of the body from different angles and heights. A few pictures also showed the other twin bed with its rumpled bedding.

A final photograph showed the bedroom door hanging from one hinge at a canted angle. It was obvious that force had been used to gain entrance into the room. A key in the door's inner lock was still visible.

The next item the headmaster examined was a signed statement by the deceased's wife, Mrs. Braxton Lovelace.

"My husband and I dined at nine with our house guest, his nephew, Roger Thornberry. We lingered over coffee, but since I had a headache, I retired at 11:00 P.M. and shortly fell asleep. I heard no sound or movement during the night as I am a heavy sleeper.

"When I awakened, at approximately 7:00 A.M., I noticed that William was quite still. When I approached the bed I saw that . . . that thing sticking out of his chest.

"It was quite obvious that he was dead. I was so shocked that I stood in the center of the floor and began to scream. Shortly, Mr. Thornberry and our butler, Mr. Bowman, heard my cries and began to pound on the door. I was quite hysterical and continued screaming. They broke into our bedroom and someone immediately called the police.

"I did not lock the door when I retired as there is only one key. I assume that my husband locked it when he came to bed."

The headmaster began to leaf through the other documents. The majority of the statements were corroborations of Mrs. Lovelace's initial affidavit. Several servants testified that there was only one key to the master-bedroom door and also that there was no other entrance to the room. The nephew, Roger Thornberry, swore that he awoke on hearing Mrs. Lovelace's screams. He tried the master-

bedroom door, found it locked, and with the aid of the butler broke the door off a hinge in their effort to gain access
to the murder room.

A copy of William Lovelace's last will and testament indicated that his sizeable estate would be equally divided between his widow Helen Braxton Lovelace and his nephew
Roger Thornberry.

The headmaster turned to the autopsy report and tried to
gain an understanding from the scientific language. Death
had been instantaneous sometime between midnight and
5:00 A.M. The cause of death was a sharp implement which
punctured the sternum and entered the left ventricle. There
had been little exterior bleeding. Marked lividity was ap-
parent in the lower extremities.

The Assistant State Prosecutor assigned to the Lovelace
case wrote a short and precise memo to the State Prosecutor:

"Helen B. Lovelace is an attractive woman interested in
money and obviously restless in her new marriage. In a moment of ill-considered rage she stabbed her husband with a
knife which we can place among the mansion's kitchen
utensils. Frightened over her act, she screamed until others
rushed to her aid. She then tried to claim that an intruder
broke into the house, stole the knife from its place in the
kitchen, and somehow entered a locked room to quietly kill
Lovelace.

"The state can positively prove that she, to the exclusion
of all others, was alone in the murder room and had motive
and opportunity for the murder.

"Recommend immediate indictment."

The headmaster piled the material back in the Chivas
Regal carton and sighed. Young Braxton would bear a
heavy cross this year and it was his job to find the boy
some relief.

He would tour the campus on his daily inspection for trash and consider the matter most carefully.

James L. Lambert popped the champagne cork, and watched it sail over the edge of the roof and fall to the ground thirty floors below.

A cheer went up from the dozen hardhats standing on the hastily planked roof of the building's final story. There was another rousing cheer as a topping-ceremony American flag was raised.

Lambert held the bubbling bottle of champagne in the air. "I hereby declare this building—"

A young workman, clutching a phone receiver with a long wire trailing behind him, climbed the ladder to the roof. "Phone call, Mr. Lambert. Some guy who claims he's the headmason."

"Headmaster," Lambert said with a sigh as he handed the champagne bottle to a construction supervisor and took the phone. "Yes, sir," he said brightly.

"I need a door," the headmaster said.

"A door, sir? Like a room door?"

"Exactly. As I recall, Lambert, you own a construction company. You must have plenty of doors."

"Of course, sir. If you give me an idea of what building or room the door is for, I can send you up something appropriate." He had a mental image of a large group of crazed sixth formers wrecking the dining-hall front door in some mad fashion.

"The murder-room door," the headmaster replied. "I want an exact duplicate of the Lovelace murder-room door along with an exact duplicate of the lock and key. You had better put the door in some sort of frame so that I can open and close it."

A cold autumn breeze blew across the rooftop. The

workmen were upending open bottles and drinking the remainder of the champagne. Lambert covered one ear and stooped over in order to hear better. "The murder-room door," he echoed.

"And don't forget the lock. That's most important. The identical lock and key. You can send it up with the man who brought the other material. Competent fellow, reminded me of Craniston, class of '36."

"Craniston, sir?" Lambert said. "A lock and door. I'll send it right up." He handed the phone receiver to the messenger and turned to find that the last of the champagne had been drunk.

The headmaster decided to take a walk and think about the problem. He donned a car coat, took his cane off the edge of the desk, and went down the Administration Building steps.

He paused at the bottom of the steps and took the rubber cap off the bottom of his cane to reveal a needle-like tip which he used to impale stray bits of trash he discovered during his walk.

It was a bright New England fall afternoon. The trees were nearly bare and the faint smell of burning leaves was vague in the air. He hunched over and deep in thought walked down the paths of Greenfield Academy. Bevies of young men and boys parted as he approached; several gave salutations but were not surprised when he didn't answer.

Helen Braxton Lovelace had a motive for murder. She was seemingly alone in a locked room with the victim during the time of the killing and there appeared to be no means of access to or egress from the room. It was what any prosecutor would term a web of circumstantial evidence. She would be tried and convicted, and young Braxton would continue to have difficulties.

It was a problem that required thought.

"Headmaster."

"Yes?" He stopped and turned to face the driver of the Lambert Construction Company pickup truck.

"I have a door and frame for you. Where do you want it?"

"Right here will be fine."

The driver looked up and down the empty walk. "Where?"

"Here. On the walk. It's level and should prove adequate."

The driver shrugged and climbed from the cab to lower the tailgate. It took him a few minutes to wrestle the heavy door in its wooden frame with supporting legs onto the pavement. His forehead was beaded with perspiration when he had finished.

"That will do nicely," the headmaster said as he approached the frame. He opened the door, turned the key in the lock on the inside, then slammed the door, and stepped around the frame to the far side. He tried turning the door handle and found it locked. "Thank you," he said. "Now you can take it back to Mr. Lambert with my thanks." ...

James L. Lambert had his pen poised over the lease agreement in the conference room of the Middleburg National Bank. Once his signature was affixed, one-half of the high-rise would be rented to an AAA tenant, the Nutmeg Insurance Company. The project would be assured of financial success.

The lawyers, bankers, and insurance men in the room around him were quiet, poised in silent tableau as if holding their mutual breath as they awaited his signature.

"Call for you, Mr. Lambert," the bright-faced secretary

said as she poked her head through the door. "It's from Mr. Headman."

Lambert sighed.

"That's the headmaster. I'll take it in your office."

"Damn it, man! Sign!" Theodore Greeley, president of the bank, said impatiently.

"In a minute," Lambert replied as he wearily walked out of the conference room into the small office where he picked up the phone. "You wanted me, sir?"

"Yes, Lambert," the headmaster said. "I want you to go to the police authorities and tell them that Mrs. Lovelace is innocent."

"I don't think they'll believe me, sir," he said.

"Of course they will, Lambert. Just tell them we have the solution to the case. Have confidence in yourself, Lambert. Never amount to anything without confidence."

"Confidence. I'll try. What's the solution?"

"You had better take notes, Lambert. Remember that history test in '49 when you forgot to answer the questions on the last page."

"I remember." He automatically reached across the desk for a pad and pencil and wondered if neatness counted.

"A locked room is a state of mind. In the Lovelace murder it was assumed that there was no way to get into the murder room. It would seem impossible to go in or out windows, and the door was locked from the inside."

"She had to be the one who did it, headmaster."

"I have discovered that the door contained a Walsh lock which can be locked from the inside while the door is open. When shut it remains in a locked position."

"I don't understand."

"The autopsy report states that there was lividity in the lower extremities. If Mr. Lovelace were killed while in a supine position in bed, the lividity would have been to his back. He was killed in a sitting position and remained in that position for some time before the body was moved. He was killed in another room, moved upstairs, and arranged on the bed. The murderer, the nephew, then locked the door on the inside and closed it from outside the room. He was able to do this without waking Mrs. Lovelace. Sedative in her after-dinner coffee, I would imagine."

"That makes a hell of a lot of sense," Lambert said.

"Of course it does. Now run over to the police immediately and tell them. I don't want young Braxton worried another night over this matter."

The young man stood before the desk in the hallway of the Administration Building and shifted restlessly from one foot to another.

The headmaster looked up. "Yes, Mr. Braxton?"

"They have dropped the charges against my mother and arrested Mr. Thornberry."

"Glad to hear that. They did the right thing."

"I want to thank you, sir."

"Nothing to thank me for, Braxton." He wrinkled his brow. "I am concerned about your not signing up for a winter sport."

"I don't know what to do, sir. The only thing I do well is play tennis and Greenfield doesn't have any indoor courts."

The headmaster looked thoughtful for a moment and then rose from his desk and walked over to a closet. He opened the door and rummaged through the cluttered interior until he found what he wanted. "I'll trade you this racket for something."

The boy took the racket. "Funny-looking tennis racket."

"Squash, Braxton. We have indoor squash courts at Greenfield. Since I thought you would be by this afternoon I have Murphy waiting for you on court two."

"Who's Murphy?"

"The boy you were fighting with. You will find squash a very aggressive sport."

"Yes, sir. I'm sure I will. Thank you, sir." Braxton turned to leave.

"You've forgotten something, young man."

"I have?"

"I said I would trade you the racket for something."

"I don't have anything to trade, headmaster."

"I'm sure you do." Their eyes met.

The boy reached into his pocket and handed the knife to the headmaster. "I guess I do."

"Very good, Braxton. You are coming right along."

MR. STRANG STUDIES EXHIBIT A

WILLIAM BRITTAIN

"The single superclue that allows the great detective to show his genius and crack the case may make for interesting detective fiction," Detective Sergeant Paul Roberts said positively, "but in real life it's plain hard work by the police acting as a team, wearing out shoeleather and following up every lead no matter how slim, that gets the crime solved."

Mr. Strang mopped the sweat from his face with a handkerchief. Although the day was a scorcher even for August, it had been necessary for the gnomelike science teacher to take time out from preparing his curriculum for the upcoming school year to shop for a belated birthday gift for his nephew, a mere lad of forty-seven. Many of the shops in downtown Aldershot were air-conditioned, but the streets themselves were a fiery furnace. And since he had to pass the Municipal Building on his walk home, Mr. Strang decided to seek respite from the blistering sun by visiting Roberts in the detective squadroom on the second floor. Now, predictably, the talk had gotten around to crime and detection, subjects on which the teacher and the detective held firm if somewhat divergent views.

"But, Paul," said Mr. Strang, fanning himself with a blank arrest report, "don't you policemen speak of getting a break in a case? What's that, if not some single fact that changes your perception of the whole problem?"

"Those breaks happen because we make 'em happen. We get out there on the streets and we talk to people. We sift and analyze every fact, no matter how unimportant it seems. We work like dogs to crack our cases. It's only in stories that a detective can solve a murder just by noticing that Lord Twiddle is using a different brand of toothpaste."

Roberts wiped a damp shirtsleeve across his forehead. "How about a can of soda, Mr. Strang? We've got some that's cold."

"Sounds good. But, Paul, even in real life, there must be crimes that are solved by taking a single object or event and inferring—" The teacher paused and stared past Roberts, who had opened the door of the small refrigerator in the corner of the squadroom. "What in blazes is that?"

"Soda," said Roberts, holding up a frosty green can. "Didn't you say you wanted some?"

"No, that other thing in the refrigerator. The one that looks like an obelisk."

"Oh, this?" Roberts took out an object about eighteen inches long, with a square base. From the base, each of the flat sides had a slight inward slant. The top had the shape of a tiny pyramid. All in all, it resembled an eighteen-inch replica of the Washington Monument constructed of galvanized sheet steel.

"It's a candle," said Roberts.

"A what?"

"A hand-poured candle. Still in its metal mold. And it's also a murder weapon. It'll be Exhibit A when Harry Robeling goes on trial next month."

"But why keep it in—"

"It's evidence. Normally we keep such stuff down in the property room in the basement, but in this weather that place gets hotter'n a two dollar pistol. So the D.A. asked if he could store it in our refrigerator so it wouldn't melt. Go ahead, have a look. The lab boys are done with it so there's no risk of altering evidence. Here, take it."

Mr. Strang grasped the wax-filled mold and almost dropped it—it weighed more than he'd expected. Slowly he turned it about in his hands. A wick sprouted from the pointed top and the base was a flat, four-inch square of white candle wax. "Quite a weapon," he said. "It'd make a wicked club."

Roberts nodded. "Harry Robeling crushed Kirk Dansker's skull with that thing. Open-and-shut case. The trial's just a formality. But, hey!" He snapped his fingers. "This is a good example of what I was talking about, Mr. Strang. About how the police work as a team. You've read about the Dansker murder in the papers, haven't you? There wasn't an awful lot at the time, but now with the trial coming up the papers are having a field day."

Mr. Strang shook his head. "I've been out of state most of the summer visiting friends," he replied. "And since returning, I've had little time for the news, with the new school year to get ready for. Why don't you tell me about it?"

"O.K." Roberts relaxed contentedly in his chair and took a long swig of soda. "It happened last fall—the night of October second, or maybe early morning on the third. But the real start was a week or so before that, when Catherine Dansker got a note from her husband saying he was coming home."

"Slower, Paul, slower," said Mr. Strang. "Who's Catherine Dansker? And why is it so important that her husband was coming home? Don't most husbands do that from time to time?"

Roberts smiled. "I forgot you hadn't read about the case.

O.K. Catherine Dansker lives over in the Mill Valley section of Aldershot. Ten years ago she and her husband Kirk bought a house there—really not much more than a shack. Kirk Dansker did odd jobs and Catherine did some craft work at home that she sold to stores for the Christmas season—candles, mainly. The family managed to make ends meet somehow. And then three years ago Kirk up and left."

"I see. But since he was murdered, I have to suppose he returned."

Roberts nodded. "Like I said, about a week before the murder Catherine Dansker got a letter from him. He had a new job as a mechanic down South somewhere and he wanted to pick up some tools from the house. He said he was in a hurry—just passing through—and he'd be dropping by sometime around midnight on October second. Just long enough to get the tools, and then he'd be leaving again.

"But the thought of Kirk's returning scared Catherine Dansker silly. It seems she had no desire to come face to face with her husband. She contacted friends—George and Jean Greenwald, who live on the next block. They offered to let Catherine spend the night at their place. On the day before her husband was due, George picked her up in his car when he came home from work. She turned on lights, unlocked the door, and left a note for Kirk to take whatever he needed but to be gone by morning."

"I have to assume, however," said Mr. Strang, "that death prevented Mr. Dankser's departure."

"Right. Enter the villain of the piece—Harry Robeling. Harry lived next door to the Dansker house, and after Kirk had left home Harry figured that Catherine was ripe for the picking. You should see this Robeling character, Mr. Strang. What a creep. Dirty, slimy teeth, breath that would kill a cow, and a mind like an open sewer. But he thinks he's God's gift to the female sex. I guess Catherine had to put up with him because he did some repairs around her house. For my money she'd have been better off doing 'em herself or leaving 'em undone. There's no way she should have gotten in debt to that hunk of sludge. But I guess he started calling on her pretty regular, like they were lovers or something."

"The murder, Paul," Mr. Strang reminded him. "Could we get to the murder?"

"Oh! Sure. The next morning, Catherine Dansker returned to her house, hoping she'd find that her husband had come and gone. Well, Kirk Dansker had arrived, all right, but he hadn't left. When Catherine entered the house, she found his body in the workroom in back, where she made the candles. The side of his skull was crushed. And beside the body was that candle, still in its mold. It was pretty obvious to the lab boys the thing had been used as a club. There was hair and blood and even bits of bone on it. All now neatly scraped into little envelopes for presentation in court."

"But how did you come to the conclusion that Harry Robeling was the killer?" asked Mr. Strang.

"Well, for one thing, we found several sets of his fingerprints in the living room—just *after* Catherine Dansker had cleaned it. No other prints at all, just his."

"But was there something else?"

"Yep. Y'see, Catherine Dansker had one piece of valuable jewelry—a gold necklace with a small emerald in it. It had been her mother's, and even when money was tight she'd never sold it. Anyway, when she called the police they asked her if anything was missing, and it didn't take her long to discover that the necklace was gone.

"We've got a set procedure for locating stolen goods. We put out a bulletin to every pawnshop for miles around saying we're looking for some article. And guess what? Six weeks after the murder, Harry turned up at a shop over in Holtsville and wanted to pawn the necklace. The proprietor called us, and we were able to pick Harry up before he'd even left the shop. And y'know what he told us? Get this, Mr. Strang. He denied ever coming near the Dansker house that night. He said he'd found the necklace hanging on the front doorknob of his own place. Man oh man! Did you ever hear such a yarn?

"Here's the way the case shapes up. Late at night on October second, Harry looks over and sees lights still on in the Dansker house. Aha, he thinks, Catherine's having a little trouble getting to sleep. So he goes over, planning on 'relaxing' her a bit, not knowing she's at the Greenwalds' and the house is empty. But when he gets there and opens the unlocked door, there's nobody home. He gets to looking around, spots that necklace, and grabs it, figuring nobody'll be the wiser.

"But just about then, Kirk Dansker walks in, looking for his tools. He sees Harry Robeling with the necklace. Robeling runs into the workroom to get away, and when Kirk Dansker follows Robeling hits him with the candle and returns home with the necklace still on him. Like I said, an open-and-shut case.

"But the whole point, Mr. Strang, is that even a case as simple and straightforward as this one took a lot of police teamwork and attention to detail to get it ready to be presented in court. Harry Dobbs and I interviewed Catherine Dansker four times just to make sure her story was coherent. We had to question the Greenwalds. A couple of men from the homicide division interrogated Robeling for days, with his lawyer objecting to everything. Naturally, Robeling lied through his teeth the whole time. Then there was the pawnshop bulletin to get ready and distribute. Hundreds of hours put in by the uniformed patrolmen. Reports and reports and more reports on everything. Teamwork and attention to detail, Mr. Strang. That's the reason Harry Robeling's going to be pronounced guilty next month."

"You seem pretty sure of that." Mr. Strang tossed off the last of the soda from the green can. "The case is still a little unclear in my mind, Paul. Let's start with the Greenwalds. You interviewed them. How did they react when Catherine Dansker first contacted them?"

Roberts reached into a desk drawer and took out a folder with a thick sheaf of official police reports. He glanced through them before answering. "Well, they were surprised when Mrs. Dansker asked them, they said, but they were happy to offer her a place to stay for the night. After work, George Greenwald stopped by the workshop to pick her up and—huh, here's a funny thing. Kind of ironic, really."

"What's that, Paul?"

"When George came by to pick Catherine up, he watched her take a panful of melted wax from the stove and pour it into that candle mold. She filled it right up to the top. Greenwald said he even remembered a little wax dribbling down the outside of the mold. Catherine told him she wanted the wax to cool overnight so she could decorate the candle the next day. Imagine that. Greenwald actually saw the murder weapon being made."

"Anything else?" asked the teacher.

"Not much. Catherine was the perfect guest. The Greenwalds wanted her to sleep in the guest room upstairs, but she insisted that was too much bother and used the couch in the living room. An argument almost started, but Catherine got her way."

"I see. You mentioned that in your investigation you found Harry Robeling's fingerprints in the living room.

What's the significance, Paul? Wouldn't you expect to find them there if he was a frequent visitor?"

Roberts shook his head. "Like I said, Mr. Strang, Catherine Dansker had spent several hours cleaning that room just before Greenwald picked her up. Any prints that were there previously would have been wiped away. But during the investigation, the fingerprint crew found Robeling's prints on the lamp, an ashtray, and the polished wood arms of the easy chair. No other prints—just Harry Robeling's.

"It's pretty clear that when he entered the house that night he sat down a while and handled some things in the living room—*after* Catherine had done her cleaning. Police teamwork again, Mr. Strang. No miracle clues. Just doing things by the book."

"Uh huh," replied the teacher absently. "One last thing, Paul. Just to get things straight in my mind. Earlier on you mentioned the Dansker 'family.' That word implies one or more children. A couple is almost always referred to as 'husband and wife'—or their given names if they're not married. Did the Danskers have children?"

"That has nothing to do with the case, Mr. Strang, and—"

"Paul, it's a simple question. Did the Danskers have children?"

Roberts sighed and nodded. "They had a little girl. Now, for Pete's sake, don't let on to Catherine Dansker that I told you this."

"Why not, Paul? What happened?"

"That's the reason Kirk Dansker left his wife. Yeah, you're right. The Danskers had a little girl. Just a toddler. One day Catherine was melting down a big pot of candle wax on her stove in the workroom. Her attention was distracted, and the kid managed to reach the handle of the pot. She pulled the whole thing over and the hot wax poured over her. Burned her horribly. She died the next day in the hospital.

"Kirk never got over it. He blamed his wife. According to the neighbors, they screamed at one another for two weeks. Then Kirk left and Catherine was left alone. But that was years ago."

Roberts stared ruefully into space. "I didn't mean for this to come out," he said. "I just wanted to show you how police teamwork solved the case. And I think I've made my point, Mr. Strang."

Mr. Strang leaned across the desk and spoke in a low, confidential tone. "I don't think you fully comprehend the point you have made, Paul."

"Huh? What do you mean?"

"You have a good solid case here."

"Of course we have. When Robeling goes to trial—"

"But it's not against Harry Robeling."

"You're not saying—"

Mr. Strang nodded. "On the basis of what you've told me here—and you've gone into quite some detail—I'm convinced that Catherine Dansker killed her husband."

Roberts groaned in exasperation. "But she was at the Greenwalds' when Kirk came home. And those fingerprints in the living room weren't hers—they were Robeling's. And Robeling had the necklace. Do you want me to believe he found it hanging on his doorknob the way he said?"

"Why not, Paul?"

"O.K., O.K." Roberts got to his feet, stomped angrily to the refrigerator, and took out another can of soda. "All right, Mr. Hot-Shot Teacher who's better than the whole police force. How come you think Catherine Dansker killed her husband?"

"First, let's consider why she might do such a terrible thing. Here we have a woman whose husband is convinced her negligence killed their child. Perhaps she was afraid of how the little girl's death would affect Kirk. As the months went by and the thing preyed on his mind, might he not one day return with revenge in his heart? Were the tools simply a ruse to gain entrance to the house, where he could get his hands on Catherine herself?

"Again, maybe Catherine could never forgive her husband for leaving her because of an accident that anyone might cause. Might not Catherine seek revenge for such a slight? We don't know. But it could be that Catherine Dansker herself felt incredible guilt because of the accident. And the embodiment of that guilt was her husband, who had accused her so cruelly and then walked out. Perhaps she sought expiation in his death.

"Fear? Revenge? Guilt? Or a combination of all three? Yes, Catherine Dansker might well wish her husband dead."

"But you're still not giving any solid evidence, Mr. Strang. Remember the fingerprints—"

"Oh, yes, those telltale fingerprints of Harry Robeling's. Paul, earlier on you told me Catherine Dansker had cleaned the living room just before Greenwald got there. And the way you said it disturbed me. You asserted it as an absolute fact. But you weren't there. The only way you could have gotten that information was by questioning Mrs. Dansker."

Roberts' face turned a brilliant red. "Of course she told us!" he snapped. "But—"

"But I don't think she told the truth, Paul. If I'm correct Catherine Dansker cleaned the room, all right, but she did it several hours—or even days—beforehand. And after she'd cleaned she talked Harry Robeling into paying another of his visits. It shouldn't have been too difficult to talk him into it from what you tell me about him. He came inside, he sat in the chair, he rested his hands on the arms. He touched several other objects as well. Meanwhile Catherine was taking great pains to touch nothing. Only Robeling's fingerprints were to be in that room."

Mr. Strang settled back in his chair. "And once he'd left, the whole area was off limits to everyone—even Catherine herself. It wouldn't be too hard. Robeling seems to have been the only outsider who entered the house regularly. Even Greenwald mentioned picking Catherine up at the rear workroom. I suspect Catherine insisted on that. She didn't want Greenwald anywhere near that living room."

"All very neat—and very wrong," said Roberts in a tired voice. "You're forgetting that Catherine was at the Greenwalds' house the night of the murder. Or were they in on the plot too?"

Mr. Strang shook his head. "No, they only provided the alibi. I was struck by Catherine's insistence that she sleep on the living room couch when the guest room had been offered. Why have even the semblance of an argument over such a simple thing? I don't think Catherine was worried about inconveniencing her hosts. But the guest room would presumably require that anyone leaving the house late at night walk about on the second floor, descend a flight of stairs, and then roam about the first floor before reaching a door. The living room, on the other hand, must have been somewhere near the front door, which could have been easily unlocked from the inside and then locked again on her return. In short, Catherine chose the couch simply so as not to wake the Greenwalds when she walked back to her own house.

"Once at home, Catherine went to her workshop and remained there, knowing full well that as soon as her husband arrived he'd go directly there."

"Yeah?" said the detective, his voice dripping with sarcasm. "Well, the front door was the one left unlocked. And the entrance to the cellar—where Kirk's tools were kept—is just inside it, to the right. Since the workroom's at the rear of the house, there'd be no reason for him to go anywhere near it."

"Oh, Catherine had a way of luring him there. And when she did she struck him down with the candle. Afterward, she took the necklace to Robeling's house and hung it on the doorknob, knowing full well the story'd sound ridiculous when Harry told it to the police. Then she returned to the Greenwalds'.

"Harry found the necklace the following day. He didn't know who owned it, but it had obvious value. I'm sure he wasn't about to let on to anyone that he had it. Still, he had to wait a few weeks to see if any claimant would advertise for it. When the owner didn't turn up, he tried to pawn it, and you caught him. End of plot, and Catherine Dansker walks away free and clear. And yet she's the one who killed Kirk Dansker."

For a long moment Roberts stared at his desk, and there was no sound in the squadroom except the whirring of the electric fan near the window.

"You're pretty positive about all this, aren't you, Mr. Strang?" he said finally.

"Yes, Paul. I am."

"But why? I'll grant, if we didn't have so much evidence against Robeling, that Catherine Dansker could—I only say could—have murdered her husband in the way you said. Maybe she could somehow have got him to the workroom where she could club him to death. But what makes you so damn sure she *did?*"

"We've come full circle," said the teacher. "At the beginning of our conversation this afternoon we talked about the single all-important clue on which an entire case may pivot. This case has such a clue. And barring some fact of which I'm not aware, that clue will put Catherine Dansker on trial as surely as it will free Harry Robeling."

"And what clue is that?" asked Roberts with a smirk.

"You have it here in this office," Mr. Strang replied. "The candle, of course. The murder weapon."

"The candle!" Roberts exploded. "But how—"

"Paul, according to George Greenwald, Catherine Dansker filled the candle mold with melted wax just before she left the house with him. 'She filled it right up to the top' were his words. Then she left the house and, according to her story, didn't return until the following day when she discovered her husband's body."

"That's right."

"That's wrong, Paul. That's wrong because the base of the candle is absolutely flat."

"Yeah, it's flat. So what?"

"When molten candle wax solidifies, it shrinks considerably. Normally the hardening wax will cling to the sides of the mold and shrink away from the areas where no metal touches it—in this case, the base. To completely fill a mold as big as this one it'd be necessary to make several pourings, letting each one cool."

"I don't—"

"If Catherine Dansker had made that candle at a single pouring, the hardening wax, contracting as it set, would have left a large depression or 'socket' at the base of the candle. But the base is quite flat. This mold had to be filled several times, the wax cooling and shrinking each time, to give the candle a flat base."

"Maybe Robeling—or Kirk—"

"Ridiculous! What reason would they have to melt candle wax?"

"Well, what reason did Catherine herself have?"

"Catherine Dansker went back to her house that evening

for the purpose of killing her husband. She concealed herself in the workroom quite some time before he was scheduled to appear. But she needed something—some bait—to get Kirk away from the front of the house where any action she took might be seen by a neighbor with insomnia. It was then she melted the wax, using it to complete the candle she'd begun earlier that day.

"Sometime in the early morning hours, Kirk Dansker came up the front walk and entered the house. He was prepared to collect his tools and leave again. But then he sensed something—something that brought back all the horror of the tragic death of his child. And because of that, he was drawn to the workroom like a moth to a flame."

"What was that?" asked Roberts.

"The stench of hot candle wax, which must have permeated the entire house, the same odor he associated with that day when his child pulled the pot off the stove. He ran to the workroom to see why that awful smell should be there in the middle of the night—and his wife struck him down."

There was a long silence in the squadroom as Roberts stared at his desk and doodled on a report form with a ball-point pen. "You—you're sure about the shrinkage of the wax, Mr. Strang?" he asked finally.

"Yes, Paul. Try it out for yourself. You don't need a candle mold and special wax. A tin can and a block of paraffin will do. Any molded candle—especially one as massive as that one—must be poured several times to fill it up."

"Oh, boy," Roberts sighed. Several minutes ticked by on the wall clock as the detective turned the problem over in his mind. Finally he looked at Mr. Strang and a series of odd sounds came from his parted lips.

He was laughing.

"Wait until I dump this into Jerry Partinger's lap," he chortled. "He's going to have a fit."

He picked up the telephone and dialed a single number. "Give me the D.A.'s office," he muttered into the receiver.

"Hello, Jerry? Paul Roberts. Look, I'm sitting here talking to a gentleman—he's a school teacher, if you must know—and, yeah, Jerry, I know you're busy, but you'd better get over here and talk to him before the Robeling case goes to trial. You see, there's this one clue, and it's got me looking at the case from a new angle.

"Hello, Jerry. Jerry?"

WAITING FOR MRS. RYDER

EDWARD D. HOCH

It was a continuing fascination with the Indian Ocean and the east coast of Africa that led Rand to remain in Cairo after his wife returned to her spring semester of lectures at the University of Reading. "I want to spend a week or so on the islands off the coast," he told Leila. "Then I'll head back home."

"It's the rainy season there," she warned him. "They call it the Long Rains."

"I know. It comes and goes."

"Like some husbands."

Rand's destination was the island of Lamu off the coast of Kenya. He learned he could reach it by flying to an airstrip on Manda Island, only a couple of kilometers away, and taking a diesel-powered launch across the channel. He did exactly that on a Monday afternoon in late April, arriving in the middle of one of the Long Rains his wife had warned him about. Leila had studied archaeology in Egypt and traveled frequently in East Africa. He had wanted to bring her with him but her lecture schedule prevented it.

The motor ferry was waiting for him at the dock and by the time it had taken him and the other two passengers across the channel the rain had started to let up. "Damned nuisance," a stout man with a white moustache muttered.

"Been coming here for ten years and the rain's always the same in the spring."

"Are you British?" Rand asked, though the accent didn't sound quite right to his ear.

"Australian, actually." He held out his hand. "James Count. I write travel books. Just now I'm updating our volume on East Africa. Lived a good bit in London, though. That's probably why you mistook me for British. You're a Brit, aren't you?"

"Yes, that's right."

"Not many people come to Lamu in this season. You here on business?"

"No," Rand assured him with a smile. "I'm a retired civil servant. This is just a holiday for me."

"Do you have a hotel?"

"Someone back in Cairo recommended the Sunrise Guest House."

"That's a good place," James Count agreed, stroking his moustache. Rand guessed him to be in his fifties. "Especially in this humidity. The rooms have ceiling fans and mosquito netting."

"Sounds fine to me."

The third passenger on the motor launch was a man in a white Muslim cap and full-length white robe, carrying a closed umbrella against the vagaries of the weather. He did not speak, and Rand suspected he did not understand English. When the ferry docked on the Lamu side of the channel he was the first one off.

"The Sunrise is at the top of this street," James Count told Rand as they came off the jetty. "After you pass through customs go up to the fort and turn right. You'll see it there."

Rand found the place without difficulty and booked a room for three nights. It seemed like a clean, well-run guesthouse with a good view of the harbor. A sign in the reception area informed him that drugs and spirits were prohibited and prostitutes and homosexuals were not allowed in the rooms.

He turned on the overhead fan as he unpacked his single suitcase. Then, seeing a bug in one of the bureau drawers, he decided to leave most of his clothing in the suitcase after all. The shuttered windows opened wide to the afternoon breeze off the Indian Ocean. It was a pleasant place despite the bugs and the humidity. Leila would have liked it.

When it was time for dinner he went off along the ancient, narrow lanes in search of a likely restaurant. He passed several Africans and white-clad Muslims on the way, some leading donkeys and carts. Private motor vehicles were not allowed on the island and donkey carts were obviously a common form of transportation. The white-walled fort with its battlements, nearly two centuries old, had been used as a prison through most of the current century, according to a brochure Rand had picked up in the guesthouse reception area. It was closed now while being converted into a museum.

There were women in the narrow lanes along with the men and he was surprised to see that they wore the traditional black wrap-around garments without the usual Muslim face veil. He was even more surprised at the cafe he chose for dining to find a pair of waitresses serving the food. His waitress was named Onyx, a brown-skinned woman with western features, possibly in her forties. She spoke fair English, enough to understand his order.

"Bring me a bottle of beer, too," he said after ordering his food.

"We have Tusker, a local beer."

"That's fine."

"Chilled or warm?" When she saw his expression of distaste she explained, "Most Africans like it warm."

"Not me. Chilled will be fine."

The food was passable and the tables were mostly filled by the time Rand finished eating. He was thinking of phoning Leila back in Reading when he thought he spotted a familiar face at a corner table. Walking over there on his way out, he saw that he was correct.

"George Ryder, isn't it? I'm Jeffrey Rand. We met in London some years ago." He kept his voice low, though the next table was empty.

Ryder was a handsome gray-haired man in his early fifties. He'd been a decade younger when Rand met him in the offices of Concealed Communications, overlooking the Thames. Rand was already retired from British Intelligence by that time, but Ryder was still quite active in the American CIA.

He looked up from his food and smiled. "You must be mistaken. My name is Watkins."

"Pardon me." Rand continued on his way out of the cafe. If George Ryder was in Lamu on an assignment, he had violated a cardinal rule of espionage in calling him by his real name. Still, Ryder had never been a case agent to his knowledge. He sat at a desk in Langley, Virginia, and shuffled papers around.

Rand thought about it as he strolled around the town, taking in the waterfront and its surprising sights. One of the most unexpected was the large number of dhows, small sailing vessels used by Arab traders. Rand had seen them before on the Arabian and Indian coasts, but never in such profusion. Staring at them in the twilight as they rode at anchor close to shore, he was not aware of the white-robed Muslim until he spoke. "The dhows are built and prepared at nearby villages. That is why there are so many here."

Rand recognized the man who'd been on the ferry that afternoon. This time he carried no umbrella. "Do you live here?" he asked.

The man nodded. "I am Amin Shade. I buy and sell these boats."

Rand introduced himself and they shook hands. "This is an unusual place, more Arab than African."

"It has a long history as an isle of fantasy and romance. It is both remote and unique, which is why it attracted your so-called hippies in the early nineteen seventies."

Rand was staring out at the boats. "I'd like to ride in a dhow," he decided, admiring the sleek craft with their distinctive sails.

"That is easily arranged. Tomorrow morning I must sail to Matondoni, one of the villages where they are built. I would be pleased to have you as a companion."

"That's very kind of you," Rand murmured. "What time do you leave?"

"Around ten o'clock," Amin Shade replied. "It is well to travel before the heat of the day, though the journey is brief. I will conduct my business, we will have a barbecued fish lunch, and return in the afternoon. I will meet you right here at ten. And bring an umbrella. It is sure to rain."

Rand left him and continued along the shore. The people of the island certainly seemed friendly enough. After a time he left the shore and headed back north, the way he had come. Almost at once he heard the laughter of a young woman and somehow knew she was British. Hurrying along the street he caught up with her and saw that she was accompanied by James Count, the travel writer who'd been his other ferry companion.

"Rand, for God's sake!" Count put a heavy arm around his shoulders and Rand could smell the beer on his breath. "Laura, this is the British chap I told you about. Laura Peters, Jeffrey Rand."

She was much younger than Count, probably still in her twenties, with the fresh attractiveness of an outdoor person. "Hello, Jeffrey Rand. You must come with us! I'm taking my uncle to see where I work."

"Your uncle?"

"Don't you think we look alike?" she asked mischievously. "If I had that moustache we'd be dead ringers!"

"Where are you two taking me?" Rand demanded with a smile.

"To something you've never seen before," she assured him, starting down the narrow lane toward the waterfront. "The Donkey Sanctuary!"

Even before they reached it the braying of the animals could be heard. If Rand had thought she was jesting he was proven wrong by the first sight of pens filled with injured, sick, and tired donkeys. "What is this? Do you round them up off the streets, Miss Peters?"

"They are brought here by their owners or we find them ourselves. We offer rest and protection until they are well."

"But whom do you work for? Who pays you for this?"

"The International Donkey Protection Trust of Sidmouth, Devon. I've been working for them the better part of a year and there's nothing like it."

"I don't imagine there is," Rand agreed.

She showed them around the place. The donkeys were interesting, but when Rand spotted a copy of the London *Times* in her small office he was more interested in that. "I haven't seen one in weeks," he admitted.

"Take it!" Laura said. "I'm finished with it. They fly

them in every week with my supplies. If you don't mind reading week-old news—"

He folded it and stuck it under his arm. "Not at all. Thank you. Can I buy you people a beer or something?"

"A capital idea!" James Count agreed. "I've already had a few but there's always room for one or two more."

"Where shall we go?" his niece asked.

Count made a face. "Only place in Lamu that serves cold beer is the Harmony Cafe. It's just a few blocks away."

"I know it," Rand told them. "I ate dinner there."

They paused at the outdoor pens while Laura petted some of her favorite donkeys, then left the Sanctuary to set off for the cafe. When they reached it Rand was pleased to see that the man who denied being George Ryder was no longer present. The owner of the place, a fat Arab named Hegad, was going over the menu with Onyx, the waitress who'd served Rand earlier. "On Tuesday evenings we serve special Indian dishes," he told her. "Some traders sail up from Zanzibar for them."

Somehow the thought of dhows docked by the jetty at Lamu like yachts on the Thames was more than Rand could imagine, but until an hour ago he'd never imagined a Donkey Sanctuary. The three of them chose a table near the door and Onyx came over to take their order. It was past the dinner hour, with only one other table occupied.

"Just beer," Count told her. "Three cold Tuskers."

Onyx went off to fill the order and Rand asked about the local economy. "What does one do for a living on Lamu?"

Laura Peters grinned. "Tend to the donkeys. Seriously, though, there is dhow building and repairing in the villages, and fabulous tourism at the right times of the year. Shela, a village south of here, has a magnificent beach. All of that brings in money. The local police will tell you illegal currency exchange is a thriving business too, but I think they exaggerate."

Over the second beer James Count and his niece turned their conversation to family matters and gossip about relatives in England and Australia. Rand glanced at the front page of the *Times,* skimming an article on the royal family. That was when his eye fell on an item at the bottom of the page. The headline read: *CIA Official Charged in Espionage Case.*

Rand quickly read the news report out of Washington: "George Ryder, longtime CIA bureau chief, and his wife Martha were both indicted on multiple counts of espionage by a federal grand jury. They are assumed to have fled the country and a worldwide search is under way. It is believed that Ryder and his wife were paid more than two million dollars over the past decade to supply CIA secrets to Moscow."

Rand lifted his eyes from the page and found himself staring at the empty table where George Ryder had been seated just a few hours earlier.

On the way back to the Sunrise Guest House Rand pondered the trick of fate that had brought him together with George Ryder at this remote outpost of civilization. They'd hardly known each other, and in truth Ryder might not even remember him. Now he was a wanted man, and Rand since his retirement was something of an unwanted man.

At the Sunrise, Rand climbed the stairs to his second-floor room and inserted the key in the lock. As he entered the darkened room he was aware of the slight swish of the ceiling fan above his head. He'd turned it off when he went out. He dropped quickly and quietly to the floor, knowing it was already too late. The red line of a laser gunsight had split the darkness and targeted the wall next to his head.

"Can't we talk about this?" Rand asked. There was a muffled sound like a dry cough and a bullet thudded into the wall above him. He slid forward under the bed, yanking off his shoe, throwing it against the side wall. The laser beam followed it, just for an instant, and Rand was out the other side of the bed, ripping the mosquito netting from its fastenings and wrapping it around the gunman before he could fire again.

He picked up the fallen gun, an awkward thing with its laser sight and silenced barrel. "Who did you expect to kill with this, Ryder? I'm retired but I'm not crippled. How'd you find me?"

"I followed you from the ferry this afternoon."

"One thing to remember, no matter how hot it gets you never turn on the ceiling fan when you're waiting in the dark to kill someone."

"Give me back the gun and we'll forget about this. It was a mistake."

"And you made it. I read your press notices in the London *Times*. I gather the Russians paid quite well."

He sighed and glared at Rand. "So you know what they're saying."

"I assume it's true, since you took a shot at me. I didn't come here looking for you, Ryder. I'm retired from British Intelligence and I certainly have no connection with your CIA."

"Then what are you doing on Lamu?"

Rand relaxed his grip on the mosquito netting but kept holding the pistol. He sat down on the edge of the bed. "I was curious about the area. An American writer, Walter Satterthwait, called Lamu the most beautiful place he'd ever seen in his life. What are *you* doing here?"

"Waiting for my wife. She was supposed to meet me three days ago."

"An odd place to meet, not exactly like Waterloo Bridge or the top of the Empire State Building."

"We were here together once, years ago. Its very remoteness made it the perfect meeting place."

"And it's on the way to Russia."

"I doubt we'll be going there. Frankly, I don't know where we'll be going." He turned his gaze on Rand, his face momentarily bathed in moonlight through the window. "Are you planning to turn me in?"

"Is there any reason why I shouldn't? If the reports are correct the Russians paid you more than I earned in my entire career with Concealed Communications. How did you and your wife get into it, anyway?"

George Ryder shifted uneasily. "If we're going to chat, I wish you'd remove this netting you've got me tangled in."

Rand turned on the light and closed the window shutters. Then he allowed Ryder to unwrap himself. "No tricks, or I'll see how this gun of yours works."

"No tricks," the CIA man promised. He sat in the room's only chair, a white wicker thing that looked uncomfortable. Rand remained seated on the bed. "Martha and I met when we were in college," he began. "I was in a play and she helped with the makeup. We started going out and were married soon after graduation. I was taking a pre-law course but in my senior year I was recruited by the CIA. We moved to Washington and took up with other young couples in government service. I like to think we were popular then. People kidded us about being George and Martha, like Washington and his wife. The nineteen seventies were a glorious time. I was advancing at the company and Martha had a nice job at a travel agency. Then came the eighties."

"What happened?" Rand asked quietly.

"I don't know. Maybe we were bored with our lives. Maybe it was simply like that spy in an Eric Ambler novel. We needed the money."

"What were you giving them for it?"

"The names of Russian double agents. I never betrayed an American."

"And your wife?"

"Martha used her position at the travel agency to arrange side trips for me. When I was out of the country on company business I'd hop over to a nearby city or country and meet with my Russian contact. That's how I delivered the material and how I was paid. The money went into a Swiss account in Martha's name, and she drew from it as we needed it."

"They never suspected you?"

"Oh, sure. I was routinely questioned a few times, especially during the great mole hunt of the mid-eighties. But things always quieted down. I managed to satisfy them and even passed the polygraph tests."

"Now you've been indicted."

He stood up and Rand shifted his grip on the pistol. "I'm being frank with you because we're in the same business, Rand. Or we were. Maybe you can understand how it is these days, with the Cold War over and the superpowers at peace with one another. Do you want to know how Martha and I managed to escape? The only close friend I still had in the company phoned me at a hotel two weeks ago and tipped me off. He said they'd been watching me and tapping my home phone for the past year. When I returned home Martha and I would both be arrested."

"What did you do?"

"I sent a fax to Martha's travel agency, tipping her off in

a prearranged code. She dispatched a ticket to Lamu, with a message that she'd join me here."

"How do you think the CIA found out about you?"

"That's the damnedest part of all. My friend said my name came down a year ago from the highest level. It just took them twelve months to prove the charges were true."

"The highest level?"

"No one will admit it. Maybe fifty years from now when the top-secret files are declassified, historians will learn about it. By that time it won't matter to anyone, especially not Martha and me. Remember what happened about a year ago? A new president of the United States met with a new president of Russia who was desperately seeking aid. The Cold War was over. Our president wanted a new beginning and the Russian president owed nothing to the former Soviet government. He owed nothing to the crumbling KGB."

"What are you telling me?" Rand asked.

"I can't prove it, but I know what happened. They held a brief private meeting without even their advisors present. The Russian president made a final appeal for more aid, and my president asked, 'What can you give me in return as a gesture of good faith?' and the Russian said, 'I can give you the name of the top Soviet agent in the CIA,' and he slipped a piece of paper across the table—a paper with my name on it."

"You really think that happened?"

"It happened. The word came down to start an intensive investigation. It took them a year, but they finally nailed me. And Martha."

"If she's not here yet she may not be coming."

"I'll wait awhile longer. Every day when the ferry comes in from the airstrip I watch for the new arrivals. I saw you today, of course, but I hoped you wouldn't run into me, or remember me. I hoped you weren't the one sent to bring me in."

"They'll only know where you are if they have Martha."

"Yes. I'm betting she's still free and on her way here by some sort of roundabout route. If anyone can shake them Martha can."

"And meanwhile you wait, and try to kill people like me. If there is an enemy here, Ryder, it could be anyone. It could be an Arab leading his donkey through the narrow lanes, or a trader sailing in on his dhow."

"I know that."

"You'll be running the rest of your life. That's why you're reluctant to go to Russia, isn't it? It's because you think the Russians betrayed you."

"I'm going," he said. "Give me back my gun."

Rand emptied the magazine onto the bedspread and cleared the chamber of the final round. Then he passed the weapon to George Ryder. "You may need it, but not against me." He returned the bullets too.

The American stuck the weapon in his belt, beneath his shirt, and left the room.

In the morning it was raining, a sudden downpour that woke Rand from a troubled sleep. He shaved and dressed and went out, borrowing one of the black umbrellas the guesthouse management kept in a stand by the front door. Although the Sunrise Guest House provided morning tea, he decided to walk to the Harmony Cafe for a full break- fast. The rain was still falling as he reached his destination and he left his umbrella inside the door. The waitress Onyx was not yet on duty but Hegad, the owner, was waiting on customers. Rand ordered banana pancakes with honey and a cup of tea. The pancakes were quite tasty but the tea was far too milky and sweet for his taste. He finally settled for a Coke.

"Has the American gentleman been around this morning?" he asked Hegad.

The fat Arab shook his head. "No Americans today. They wait for the rain to stop."

A few others drifted in and finally the waitress arrived, leaving her umbrella with the others. "You are back again," she said with a chuckle. "Does our food deserve a second or third chance?"

"This was my first time for breakfast. Those pancakes are quite good."

Onyx cast an eye on Hegad. "Sometimes he lets me make them. They are even better."

The rain was finally stopping and Rand remembered his ten o'clock appointment with Amin Shade at the dhows. He would worry about George Ryder later. He paid his bill and picked up the umbrella by the door. The humidity outside was high as the sun broke through the clouds and water vapor rose from the puddles along the lanes.

It was just before ten when he reached the mooring area for the dhows, south of the jetty. There was no sign of Shade, but he was surprised to see Laura Peters tugging on the reins of a recalcitrant donkey. She was trying, without great success, to urge him north along the shore to her Sanctuary a few hundred meters away.

"Need some help?" he asked.

"A great deal, Mr. Rand. This creature just doesn't realize what I'm doing is for its own good! Could you give me a hand, push from the rear while I pull?"

He put down the umbrella and got into position. "It's not every day I get to push donkeys."

But it seemed to work, and the beast was soon in motion

without even a parting kick. "Thank you!" she called back to him. "I'll give you a job any time you need one!"

He laughed and waved, turning back to the mooring area. There was still no sign of Amin Shade. Finally he asked an old man who seemed to be in charge of renting the dhows, "Has Amin Shade been here this morning?"

The man peered at the boats bobbing on the water. "He is out there on his vessel. He waits for you."

The dhow he indicated was moored about fifty meters offshore. Rand could see a white-robed figure hunched over one of the two masts, but there was no rowboat riding alongside. He borrowed one from the old man and rowed himself out to meet Shade.

"Did you forget your invitation?" he asked as he pulled alongside and climbed over the railing.

The figure at the mast didn't move. It was indeed Amin Shade, but he wouldn't be traveling to Shela or anywhere else. He appeared to have been shot once in the throat. There was a great deal of blood all around, attracting flies, and Rand could see that he was dead.

Before summoning help, he looked closely at the deck in front of the sagging body. Shade had not died instantly from the neck wound. He'd lived long enough to print a half-dozen letters in his own blood. *CAMERI,* it said, or possibly the final *A* was incomplete and it was meant to read *CAMERA.*

Rand searched around for a camera but there was none on the vessel. In fact there was nothing at all that might have belonged to Amin Shade. If he'd had anything with him, the killer had taken it. Although the deck was wet from the morning rain it had not washed away the man's dying word. That meant he'd been alive during the last twenty minutes, after the rain had stopped, though the shooting could have been earlier.

Rand rowed back to shore and told the old man what he'd found. "Amin Shade is dead. We must call the police." The man's eyes widened. "Did you hear a shot while you were here?"

"No, no shot! He go out to the boat with another Arab."

"Did you see the man's face?"

A shake of the head. "Raining. Shade covered the other with his umbrella. I went inside and did not see the other man row away."

Presently, as word spread and a crowd gathered on the shore, the district commissioner arrived—a towering black man wearing portions of a military uniform and driving a Land Rover, the only motor vehicle allowed on the island. He listened intently to Rand's story and noted down his name and address in Lamu. "We will talk to you further," he promised in perfect English. "Do not leave the island."

That afternoon when the ferry arrived from the airstrip on the adjoining island, he found George Ryder standing in a nearby lane watching the new arrivals. Rand could see that Martha Ryder was not among them. "Hello, Ryder," he said. "Do you still have the gun?"

The American looked at him distastefully. "Are you planning a bit of blackmail, Rand?"

"No. Someone was killed today, possibly with a silenced pistol. No shot was heard. Can you imagine two silenced pistols in a place like Lamu?"

"I can imagine ten silenced pistols if I put my mind to it. I had nothing to do with any killing. I don't even know who died."

"An Arab named Amin Shade who bought and sold dhows."

"The name means nothing to me."

"If you were watching yesterday's ferry, he got off with

that travel writer and me. He was wearing a white robe and cap, carrying a furled umbrella."

"I may have noticed him but I didn't know him."

"Has there been any word from your wife?"

"None. I am beginning to fear she's been arrested. She would be here by now otherwise." He started to turn away.

"Do you know anything about a camera?"

The American shrugged. "Tourists and spies always carry them. Sometimes the tourists have more expensive cameras than the spies."

Rand watched him walk away. Then he went back to the Sunrise Guest House and dug the bullet out of the wall of his room.

The district commissioner was named Captain Chegga and he remembered Rand from their morning encounter at the scene of Shade's murder. He used a small room at the post office when official business summoned him to Lamu, and in the confined space he seemed hemmed in and uncomfortable. "It's much too humid here on the coast," he grumbled. "Do you have more information about the killing of Mr. Shade?"

"Perhaps," Rand answered. He took an envelope from his pocket and removed the bullet from it. "You might try matching this with the slug that killed him. I assume it was recovered?"

"It will be. There was no exit wound. Where did this come from?"

"First tell me if it came from the same gun that killed Shade."

The district commissioner smiled sadly. "There are no facilities here in Lamu. The bullets must be sent to the mainland."

"How long will that take? A few hours?"

"Ah, you Englishmen! You expect everything to happen instantly."

"How long?"

"Twenty-four hours, at the very least. It will be morning before the bullets arrive for comparison, and afternoon before I receive a report, even by telephone."

"I'll come back then. Meanwhile, what about Shade's background? Was he involved in anything—"

"Shady?" Captain Chegga laughed at his own humor. "We are looking into it, never fear. Go now, Mr. Rand, and enjoy your vacation. Or whatever it is that has brought you to Lamu."

James Count was having a beer at the Harmony Cafe when Rand arrived there. "The only place you can get a cold one," he said, holding up his bottle of Tusker. "Come join me."

"How's the travel book going?" Rand asked, pulling out a chair for himself.

"Revisions, revisions. Even places like Lamu never stay quite the same. The guesthouses and cafes must be reevaluated, the prices adjusted."

Rand told him about encountering Laura with the balky donkey that morning. "It was just before I found that dead Arab, Amin Shade."

"I heard about that," the Australian said. "Crimes against tourists are usually limited to confidence games or muggings." He signaled to Onyx and she brought them two more cold beers. "But then Shade was not a tourist."

"Might he have been a smuggler?"

"Anything is possible."

Rand saw the body again, lying in its pool of blood on the deck of the dhow. In his mind's eye he was trying to see something else, something that wasn't there—

"They say the killer was dressed like an Arab, in white robe and cap—*khanzus* and *kofia,* I guess they're called."

"That proves nothing," Count said.

"No, I suppose not." Rand thought of something else. "Is the ferry the only way onto this island?"

"Well, yes, but there are three ferries from various points on Manda Island, where the airstrip is, and another from the mainland. In addition, of course, there are always private dhows for hire."

In the end Rand was no closer to learning anything than he'd been before. He declined Count's invitation to dinner, deciding he needed to be by himself. His long conversation with George Ryder the previous night had cut drastically into his sleeping time and he was beginning to feel the effects of it. He went back to his room and put in a call to Leila, trying not to alarm her with too much detail about the journey.

"It's beautiful here," he said. "A little paradise."

"Will you be home soon?"

"I'm only booked here for three nights. We'll see what happens then."

He thought about telling someone in London or Washington about George Ryder's presence in Lamu but decided against it. He was beginning to suspect that too many people knew about it already.

Rand spent Wednesday morning exploring the quaint little shops of the island, choosing a gift for his wife from among the native crafts and imported Asian items. In the afternoon he encountered George Ryder again, down by the ferry dock. James Count had told Rand that boats arrived at different times of the day, but obviously it was the ferry airline connection that interested Ryder. Today the plane had brought no one at all. The ferry carried only a man from the neighboring island with two donkeys to sell.

"No word from her yet?" Rand asked the American.

"Nothing. If they have arrested her they will be coming for me next." He glanced nervously at Rand. "You seem to be keeping an eye on me."

"You tried to kill me two nights ago," Rand reminded him. "That makes us practically brothers."

"If they come for me, could I look to my brother for help?"

In that instant Rand almost felt sorry for the man. He didn't answer directly, only asked, "Where are you staying?"

"Yumbe House, a hotel at the north end of town, a few blocks inland from the Donkey Sanctuary."

"I'll find it." The safest place for George Ryder might be a jail cell, but he didn't tell him that.

After they parted Rand left the jetty and walked to the nearby post office. Captain Chegga was in his office, relaxing beneath the slowly turning ceiling fan. "It is Mr. Rand, isn't it?"

"That's right. I came to see you yesterday. I brought you a bullet."

"I remember."

"Does it match the bullet that killed Amin Shade?"

"Yes, the bullets match, but it appears that the body does not match. The real Amin Shade is alive and well on Zanzibar."

"Then who—?"

"The dead man was an Italian ex-convict named Giacomo Verdi, a confidence man and occasional government informer. He had been known to indulge in blackmail in the past. He may have tried it again. Apparently he assumed Shade's identity to help pull off some sort of swindle involving the sale of used dhows."

"Then he wasn't an Arab at all?"

"No, no." Captain Chegga played with the papers on his desk. "Now if you will please tell me where you obtained that bullet—"

"It was fired at me two nights ago by a sneak thief I discovered in my room at the Sunrise Guest House. He escaped before I could raise the alarm, and since he took nothing I didn't report it. That was the bullet I dug out of the wall."

"Interesting. The thief could have been an accomplice of Verdi's. They may have had a falling-out."

Suddenly the rain was back, with drops dancing against the windows of the little office. They reminded Rand of what he'd forgotten earlier. "Did you find Shade's umbrella anywhere?"

"It was onshore. His initials were on the handle. He must have left it there when he rowed out to the dhow."

"And now I find myself without one," Rand said, looking out at the rain.

"It never lasts long, but you may borrow one of mine if you wish. I'm sure I'll be seeing you again, Mr. Rand." It sounded more like a threat than a promise.

The district commissioner had been right. The rain stopped within five minutes and Rand closed the borrowed umbrella. Up ahead he saw the man with the two donkeys who'd been aboard the ferry. He'd been joined now by James Count's niece from the Donkey Sanctuary, who was attempting to examine the animals.

"Need any help pushing?" Rand asked with a smile.

"No, but I'm trying to tell this man these animals are sick. I want to treat them at my place before he sells them."

There was more talk in a language Rand did not understand, then Laura Peters seemed to end the discussion by taking a small camera from the pocket of her jeans and snapping a picture of the donkeys' heads. The trader was furious, trying to grab it from her, but Rand intervened. Finally he relented, and Laura smiled as she put away the camera and took hold of the donkeys' reins.

"Thank you for your help once again!" she told Rand. She set off toward the Sanctuary with the trader following meekly along.

Rand smiled and went on his way. He'd almost reached the Sunrise Guest House when an African man wearing a uniform similar to the district commissioner's appeared from a side lane to intercept him. "Mr. Rand, Captain Chegga wishes to see you."

"I just saw him less than an hour ago. Is he worried about getting his umbrella back?"

The officer did not smile. "You will come with me."

Rand saw that he had no choice, and he fell into step beside the man. "Where are we going? Back to the post office?"

"To Yumbe House."

Rand recognized the name. It was the hotel where George Ryder was staying. He asked no more questions. It was a five-minute walk through the narrow lanes, and when they reached the little hotel the district commissioner's Land Rover was parked in front. They went up to the second floor where Captain Chegga was standing grim-faced with several others in the hall outside an open door.

"May I go in?" Rand asked.

The commissioner nodded. "Touch nothing. We are waiting for the photographer."

George Ryder was seated in a chair by the window. There was a bullet hole in his right temple and the gun was lying on the floor beneath his right hand, minus its silencer and laser scope. "Did anyone hear the shot?" Rand asked.

"No one. The maid found him. When did you last see Mr. Ryder?"

Rand knew the question was a trick. He'd never mentioned Ryder to the commissioner, but anyone might have seen them conversing at the jetty. "Just before I stopped at your office. He was meeting the ferry from the airstrip."

"Was there someone he knew on it?"

"No, only a trader with a pair of sick donkeys. The woman from the Sanctuary has them now."

"Do you have any ideas about this?" Captain Chegga asked, gesturing towards the body in the chair.

"Just one. It wasn't suicide."

"How so?"

"This place has thin walls, yet no one heard a shot. If you'll look closely at the barrel of that gun you'll see scratch marks where a silencer was attached. If he shot himself with a silenced gun, where's the silencer? Without the silencer this gun would have made more noise and left more powder burns around the wound."

Chegga was impressed. "You have done some detective work back in England, Mr. Rand."

"Not this sort. A bit of work with codes, but I suppose in a way it's all the same."

"Do you know who killed him and the other one?"

"Yes." He did know, now that it was too late.

"Will you tell me?"

"Suppose we discuss it over dinner tonight, Captain."

"Where would you suggest?"

"The only place in Lamu that serves cold beer."

Rand was not surprised to see James Count and his niece Laura at one of the tables when they entered the Harmony Cafe a couple of hours later. The owner, Hegad, hurried over to take their order, obviously a bit intimidated at having the district commissioner as a customer. Rand waved to Count and Laura and ordered a Tusker. Captain Chegga chose a glass of wine.

"I have spent too much time in Lamu," the captain complained. "There are duties on the mainland."

"I was told nothing happens in a hurry here."

"That is part of Lamu's charm," Chegga agreed. "But it can be carried too far. Will you tell me what you know?"

"All in good time."

The beer tasted fine. Rand ordered from the chalked menu on the wall, choosing a beef dish as the safest. The captain ordered mutton. Onyx served them both in a reasonable time and Rand could see Hegad relax behind his cash register. "Now will you tell me?" the captain asked.

Rand nodded. "I think the time has come."

Onyx had cleared the table of dishes and returned with the check. That was when Rand gripped her wrist and held it tight. "What is this?" she asked.

"Captain Chegga, let me introduce you to the killer of Amin Shade and George Ryder—the elusive Mrs. Ryder."

Later, back at the little room in the post office, Rand told Captain Chegga, "There were at least five clues pointing to Onyx as Mrs. Ryder and the double killer of Shade and Ryder. For dramatic effect I might call them the clues of the borrowed gun, the wrong umbrella, the dangerous rain, the menu lesson, and the dying message."

"I think you Englishmen sometimes read too much of Sherlock Holmes, but go on."

"First, the borrowed gun. We established through the bullet comparison that Amin Shade, whatever his true name, was killed by George Ryder's gun. He'd tried to use it on me less than twelve hours earlier, and it was back at his side this afternoon. Conclusion: either Ryder killed Shade and then himself or he loaned the weapon to someone else. Since I'd shown that he didn't kill himself, we can conclude that he loaned the weapon to someone. Obviously that would have to be someone very close. Martha Ryder, as his coconspirator, was the most likely person."

The commissioner grunted. "Except that she wasn't yet here on the island."

"I had only his word for that, the word of a spy and traitor. He had a very good reason for keeping her presence on the island a secret. If I or someone else had come here to arrest him for extradition back to America, we'd be most likely to wait until Martha Ryder arrived too. So long as he went through the daily charade of waiting for her at the ferry dock, he was safe."

"Go on."

"The clue of the wrong umbrella. I had an umbrella with me yesterday morning. I left it by the door at the Harmony Cafe where I had breakfast. While I was there the waitress Onyx came in with another umbrella and left it by the door. I took an umbrella, thinking it was mine, when I left and went down to the dhow moorings to meet Amin Shade. I left the umbrella on shore to row out to his vessel and discover the body. The man who rents the dhows told me Shade was carrying an umbrella when he went out to his vessel, obscuring the face of his companion. Yet there was no umbrella on the dhow. There was nothing belonging to Shade. Obviously the killer took it as protection against the rain. You told me you found it on shore, with his initials on the handle. Had the killer left it there? No, the umbrella would have provided virtually no protection while he was rowing the boat to shore. It was taken because it was needed after landing, so it would not have been left on shore. I brought it there myself, because I picked up the wrong umbrella at the Harmony Cafe—the umbrella Onyx brought in with her."

"But how could Onyx be Martha Ryder? Her skin color—"

"Which brings us to the clue of the dangerous rain. Why was an umbrella so necessary to the killer? Because the rain was dangerous. It would cause her body makeup to run! Ryder told me earlier he met his wife while performing in a college play for which she helped with the makeup. She used body makeup to give herself a brown skin and a perfect disguise. Onyx was not young, remember. Even in her makeup she was clearly middle-aged, with Western features. Something else—my clue of the menu lesson. Monday at the Harmony Cafe I overheard the owner explaining to Onyx that they featured special Indian dishes on Tuesday nights. The implication was that Onyx had been employed at the Harmony for less than a week."

"She was new," the commissioner confirmed. "But your final clue, the dying message—"

"*CAMERI.* I thought he was trying to write *camera* until you told me that Shade wasn't Shade but an Italian confidence man named Verdi. In his dying moments he reverted to his native tongue. He was trying to write *CAMERIERA,* the Italian word for waitress. Because she was new, he didn't know the name she was using. He only knew that Martha Ryder was posing as a waitress, and when he tried to blackmail her, she took her husband's silenced pistol and shot him."

"Why would she kill Ryder?"

"There could only be one reason. When he escaped arrest his continued freedom was too embarrassing for the governments involved."

Rand went to the jetty a bit later when the commissioner

and his Land Rover were leaving the island. He watched while Martha Ryder was led to the ferry in handcuffs. With the makeup gone she seemed simply a lonely middle-aged woman. He walked over to meet her and said, "Tell me one thing, Mrs. Ryder. Which side paid you to kill your husband?"

She stared at him for an instant before replying. "Does it really matter? It's all politics."

PROFESSIONAL RIPOSTE

MICHAEL GILBERT

In the long years of his retirement, Doctor Arnold Lethbury sometimes felt an overmastering desire to discuss the facts of his last case. But he refrained. It involved three deaths, two different and equally undetectable methods of committing murder, and an accusation against a man still living. It also involved one of his own rare indiscretions . . .

At the time of his retirement Dr. Lethbury had been County Pathologist for twenty years. Forensic medicine is not a subject which can be learned out of books. "It's partly experience, partly instinct," he explained to his friend and former pupil, Dr. Richard Tanner. "After you've cut up a thousand bodies you get a sort of feeling about death. You get so that you can tell what *ought* to have killed someone. An autopsy is unnecessary. You do it to please the coroner."

"You do it to earn your fee," said Dr. Tanner. He had known Dr. Lethbury long enough to pull his leg. "Have you ever been baffled?"

"Until very recently I should have said that I'd often been puzzled, but never baffled."

"And now you *are* baffled?"

"Listen to this," said Dr. Lethbury. "Three days ago Sergeant Hefflin collapsed and died five minutes after coming on duty at the Docks Police Station. The snap diagnosis made by the Police Surgeon was occlusion of the coronary artery—in other words, a thrombosis. Now—what do you visualize?"

Dr. Tanner smiled and said, "I see a red-faced, burly man, overweight from too much desk work."

Doctor Lethbury said, "Sergeant Hefflin was twenty-four. He had just been promoted to desk work from the beat. He was a first-class football player, he rarely smoked, and he never touched alcohol."

"Then the Police Surgeon must have been daft."

"I have just concluded the autopsy, and shall have to report that there was every sign of occlusion of the coronary artery—and no other discernible cause of death."

Dr. Tanner gasped. "Thrombosis—in a youngster of twenty-four?"

"It's a very odd case," agreed Dr. Lethbury, "and I've still got some inquiries to make. Call round for coffee this evening and I may be able to tell you more."

"I'd like to do that," said Dr. Tanner. "My wife will be out—some committee or other."

"Anthea's a busy woman."

"She's so damned busy I scarcely see her. Meetings and committees nearly every evening, and her garden every weekend."

"She certainly keeps that garden of yours in apple-pie order."

"I'd hate to be a slug in one of *her* roses," said Dr. Tanner, and then blushed, as if he had made an indecent remark . . .

A man who spends a large part of his work day following the tiny footprints of death through the corridors of the human body must develop a talent for observation. Discretion was Doctor Lethbury's watchword. But he could not help reflecting on the sad trick which fate had played on his friend and former pupil. Dick Tanner was rich, talented, and over forty when he met Anthea, who was strikingly beautiful, and who married him for all the wrong reasons—because of the prestige which being the wife of a successful doctor would bring, because she was younger than Dick, and because she would inherit his wealth.

Dr. Lethbury had thought it all a great pity, but he had not worried about it until two things happened. First, Dick Tanner's young partner, David Maxwell, appeared on the scene; and second, Anthea developed anemia. It was only a mild form of anemia, but it was a threat. Dr. Lethbury, meeting her on social occasions and talking polite trivialities, had read a disturbing message in her flat green eyes. It was the look of someone who saw a rich prize ahead of her—and saw time running out before she could grasp it . . .

Reflecting on the perversity of life and the diversity of death, Dr. Lethbury made his way to the Docks Police Station. He had an appointment with Inspector Frost.

"To be honest with you," said Frost, "I wouldn't have called Hefflin popular. A good footballer like him should've been popular. But he was ambitious—not too much harm in that. And he was a bit mean."

"Mean?"

"When he broke training after a big match, he'd cadge a cigarette to save buying himself a packet."

"I see," said Dr. Lethbury. That seemed a fairly harmless failing. "Where did you put his things?"

"They're in a room at the back. Would you like to look at them?"

The total of the late Sergeant Hefflin's worldly goods hardly filled one corner. Two big suitcases, a kit bag, a squash racquet. A briefcase full of personal papers. A cardboard box full of oddments. On top of the box, the first thing that caught Dr. Lethbury's eye was a packet of cigarettes. The torn cellophane showed that it had been opened.

"So he did buy his own sometimes. Expensive taste too. Handmade Turkish."

"I've never known him to smoke anything but Virginians," said the Inspector. "Maybe they were a present from some girl."

Dr. Lethbury opened the packet. There were eighteen cigarettes in it. Now a very faint suspicion was niggling at the back of his mind.

"You say he only smoked occasionally?"

"That's right. After a big match. One to celebrate, as you might say. Why?"

"The only thing I noticed when doing the autopsy—the only thing out of the way, that is—was the smell of nicotine. You'd have expected it with a heavy smoker, but not with a chap like Hefflin. Do you mind if I borrow these?"

"I shouldn't think anyone'd object if you kept them," said the Inspector.

When Doctor Tanner called that evening he found his host emerging from his private laboratory.

"You've timed it well," said Dr. Lethbury. "The coffee's almost ready."

"Are you working on something?"

"I've just finished. Sit down."

"What have you been doing?"

Dr. Lethbury said, "As a matter of fact, I've been analyzing a packet of cigarettes."

"And what did you find in them?"

"Nicotine."

Dr. Tanner laughed, and said, "You surprise me."

"It was the quantity of nicotine that was surprising," said Dr. Lethbury. "Between forty and fifty times as much as there should have been. I wonder if you recognize this packet?"

Dr. Tanner turned his head. There was a note in Dr. Lethbury's voice that he found disturbing.

"Certainly," he said. "They're Giaour Turks. Rather an acquired taste. I thought I was the only person in these parts who smoked them. *What* was that you said—?"

"I said that there was nearly fifty times as much nicotine in them as there should have been. I'm not sure how it got there but my guess would be that someone took a hypodermic syringe and injected a drop or two of pure nicotine into each cigarette."

There was a longish silence while the two doctors looked at each other, and the percolator bubbled. Then Doctor Tanner said unexpectedly, "Hefflin—Hefflin! When you said it, I knew I'd heard the name before. He was the policeman who picked us up when we had our crash. Just before Christmas. I heard his name when he gave evidence at the Inquest."

There was another pause. Dr. Lethbury could see his colleague's mind sprinting along the same track that he himself had followed so laboriously.

Dr. Lethbury said, "You're talking about your father-in-law's death, aren't you? What exactly did happen?"

"It was just before Christmas. I was driving the old boy down to the station. He wanted a cigarette. I was smoking the last one in my own case, but there was a new packet of Giaour Turks in the glove compartment. I told him to help himself. A minute later he grabbed at his chest with both hands, keeled over, and fell on top of me. I lost control, hit a lamppost, and woke up in the General Infirmary."

"Your father-in-law's death was brought in as thrombosis?"

"Certainly. No one had the least doubt about it."

"And so, in a sense, it was," said Dr. Lethbury. "A large overdose of nicotine, taken in that way, would immediately occlude the coronary artery."

"There's something I can't quite understand," said Dr. Tanner. "Assume that Sergeant Hefflin picked up the packet of cigarettes after the crash, and pocketed it. Why didn't *he* run into trouble sooner?"

Dr. Lethbury explained about Hefflin's training methods. He took his time over it. It helped to fill a silence which was becoming awkward. As he spoke, Doctor Lethbury was seeing a woman with flat green eyes. He saw her going to the garden shed where she kept her nicotine sprays—she was an inveterate gardener. He saw her going into her husband's surgery, where the hypodermics were kept—softly, softly—and he saw her tearing the cellophane on a new packet of Turkish cigarettes . . .

Dr. Tanner got abruptly to his feet, and hurried out.

Dr. Lethbury gave a cocktail party to celebrate his retirement. Dick Tanner and Anthea excused themselves from attending—indeed, Dr. Lethbury had seen little of either of them since the chat over the coffee cups.

But young Dr. David Maxwell was there, and he was full of his own troubles—too many patients, too little spare time, too little money.

"It's all right for you," he said. "You were in the racket in the old days when a doctor could put a bit of money by. What's a G.P. nowadays? A slot machine for prescriptions. I share a surgery and a dispenser with three other doctors—"

The handsome face was petulant. Dr. Lethbury was only

half listening—when something the young man said made him prick up his ears.

"I can't even look after my own drugs. Why, the other day I lost a whole bottle of Nor-adrenalin. God knows what happened to it. The dispenser probably broke it—but of course she won't admit it . . ."

Dr. Lethbury was thinking of that conversation as he lay on the beach at Petalidion, listening to the soft slapping of the Ionian Sea on white sands.

Nor-adrenalin. A neat answer! A professional riposte!

He extracted from his wallet, and reread, the news clipping which a friend in England had sent to him.

It was headlined: *Tragedy Strikes Again,* and it recorded the unexpected death of Anthea Tanner, wife of Dr. Richard Tanner, from a contraction of the heart, tentatively diagnosed as thrombosis. The coincidence, which had caught the attention of an alert journalist, was that Anthea Tanner's father had succumbed to a similar attack only six months before.

Dr. Lethbury stretched out a bare foot and scratched a line in the sand. His thought assumed, momentarily, a logical pattern.

Anthea was having injections for her anemia. The substitution of a single shot of Nor-adrenalin would have done the trick. And if anyone had been suspicious—which they weren't—the adrenalin would have been traced back to young Dr. Maxwell, not to her husband.

"If that's the way Dick did it," said Dr. Lethbury, "it was the safest murder ever committed."

A long shadow slid down the beach as the sun touched the top of Mount Likodimos.

Dr. Lethbury wondered if it could ever be right to approve of a husband murdering his wife. Anthea had attempted to kill Dick. She had succeeded in killing her own father and a policeman. If Dr. Lethbury hadn't shoved his oar in, she would surely have tried again, and would no doubt, ultimately, have succeeded. She would then have used Dick's money to ensnare young Dr. Maxwell.

And when she had got tired of *him*—?

Dr. Lethbury rolled over. It was getting cold. He wondered who had done the autopsy on Anthea. No matter. He was retired. It had nothing to do with him—not any more.